P9-ECY-745

PUFFIN CLASSICS

LORNA DOONE

'My dear father had been killed by the Doones of Bagworthy, while riding home from Porlock market, on the Saturday evening.' And from that moment on, John Ridd's life became increasingly influenced by the Doone family, especially when he fell in love with the beautiful Lorna Doone. Lorna had been a captive of the wild, outlawed Doone family since childhood and John Ridd determined to rescue her and take her home as his bride, much against the wishes of his own family. For generations the Doone family had been feared for their savage, marauding raids on innocent travellers crossing Exmoor and it had long been the family's intention that Lorna should marry the ruthless Carver Doone. When John Ridd stole her away he brought down upon his head the enmity of the entire Doone family, bent upon revenge.

The story of *Lorna Doone* has been loved by generations of readers and this edition will find thousands more. It has been specially abridged for Puffin by Stephanie Nettell.

Richard Doddridge Blackmore was born at Longworth in Berkshire in 1825. After studying at Oxford he became a barrister, but gradually gave more of his time to writing. He wrote a great deal of verse and many novels, of which *Lorna Doone* is the most famous. He died in 1900.

Lorna Doone

R. D. BLACKMORE

ABRIDGED BY

STEPHANIE NETTELL

*

PUFFIN BOOKS

PUFFIN BOOKS

Penguin Books Ltd, 27 Wrights Lane, London W8 5TZ (Publishing and Editorial)
and Harmondsworth, Middlesex, England (Distribution and Warehouse)
Viking Penguin Inc., 40 West 23rd Street, New York, New York 10010, USA
Penguin Books Australia Ltd, Ringwood, Victoria, Australia
Penguin Books Canada Ltd, 2801 John Street, Markham, Ontario, Canada L3R 1B4
Penguin Books (NZ) Ltd, 182–190 Wairau Road, Auckland 10, New Zealand

First published 1869
This edition first published 1976
Reprinted 1981, 1984, 1985, 1986, 1987

Set, printed and bound in Great Britain by
Cox & Wyman Ltd, Reading
Set in Linotype Pilgrim

Contents

Introduction

THIS is an abridged version (about one third) of a story that blends adventure and romance with history. Although Blackmore published it in 1869, he wanted it to appear as if it had been written by John Ridd himself in the language of about 1700. In this edition, a few of the more obscure archaic words have been changed, though the place names, most of which you will still find easily on a map, retain their old spelling. The Bagworthy forest, where the Doones lived, is always pronounced 'Badgery'.

The War-Path of the Doones

My father being of good substance, at least as we reckon in Exmoor, and seized in his own right, from many generations, of the best and largest of the three farms into which our parish is divided, he, John Ridd, the elder, churchwarden and overseer, being a great admirer of learning, and well able to write his name, sent me his only son to be schooled at Tiverton, in the county of Devon. For the chief boast of that ancient town (next to its woollen-staple) is a worthy grammar-school, the largest in the west of England, founded and handsomely endowed in the year 1604, by Master Peter Blundell, of that same place, clothier.

And so it came about that on the 29th day of November, in the year of our Lord 1673, the very day when I was twelve years old, and had spent all my substance in sweetmeats, with which I made treat to the little boys, till the large boys ran in and took them, we were just coming out of school at five o'clock, as the rule is upon Tuesdays, when John Fry came riding up to us, leading a pony.

'Plaise ye, worshipful masters,' he said, being feared of the gateway, 'carn 'e tull whur our Jan Ridd be?'

'Hyur a be, Jan Ridd,' answered a sharp little chap, making game of John Fry's language.

'Zhow un up, then,' says John Fry.

The other little chaps pointed at me, and some began to holla; but I knew what I was about.

'Oh, John, John,' I cried; 'what's the use of your coming now, and bringing Peggy over the moors, too, and it is so cruel cold for her? The holiday don't begin till Wednesday fortnight, John. To think of your not knowing that!'

John Fry leaned forward in the saddle, and turned his eyes

away from me; and then there was a noise in his throat, like a snail crawling on a window-pane.

'Oh, us knaws that wull enough, Maister Jan; reckon every Oare-man knaw that. Your moother have kept arl the apples up, and old Betty toorned the black puddens, and none dare set trap for a blagbird. Arl for thee, lad; every bit of it now for thee!'

He checked himself suddenly, and frightened me. I knew that John Fry's way so well.

'And father, and father – oh, how is father?' I pushed the boys right and left as I said it. 'John, is father up in town! He always used to come for me, and leave nobody else to do it.'

'Vayther 'll be at the crooked post, t'other side o' telling-house.* Her coodn't lave 'ouze by raison of the Christmas bakkon comin' on, and zome o' the cider welted.'

He looked at the nag's ears as he said it; and, being up to John Fry's ways, I knew that it was a lie. And my heart fell, like a lump of lead, and I leaned back on the stay of the gate. A sort of dull power hung over me, like the cloud of a brooding tempest, and I feared to be told anything. I did not even care to stroke the nose of my pony Peggy, although she sniffed at me, and began to crop gently after my fingers.

Now from Tiverton town to the town of Oare in Somerset is a very long and painful road, and in good truth the traveller must make his way, as the saying is; for the way is still unmade, at least, on this side of Dulverton, although there is less danger now than in the time of my schooling. In those days, when I came from school (and good times they were, too, full of a warmth and fine hearth-comfort, which now are dying out), it was a sad and sorry business to find where lay the highway. And though still John Fry was dry with me of the reason of his coming, and only told lies about father, and could not keep them agreeable, I hoped for the best, as

*The 'telling-houses' on the moor are rude cots where the shepherds meet, to 'tell' their sheep at the end of the pasturing season.

all boys will. And I thought, perhaps father had sent for me, because he had a good harvest, and the rats were bad in the corn-chamber.

It was high noon before we were got to Dulverton that day, near to which town the river Exe and its big brother Barle have union. My mother had an uncle living there, but we were not to visit his house this time, at which I was somewhat astonished, since we needs must stop for at least two hours, to bait our horses thorough well, before coming to the black bogway.

Now hot mutton pasty was a thing I had often heard of from very wealthy boys and men, who made a dessert of dinner; and to hear them talk of it made my lips smack, and my ribs come inwards.

And now John Fry strode into the hostel, with the air and grace of a short-legged man, and shouted as loud as if he was calling sheep upon Exmoor –

'Hot mootton pasty for twoo trarv'lers, at number vaive, in vaive minnits! Dish un up in the tin with the grahvy, zame as I hardered last Tuesday.'

Of course it did not come in five minutes, nor yet in ten or twenty; but that made it all the better when it came to the real presence; and the smell of it was enough to make an empty man thank God for the room there was inside him. Fifty years have passed me quicker than the taste of that gravy.

When the mutton pasty was done, and Peggy and Smiler had dined well also, out I went to wash at the pump, being a lover of soap and water, at all risk, except of my dinner.

Then a lady's-maid came out, and the sun was on her face, and she turned round to go back again; but put a better face upon it, and gave a trip and hitched her dress, and looked at the sun full body, lest the hostlers should laugh that she was losing her complexion. With a long Italian glass in her fingers very daintily, she came up to the pump in the middle of the yard, where I was running the water off all my head and shoulders, and arms, and some of my breast even, and though I had glimpsed her through the sprinkle, it gave me quite a turn to see her, child as I was, in my open aspect. But she looked at me, no whit abashed, making a baby of me, no doubt, as a woman of thirty will do, even with a very big boy when they catch him on a hayrick, and she said to me, in a brazen manner, as if I had been nobody, while I was shrinking behind the pump, and craving to get my shirt on, – 'Good leetle boy, come hither to me. Fine heaven! how blue your eyes are, and your skin like snow.'

All this time she was touching my breast, here and there, very lightly, with her delicate brown fingers, and I understood from her voice and manner that she was not of this country, but a foreigner by extraction. And then I was not so shy of her, because I could talk better English than she; and yet I longed for my jerkin, but liked not to be rude to her.

'If you please, madam, I must go. John Fry is waiting by the tapster's door, and Peggy neighing to me. If you please, we must get home tonight; and father will be waiting for me this side of the telling-house.'

'There, there, you shall go, leetle dear, and perhaps I will go after you. I have taken much love of you. But the Baroness is hard to me. How far you call it now to the bank of the sea at Wash – Wash – '

'At Watchett, likely you mean, madam. Oh, a very long way, and the roads as soft as the road to Oare.'

'Oh-ah, oh-ah, – I shall remember; that is the place where my leetle boy live, and some day I will come seek for him. Now make the pump to flow, my dear, and give me the good water. The Baroness will not touch, unless a nebule be formed outside the glass.'

When she was satisfied, she retreated up the yard, with a certain dark dignity, and a foreign way of walking.

Now, up to the end of Dulverton town, on the northward side of it, where the two new pig-sties be, the Oare folk and the Watchett folk must trudge on together, until we come to a broken cross, where a murdered man lies buried. Peggy and Smiler went up the hill, as if nothing could be too much for them, after the beans they had eaten, and suddenly turning a corner of trees, we happened upon a great coach and six horses labouring very heavily. John Fry rode on with his hat in his hand, as became him towards the quality; but I was amazed to that degree that I left my cap on my head, and drew bridle without knowing it.

For in the front of the coach, which was halfway open, being of new city-make, and the day in want of air, sate the foreign lady, who had met me at the pump and offered to salute me. By her side was a little girl, dark-haired and very wonderful, with a wealthy softness on her, as if she must have her own way. I could not look at her for two glances, and she did not look at me for one, being such a little child, and busy with the hedges. But in the honourable place sate a handsome lady, very warmly dressed, and sweetly delicate of colour. And close to her was a lively child, two or it may be three years old, bearing a white cockade in his hat, and staring at all and everybody. Now, he saw Peggy, and took such a liking to her, that the lady his mother – if so she were – was forced to look at my pony and me. And, to tell the truth, although I am not of those who adore the high folk, she looked at us very kindly, and with a sweetness rarely found in the women who milk the cows for us.

Then I took off my cap to the beautiful lady, without asking wherefore; and she put up her hand and kissed it to me, thinking perhaps, that I looked like a gentle and good little boy; for folk always called me innocent, though God knows I never was that.

We saw no more of them after that, but turned into the sideway, and soon had the fill of our hands and eyes to look to our own going. For the road got worse and worse, until there was none at all, and perhaps the purest thing it could do was to be ashamed to show itself. But we pushed on as best we might, with doubt of reaching home any time, except by special grace of God.

The fog came down upon the moors as thick as ever I saw it; and there was no sound of any sort, nor a breath of wind to guide us. The little stubby trees that stand here and there, like bushes with a wooden leg to them, were drizzled with a mass of wet, and hung their points with dropping. But soon it was too dark to see that, or anything else, I may say, except the creases in the dusk, where prisoned light crept up the valleys.

After awhile even that was gone, and no other comfort left to us, except to see our horses' heads jogging to their footsteps, and the dark ground pass below us, lighter where the wet was, and then the splash, foot after foot, more clever than we can do it, and the orderly jerk of the tail, and the smell of what a horse is.

John Fry was bowing forward with sleep upon his saddle, and now I could no longer see the frizzle of wet upon his beard. But still I could see the jog of his hat – a Sunday hat with a top to it – and some of his shoulder bowed out in the mist, so that one could say, 'Hold up, John,' when Smiler put his foot in.

'Mercy of God! Where be us now?' said John Fry, waking suddenly; 'us ought to have passed hold hash, Jan. Zeen it on the road, have 'ee?'

'No indeed, John; no old ash. Nor nothing else to my knowing; nor heard nothing, save thee snoring.'

'Watt a vule thee must be then, Jan; and me myzell no better. Harken, lad, harken!'

We drew our horses up and listened, through the thickness of the air, and with our hands laid to our ears. At first there was nothing to hear, except the panting of the horses, and the trickle of the eaving drops from our head-covers and clothing, and the soft sounds of the lonely night, that make us feel, and try not to think. Then there came a mellow noise, very low and mournsome, not a sound to be afraid of, but to long to know the meaning, with a soft rise of the hair. Three times it came and went again, as the shaking of a thread might pass away into the distance; and then I touched John Fry to know that there was something near me.

'Doon't 'e be a vule, Jan! Vaine moozick as iver I 'eer. God bless the man as made un doo it.'

'Have they hanged one of the Doones then, John?'

'Hush, lad; never talk laike o' thiccy. Hang a Doone! God knoweth, the King would hang pretty quick, if her did.'

'Then who is it in the chains, John?'

I felt my spirit rise as I asked; for now I had crossed Exmoor so often as to hope that the people sometimes deserved it, and think that it might be a lesson to the rogues who unjustly loved the mutton they were never born to. But, of course, they were born to hanging, when they set themselves so high.

'It be nawbody,' said John, 'vor as to make a fush about. Belong to t'other zide o' the moor, and come staling shape to our zide. Red Jem Hannaford his name. Thank God for him to be hanged, lad; and good cess to his soul, for craikin' zo.'

So the sound of the quiet swinging led us very modestly, as it came and went on the wind, loud and low pretty regularly, even as far as the foot of the gibbet where the four cross-ways are.

'Vamous job this here,' cried John, looking up to be sure of it, because there were so many; 'here be my own nick on the post. God bless them as discovered the way to make a rogue so useful. Good naight to thee, Jem, my lad; and not break thy drames with the craikin'.'

John Fry shook his bridle-arm, and smote upon Smiler

merrily, as he jogged into the homeward track from the guiding of the body. But I was sorry for Red Jem, and wanted to know more about him, and whether he might not have avoided this miserable end, and what his wife and children thought of it, if, indeed, he had any. But John would talk no more about it; and perhaps he was moved with a lonesome feeling, as the creaking sound came after us.

'Hould thee tongue, lad,' he said sharply; 'us be naigh the Doone-track now, two maile from Dunkery Beacon hill, the haighest place of Hexmoor. So happen they be abroad tonaight, us must crawl on our belly-places, boy.'

I knew at once what he meant, – those bloody Doones of Bagworthy, the awe of all Devon and Somerset, outlaws, traitors, murderers. My little legs began to tremble to and fro upon Peggy's sides, as I heard the dead robber in chains behind us, and thought of the live ones still in front.

'But, John,' I whispered, warily, sidling close to his saddle-bow; 'dear John, you don't think they will see us in such a fog as this?'

'Never God made vog as could stop their eyesen,' he whispered in answer, fearfully; 'here us be by the hollow ground. Zober, lad, goo zober now, if thee wish to see thy moother.'

For I was inclined, in the manner of boys, to make a run of the danger, and cross the Doone-track at full speed; to rush for it, and be done with it. But even then I wondered why he talked of my mother so, and said not a word of father.

We were come to a long deep 'goyal', as they call it on Exmoor, a long trough among wild hills, falling towards the plain country, rounded at the bottom, perhaps, and stiff, more than steep, at the side of it.

We rode very carefully down our side, and through the soft grass at the bottom, and all the while we listened as if the air was a speaking-trumpet. Then gladly we breasted our nags to the rise, and were coming to the comb of it, when I heard something, and caught John's arm, and he bent his hand to the shape of his ear. It was the sound of horses' feet, knocking up through splashy ground, as if the bottom sucked them. Then a grunting of weary men, and the lifting noise of stirrups, and sometimes the clank of iron mixed with the wheezy croning of leather, and the blowing of hairy nostrils.

'God's sake, Jack, slip round her belly, and let her go where she wull.'

As John Fry whispered, so I did, for he was off Smiler by this time; but our two pads were too fagged to go far, and began to nose about and crop, sniffing more than they need have done. I crept to John's side very softly, with the bridle on my arm.

'Let goo braidle; let goo, lad. Plaise God they take them for forest-ponies, or they'll zend a bullet through us.'

I saw what he meant, and let go the bridle; for now the mist was rolling off, and we were against the sky-line to the dark cavalcade below us. John lay on the ground by a barrow of heather, where a little gullet was, and I crept to him, afraid of the noise I made in dragging my legs along, and the creak of my cord breeches. John bleated like a sheep to cover it – a sheep very cold and trembling.

Then just as the foremost horseman passed, scarce twenty yards below us, a puff of wind came up the glen, and the fog rolled off before it. And suddenly a strong red light cast by the cloud-weight downwards, spread like fingers over the moorland, opened the alleys of darkness, and hung on the steel of the riders.

'Dunkery Beacon,' whispered John, so close into my ear, that I felt his lips and teeth shake; 'dursn't fire it now, no more than to show the Doones way home again, since the naight as they went up, and throwed the watchman atop of it. Why, wutt be 'bout, lad? God's sake – '

For I could keep still no longer, but wriggled away from his arm, and along the little gullet, still going flat on my breast and thighs, until I was under a grey patch of stone, with a fringe of dry fern round it; there I lay, scarce twenty feet above the heads of the riders, and I feared to draw my breath, though prone to do it with wonder.

For now the beacon was rushing up, in a fiery storm to heaven, red, deep in twisted columns, and then a giant beard of fire streamed throughout the darkness. The sullen hills were flanked with light, and the valleys chined with shadow, and all the sombrous moors between awoke in furrowed anger.

But most of all, the flinging fire leaped into the rocky mouth of the glen below me, where the horsemen passed in silence, scarcely deigning to look round. Heavy men, and large of stature, reckless how they bore their guns, or how they sate their horses, with leathern jerkins, and long boots, and iron plates on breast and head, plunder heaped behind their saddles, and flagons slung in front of them; more than thirty went along, like clouds upon red sunset. Some had carcases of sheep swinging with their skins on, others had deer, and one had a child flung across his saddle-bow. Whether the child were dead, or alive, was beyond my vision, only it hung head downwards there, and must take the chance of it. They had got the child, a very young one, for the sake of the dress, no doubt, which they could not stop to pull off from it; for the dress shone bright, where the fire struck it, as if with gold and jewels. I longed in my heart to know most sadly, what they would do with the little thing, and whether they would eat it.

It touched me so to see that child, a prey among those vultures, that in my foolish rage and burning I stood up, and shouted to them, leaping on a rock, and raving out of all possession. Two of them turned round, and one set his carbine at me, but the other said it was but a pixie, and bade him keep his powder. Little they knew, and less thought I, that the pixie then before them would dance their castle down one day.

John Fry, who in the spring of fright had brought himself down from Smiler's side, as if he were dipped in oil, now came up to me, danger being over, cross, and stiff, and aching sorely from his wet couch of heather.

'Small thanks to thee, Jan, as my new waife bain't a widder. And who be you to zupport of her, and her son, if she have one? Zarve thee right, if I was to chuck thee down into the Doone-track.'

My father never came to meet us, at either side of the telling-house, neither at the crooked post, nor even at home-linhay, although the dogs kept such a noise that he must have heard us. All at once my heart went down, and all my breast was hollow. There was not even the lanthorn light on the peg against the cow's house, and nobody said 'Hold your noise!' to the dogs, or shouted 'Here our Jack is!'

I looked at the posts of the gate, in the dark, because they were tall, like father, and then at the door of the harness-room, where he used to smoke his pipe and sing. Then I thought he had guests perhaps – people lost upon the moors – whom he could not leave unkindly, even for his son's sake. And yet about that I was jealous, and ready to be vexed with him, when he should begin to make much of me. And I felt in my pocket for the new pipe which I had brought him from Tiverton, and said to myself, 'He shall not have it until tomorrow morning.'

Woe is me! I cannot tell. How I knew I know not now – only that I slunk away, without a tear, or thought of weeping, and hid me in a saw-pit. All I wanted was to hide, and none to tell me anything.

By and by, a noise came down, as of woman's weeping; and there my mother and sister were, choking and holding together. Although they were my dearest loves, I could not bear to look at them, until they seemed to want my help, and turned away, that I might come.

A Rash Visit

MY dear father had been killed by the Doones of Bagworthy, while riding home from Porlock market, on the Saturday evening. With him were six brother-farmers, all of them very sober; for father would have no company with any man who went beyond half-a-gallon of beer, or a single gallon of cider.

These seven farmers were jogging along, helping one another in the troubles of the road, and singing goodly hymns and songs, to keep their courage moving, when suddenly a horseman stopped in the starlight full across them.

By dress and arms they knew him well, and by his size and stature, shown against the glimmer of the evening star; and though he seemed one man to seven, it was in truth one man to one. Of the six who had been singing songs and psalms, about the power of god, and their own regeneration – such psalms as went the round, in those days, of the public-houses – there was not one but pulled out his money, and sang small beer to a Doone.

But father had been used to think, that any man, who was comfortable inside his own coat and waistcoat, deserved to have no other set, unless he would strike a blow for them. And so, while his gossips doffed their hats, and shook with what was left of them, he set his staff above his head, and rode at the Doone robber. With a trick of his horse, the wild man escaped the sudden onset; although it must have amazed him sadly, that any durst resist him. Then when Smiler was carried away with the dash and the weight of my father (not being brought up to battle, nor used to turn, save in plough harness), the outlaw whistled upon his thumb, and plundered the rest of the yeomen. But father, drawing at Smiler's head, to try to come back and help them, was in the midst of a dozen men, who seemed to come out of a turf-rick, some on horse, and some a-foot. Nevertheless, he smote lustily, so far as he could see; and being of great size and strength, and his blood well up, they had no easy job with him. With the play of his wrist, he cracked three or four crowns, being always famous at single-stick; until the rest drew their horses away, and he thought that he was master, and would tell his wife about it.

But a man beyond the range of staff was crouching by the peat-stack, with a long gun set to his shoulder, and he got poor father against the sky, and I cannot tell the rest of it. Only they knew that Smiler came home, with blood upon his withers, and father was found in the morning dead on the moor, with his ivy-twisted cudgel lying broken under him. Now, whether this were an honest fight, God judge betwixt the Doones and me.

It was more of woe than wonder, being such days of violence, that mother knew herself a widow, and her children fatherless. Of children there were only three, none of us fit to be useful yet, only to comfort mother, by making her to work for us. I, John Ridd, was the eldest, and felt it a heavy thing on me; next came sister Annie, with about two years between us; and then the little Eliza.

Now, before I got home and found my sad loss – and no boy ever loved his father better than I loved mine – mother had done a most wondrous thing, which made all the neighbours say that she must be mad, at least. Upon the Monday morning, while her husband lay unburied, she cast a white hood over her hair, and gathered a black cloak round her, and, taking counsel of no one, set off on foot for the Doone-gate.

In the early afternoon she came to the hollow and barren

entrance; where in truth there was no gate, only darkness to go through. No gun was fired at her, only her eyes were covered over, and somebody led her by the hand, without any wish to hurt her.

A very rough and headstrong road was all that she remembered, for she could not think as she wished to do, with the cold iron pushed against her. At the end of this road they delivered her eyes, and she could scarce believe them.

For she stood at the head of a deep green valley, carved from out the mountains in a perfect oval, with a fence of sheer rock standing round it, eighty feet or a hundred high; from whose brink black wooded hills swept up to the sky-line. By her side a little river glided out from underground with a soft dark babble, unawares of daylight; then growing brighter, lapsed away, and fell into the valley. There, as it ran down the meadow, alders stood on either marge, and grass was blading out upon it, and yellow tufts of rushes gathered, looking at the hurry. But further down, on either bank, were covered houses, built of stone, square and roughly cornered, set as if the brook were meant to be the street between them. Only one room high they were, and not placed opposite each other, but in and out as skittles are; only that the first of all, which proved to be the captain's, was a sort of double house, or rather two houses joined together by a plank-bridge over the river.

Fourteen cots my mother counted, all very much of a pattern, and nothing to choose between them, unless it were the captain's. Deep in the quiet valley there, away from noise, and violence, and brawl, save that of the rivulet, any man would have deemed them homes of simple mind and innocence. Yet not a single house stood there but was the home of murder.

Two men led my mother down a steep and gliddery stairway, like the ladder of a hay-mow; and thence, from the break of the falling water, as far as the house of the captain.

And there at the door, they left her trembling, strung as she was, to speak her mind.

Now, after all, what right had she, a common farmer's widow, to take it amiss that men of birth thought fit to kill her husband? And the Doones were of very high birth, as all we clods of Exmoor knew; and we had enough of good teaching now – let any man say the contrary – to feel that all we had belonged of right to those above us. Therefore my mother was half-ashamed that she could not help complaining.

But after a little while, as she said, remembrance of her husband came, and the way he used to stand by her side and put his strong arm round her, and how he liked his bacon fried, and praised her kindly for it, – and so the tears were in her eyes, and nothing should gainsay them.

A tall old man, Sir Ensor Doone, came out with a bill-hook in his hand, and hedger's gloves going up his arms, as if he were no better than a labourer at ditch-work. Only in his mouth and eyes, his gait, and most of all his voice, even a child could know and feel, that here was no ditch-labourer. Good cause he has found since then, perhaps, to wish that he had been one.

With his white locks moving upon his coat, he stopped and looked down at my mother, and she could not help herself but courtesy under the fixed black gazing.

'Good woman, you are none of us. Who has brought you hither? Young men must be young – but I have had too much of this work.'

And he scowled at my mother, for her comeliness; and yet looked under his eyelids, as if he liked her for it. But as for her, in the depth of love-grief, it struck scorn upon her womanhood; and in the flash she spoke.

'What you mean, I know not. Traitors! cut-throats! cowards! I am here to ask for my husband.' She could not say any more, because her heart was now too much for her, coming hard in her throat and mouth; but she opened up her eyes at him.

'Madam,' said Sir Ensor Doone – being born a gentleman, although a very bad one – 'I crave pardon of you. My eyes are old, or I might have known. Now, if we have your husband prisoner, he shall go free without ransom, because I have insulted you.'

'Sir,' said my mother, being suddenly taken away with sorrow, because of his gracious manner, 'please to let me cry a bit.'

He stood away, and seemed to know that women want no help for that. And by the way she cried, he knew that they had killed her husband. Then, having felt of grief himself, he was not angry with her, but left her to begin again.

'Loth would I be,' said mother, sobbing with her new red handkerchief, and looking at the pattern of it, 'loth indeed, Sir Ensor Doone, to accuse any one unfairly. But I have lost the very best husband God ever gave to a woman, and I knew him when he was to your belt, and I not up to your knee, sir; and never an unkind word he spoke, nor stopped me short in speaking. All the herbs he left to me, and all the bacon-curing, and when it was best to kill a pig, and how to treat maidens. Not that I would ever wish – oh, John, it seems so strange to me, and last week you were everything.'

Here mother burst out crying again, not loudly, but turning quietly, because she knew that no one now would ever care to wipe the tears. And fifty or a hundred things, of weekly and daily happening, came across my mother, so that her spirit fell, like slackening lime.

'This matter must be seen to; it shall be seen to at once,' the old man answered, moved a little in spite of all his knowledge. 'Madam, if any wrong has been done, trust the honour of a Doone; I will redress it to my utmost. Come inside and rest yourself, while I ask about it. What was your good husband's name, and when and where fell this mishap?'

'Deary me,' said mother, as he set a chair for her very politely, but she would not sit upon it; 'Saturday morning I was a wife, sir; and Saturday night I was a widow, and my children fatherless. My husband's name was "John Ridd", sir, as everybody knows; and there was not a finer or better man, in Somerset or Devon. He was coming home from Porlock market, and a new gown for me on the crupper, and a shell to put my hair up, – oh, John, how good you were to me!'

Of that she began to think again, and not to believe her sorrow, except as a dream from the evil one, because it was too bad upon her, and perhaps she would awake in a minute, and her husband would have the laugh of her. And so she wiped her eyes and smiled, and looked for something.

'Madam, this is a serious thing,' Sir Ensor Doone said graciously, and showing grave concern: 'my boys are a little wild, I know. And yet I cannot think that they would willingly harm anyone. And yet – and yet, you do look sad. Send Counsellor to me,' he shouted, from the door of his house; and down the valley went the call, 'send Counsellor to Captain.'

Counsellor Doone came in, ere yet my mother was herself again; and if any sight could astonish her, when all her sense of right and wrong was gone astray with the force of things, it was the sight of the Counsellor. A square-built man of enormous strength, but a foot below the Doone stature, he carried a long grey beard descending to the leather of his belt. Great eyebrows overhung his face, like ivy on a pollard oak, and under them two large brown eyes, as of an owl when muting. And he had a power of hiding his eyes, or showing them bright, like a blazing fire. He stood there with his beaver hat off, and mother tried to look at him; but he seemed not to descry her.

'Counsellor,' said Sir Ensor Doone, standing back in his height from him, 'here is a lady of good repute – '

'Oh, no, sir; only a woman.'

'Allow me, madam, by your good leave. Here is a lady, Counsellor, of great repute in this part of the country, who charges the Doones with having unjustly slain her husband – '

'Murdered him! murdered him!' cried my mother; 'if ever there was a murder. Oh, sir! oh, sir! you know it.'

'The perfect right and truth of the case is all I wish to know,' said the old man, very loftily; 'and justice shall be done, madam.'

'Oh, I pray you – pray you, sirs, make no matter of business of it. God from heaven, look on me!'

'Put the case,' said the Counsellor.

'The case is this,' replied Sir Ensor, holding one hand up to mother: 'This lady's worthy husband was slain, it seems, upon his return from the market at Porlock, no longer ago than last Saturday night. Madam, amend me if I am wrong.'

'No longer, indeed, indeed, sir. Sometimes it seems a twelve-month, and sometimes it seems an hour.'

'Cite his name,' said the Counsellor, with his eyes still rolling inwards.

' "Master John Ridd", as I understand. Counsellor, we have heard of him often; a worthy man and a peaceful one, who meddled not with our duties. Now, if any of our boys have been rough, they shall answer it dearly. And yet I can scarce believe it. For the folks about these parts are apt to misconceive of our sufferings, and to have no feeling for us. Counsellor, you are our record, and very stern against us; tell us how this matter was.'

'Oh, Counsellor!' my mother cried; 'Sir Counsellor, you will be fair; I see it in your countenance. Only tell me who it was, and set me face to face with him; and I will bless you, sir; and God shall bless you, and my children.'

The square man with the long grey beard, quite unmoved by anything, drew back to the door, and spoke, and his voice was like a fall of stones in the bottom of a mine.

'Few words will be enow for this. Four or five of our best-behaved and most peaceful gentlemen went to the little market at Porlock, with a lump of money. They bought some household stores and comforts at a very high price, and pricked upon the homeward road, away from vulgar revellers. When they drew bridle to rest their horses, in the shelter of a peat-rick, the night being dark and sudden, a robber of great size and strength rode into the midst of them, thinking to kill or terrify. His arrogance, and hardihood, at the first amazed them, but they would not give up without a blow goods which were on trust with them. He had smitten three of them senseless, for the power of his arm was terrible; whereupon the last man tried to ward his blow with a pistol. Carver, sir, it was, our brave and noble Carver, who saved the lives of his brethren and his own; and glad enow they were to escape. Notwithstanding, we hoped it might be only a flesh-wound, and not to speed him in his sins.'

As this atrocious tale of lies turned up joint by joint before her, like a 'devil's coach-horse',* mother was too much amazed to do any more than look at him, as if the earth must open. But the only thing that opened was the great brown eyes of the Counsellor, which rested on my mother's face, with a dew of sorrow, as he spoke of sins.

She, unable to bear them, turned suddenly on Sir Ensor, and caught (as she fancied) a smile on his lips, and a sense of quiet enjoyment.

'All the Doones are gentlemen,' answered the old man, gravely, and looking as if he had never smiled since he was a baby. 'We are always glad to explain, madam, any mistake which the rustic people may fall upon us; and we wish

*The cock-tailed beetle has earned this name in the West of England.

you clearly to conceive, that we do not charge your poor husband with any set purpose of robbery; neither will we bring suit for any attainder of his property. Is it not so, Counsellor?'

'Without doubt his land is attainted; unless in mercy you forbear, sir.'

'Counsellor, we will forbear. Madam, we will forgive him. Like enough he knew not right from wrong, at that time of night. The waters are strong at Porlock, and even an honest man may use his staff unjustly, in this unchartered age of violence and rapine.'

The Doones to talk of rapine! Mother's head went round so, that she courtesied to them both, scarcely knowing where she was, but calling to mind her manners. All the time she felt a warmth, as if the right was with her, and yet she could not see the way to spread it out before them. With that, she dried her tears in haste, and went into the cold air, for fear of speaking mischief.

But when she was on the homeward road, and the sentinels had charge of her, blinding her eyes, as if she were not blind enough with weeping, someone came in haste behind her, and thrust a heavy leathern bag into the limp weight of her hand.

'Captain sends you this,' he whispered; 'take it to the little ones.'

But mother let it fall in a heap, as if it had been a blind worm; and then for the first time crouched before God, that even the Doones should pity her.

An Illegal Settlement

GOOD folk, who dwell in a lawful land, if any such there be, may judge our neighbourhood harshly, unless the whole truth is set before them. In bar of such prejudice, many of us ask leave to explain how, and why, the robbers came to that head in the midst of us. We would rather not have had it so, and were wise enough to lament it; but it grew upon us gently, in the following manner. Only let all who read observe that here I enter many things which came to my knowledge in later years.

In or about the year of our Lord 1640, when all the troubles of England were swelling to an outburst, great estates in the north country were suddenly confiscated, through some feud of families, and strong influence at Court, and the owners were turned upon the world, and might think themselves lucky to save their necks. These estates were in co-heirship, joint tenancy I think they called it, although I know not the meaning, only so that if either tenant died, the other living, all would come to the live one, in spite of any testament.

One of the joint owners was Sir Ensor Doone, a gentleman of brisk intellect; and the other owner was his cousin, the Earl of Lorne and Dykemont.

Lord Lorne was some years the elder of his cousin Ensor Doone, and was making suit to gain severance of the cumbersome joint-tenancy, by any fair apportionment, when suddenly this blow fell on them, and instead of dividing the land, they were divided from it.

The nobleman was still well-to-do, though crippled in his expenditure; but as for the cousin, he was left a beggar, with many to beg from him. He thought that the other had wronged him, and that all the trouble of law befell through his unjust petition. Many friends advised him to make interest at Court, for, having done no harm whatever, and being a good Catholic, which Lord Lorne was not, he would be sure to find hearing there, and probably some favour. But he, like a very hot-brained man, although he had long been married to the daughter of his cousin (whom he liked none the more for that), would have nothing to say to any attempt at making a patch of it, but drove away with his wife and sons, and the relics of his money, swearing hard at everybody. In this he may have been quite wrong; probably, perhaps he was so; but I am not convinced at all, but what most of us would have done the same.

Some say that, in the bitterness of that wrong and outrage, he slew a gentleman of the Court, whom he supposed to have borne a hand in the plundering of his fortunes. Others say that he bearded King Charles the First himself, in a manner beyond forgiveness. One thing, at any rate, is sure – Sir Ensor was attainted, and made a felon outlaw, through some violent deed ensuing upon his dispossession.

In great despair at last, he resolved to settle in some outlandish part, where none could be found to know him; and so, in an evil day for us, he came to the West of England. Not that our part of the world is at all outlandish, according to my view of it (for I never found a better one), but that it was known to be rugged and large, and desolate. And here, when he had discovered a place which seemed almost to be made for him, so withdrawn, so self-defended, and uneasy of access, some of the country-folk around brought him little offerings – a side of bacon, a keg of cider, hung mutton, or a brisket of venison; so that for a little while he was very honest. But when the newness of his coming began to wear away, and our good folk were apt to think, that even a gentleman ought to work, or pay other men for doing it, and many farmers were grown weary of manners without discourse to them, and all cried out to one another, how unfair it was that owning such a fertile valley, young men would not spade or plough by reason of noble lineage – then the young Doones, growing up, took things they would not ask for.

There was not more than a dozen of them, counting a few retainers, who still held by Sir Ensor; but soon they grew and multiplied in a manner surprising to think of. Whether it was the venison, which we call a strengthening victual, or whether it was the Exmoor mutton, or the keen soft air of the moorlands, anyhow the Doones increased much faster than their honesty. At first they had brought some ladies with them, of good repute with charity; and then, as time went on, they added to their stock by carrying. They carried off many good farmers' daughters, who were sadly displeased at first; but took to them kindly after awhile, and made a new home in their babies. For women, as it seems to me, like strong men more than weak ones, feeling that they need some staunchness, something to hold fast by.

Perhaps their den might well have been stormed, and themselves driven out of the forest, if honest people had only agreed to begin with them at once, when first they took to plundering. But having respect for their good birth, and pity for their misfortunes, and perhaps a little admiration at the justice of God, that robbed men now were robbers, the squires, and farmers and shepherds, at first did nothing more than grumble gently, or even make a laugh of it, each in the case of others. After a while they found the matter gone too far for laughter, as violence and deadly outrage stained the hand of robbery, until every woman clutched her child, and every man turned pale at the very name of 'Doone'. For the sons, and grandsons, of Sir Ensor, grew up in foul liberty, and haughtiness, and hatred, to utter scorn of God and man, and brutality towards dumb animals. There was only one good thing about them, if indeed it were good, to wit, their faith to one another, and truth to their wild eyry. But this only made them feared the more, so certain was the revenge they wreaked upon any who dared to strike a Doone. One night, soon after I was born, when they were sacking a rich man's house, not very far from Minehead, a shot was fired at them in the dark, of which they took little notice, and only one of them knew that any harm was done. But when they were well on the homeward road, not having slain either man or woman, or even burned a house down, one of their number fell from his saddle, and died without so much as a groan. The youth had been struck, but would not complain, and perhaps took little heed of the wound, while he was bleeding inwardly. His brothers and cousins laid him softly on a bank of whortle-berries, and just rode back to the lonely hamlet, where he had taken his death-wound. No man, nor woman, was left in the morning, nor house for any to dwell in, only a child with its reason gone.*

Not to mention the strength of the place, which I shall describe in its proper order, when I come to visit it, there was not one among them but was a mighty man, straight and tall, and wide, and fit to lift four hundred-weight. If son or grandson of old Doone, or one of the northern retainers, failed at the age of twenty, while standing on his naked feet, to touch with his forehead the lintel of Sir Ensor's door, and to fill the door-frame with his shoulders from sidepost even to sidepost, he was led away to the narrow pass, which made their valley so desperate, and thrust from the crown with ignominy, to get his own living honestly. Now, the measure of that doorway is, or rather was, I ought to say, six feet and one inch lengthwise, and two feet all but two inches taken crossways in the clear. Yet I not only have heard, but know, being so closely mixed with them, that no descendants of old Sir Ensor, neither relative of his (except, indeed, the Counsellor, who was kept by them for his

*This vile deed was done, beyond all doubt.

wisdom), and no more than two of their following, ever failed of that test, and relapsed to the difficult ways of honesty.

Hard it is to Climb

WHEN I was turned fourteen years old, and put into good small-clothes, buckled at the knees, and strong blue worsted hosen, knitted by my mother, it happened to me without choice, I may say, to explore the Bagworthy water. And it came about in this wise.

My mother had long been ailing, and not well able to eat much; and there is nothing that frightens us so much as for people to have no love of their victuals. Now I chanced to remember, that once at the time of the holidays, I had brought dear mother from Tiverton a jar of pickled loaches, caught by myself in the Lowman river, and baked in the kitchen oven, with vinegar, a few leaves of bay, and about a dozen peppercorns. And mother had said that, in all her life, she had never tasted anything fit to be compared with them.

So now, being resolved to catch some loaches, whatever trouble it cost me, I set forth without a word to any one, in the forenoon of St Valentine's day, 1675–6, I think it must have been.

I never could forget that day, and how bitter cold the water was. For I doffed my shoes and hose, and put them into a bag about my neck; and left my little coat at home, and tied my shirt-sleeves back to my shoulders. Then I took a three-pronged fork firmly bound to a rod with cord, and a piece of canvas kerchief, with a lump of bread inside it; and so went into the pebbly water, trying to think how warm it was. When I had travelled two miles or so, suddenly, in an open space, where meadows spread about it, I found a good stream flowing softly into the body of our brook, gliding smoothly and forcibly, as if upon some set purpose.

Hereupon I drew up, and thought, and reason was much inside me; because the water was bitter cold, and my little toes were aching. So on the bank I rubbed them well with a sprout of young sting-nettle, and having skipped about awhile, was kindly inclined to eat a bit.

Now all the turn of all my life hung upon that moment.

It seemed a sad business to go back now, and tell Annie there were no loaches; and yet it was a frightful thing, knowing what I did of it, to venture, where no grown man durst, up the Bagworthy water.

However, as I ate more and more, my spirit arose within me. So I put the bag round my neck again, and buckled my breeches far up from the knee, expecting deeper water, and crossing the Lynn, went stoutly up under the branches which hang so dark on the Bagworthy river.

I found it strongly over-woven, turned, and torn with thicket-wood, but not so rocky as the Lynn, and more inclined to go evenly.

Here, although affrighted often by the deep, dark places, and feeling that every step I took might never be taken backward, on the whole I had very comely sport of loaches, trout, and minnows, forking some, and tickling some, and driving others to shallow nooks, whence I could bail them ashore. Till suddenly I saw that the day was falling fast behind the brown of the hill-tops; and the trees, being void of leaf and hard, seemed giants ready to beat me. And every moment, as the sky was clearing up for a white frost, the cold of the water got worse and worse, until I was fit to cry with it. And so, in a sorry plight, I came to an opening in the bushes, where a great black pool lay in front of me, whitened with snow (as I thought) at the sides, till I saw it was only foam-froth.

I shuddered and drew back; not alone at the pool itself, and the black air there was about it, but also at the whirling manner, and wisping of white threads upon it, in stripy circles round and round; and the centre still as jet.

But soon I saw the reason of the stir and depth of that great pit, as well as of the roaring sound which long had made me wonder. For skirting round one side, with very little comfort, because the rocks were high and steep, and the ledge at the foot so narrow, I came to a sudden sight and marvel, such as I never dreamed of. For, lo! I stood at the foot of a long pale slide of water, coming smoothly to me, without any break or hindrance, for a hundred yards or more, and fenced on either side with cliff, sheer, and straight, and shining. The water neither ran nor fell, nor leaped with any spouting, but made one even slope of it, as if it had been combed or planed, and looking like a plank of deal laid down a deep black staircase. However there was no side-rail, nor any place to walk upon, only the channel a fathom wide, and the perpendicular walls of crag shutting out the evening.

What prevented me from turning back was a strange inquisitive desire, very unbecoming in a boy of little years; in a word, I would risk a great deal to know, what made the water come down like that, and what there was at the top of it.

Therefore, seeing hard strife before me, I girt up my breeches anew, with each buckle one hole tighter, for the sodden straps were stretching and giving, and mayhap my legs were grown smaller from the coldness of it. Then I bestowed my fish around my neck more tightly, and not stopping to look much, for fear of fear, crawled along over the fork of rocks, where the water had scooped the stone out; and shunning thus the ledge from whence it rose, like the mane of a white horse, into the broad black pool, softly I let my feet into the dip and rush of the torrent.

The green wave came down, like great bottles upon me, and my legs were gone off in a moment, and I had not time to cry out with wonder, only to think of my mother and Annie. But all in a moment, before I knew aught, except that I must die out of the way, with a roar of water upon me, my fork, praise God, stuck fast in the rock, and I was borne up upon it. And presently the dash of the water upon my face revived me, and my mind grew used to the roar of it.

Therefore I gathered my legs back slowly, as if they were fish to be landed, stopping whenever the water flew too strongly off my shin-bones, and coming along, without sticking out to let the wave get hold of me. Then I said to myself, 'John Ridd, the sooner you get yourself out by the way you came, the better it will be for you.' But to my great dismay and affright, I saw that no choice was left me now, except that I must climb somehow up that hill of water, or else be washed down into the pool, and whirl around till it drowned me.

Having said the Lord's Prayer (which was all I knew), and made a very bad job of it, I grasped the good loach-stick under a knot, and steadied me with my left hand, and so with a sigh of despair began my course up the fearful torrent-way.

How I went carefully, step by step, keeping my arms in front of me, and never daring to straighten my knees, is more than I can tell clearly, or even like now to think of, because it makes me dream of it. Only I must acknowledge, that the greatest danger of all was just where I saw no jeopardy, but ran up a patch of black ooze-weed in a very boastful manner, being now not far from the summit.

Here I fell very piteously, and was like to have broken my knee-cap, and the torrent got hold of my other leg, while I was indulging the bruised one. And then a vile knotting of cramp disabled me, and for awhile I could only roar, till my mouth was full of water, and all of my body was sliding. But the fright of that brought me to again, and my elbow caught in a rock-hole; and so I managed to start again, with the help of more humility.

Now being in the most dreadful fright, because I was so near the top, and hope was beating within me, I laboured hard with both legs and arms, going like a mill, and grunting. At last the rush of forked water, where first it came over the lips of the fall, drove me into the middle, and I stuck awhile with my toe-balls on the slippery links of the popweed, and the world was green and gliddery, and I durst not look behind me. Then I made up my mind to die at last; for so my legs would ache no more, and my breath not pain my heart so; only it did seem such a pity, after fighting so long, to give in, and the light was coming upon me, and again I fought towards it; then suddenly I felt fresh air, and fell into it headlong.

A Boy and a Girl

WHEN I came to myself again, my hands were full of young grass and mould; and a little girl kneeling at my side was rubbing my forehead tenderly, with a dock-leaf and a handkerchief.

'Oh, I am so glad,' she whispered softly, as I opened my eyes and looked at her; 'now you will try to be better, won't you?'

I had never heard so sweet a sound as came from between her bright red lips, while there she knelt and gazed at me; neither had I ever seen anything so beautiful as the large dark eyes intent upon me, full of pity and wonder. And then, my nature being slow, and perhaps, for that matter, heavy, I wandered with my hazy eyes down the black shower of her hair, as to my jaded gaze it seemed; and where it fell on the turf, among it (like an early star) was the first primrose of the season. And since that day, I think of her, through all the rough storms of my life, when I see an early primrose.

'What is your name?' she said, as if she had every right to ask me; 'and how did you come here, and what are these wet things in this great bag?'

'You had better let them alone,' I said; 'they are loaches for my mother. But I will give you some, if you like.'

'Dear me, how much you think of them! Why they are only fish. But how your feet are bleeding! oh, I must tie them up for you. And no shoes nor stockings! Is your mother very poor, poor boy?'

'No,' I said, being vexed at this; 'we are rich enough to buy all this great meadow, if we chose; and here my shoes and stockings be.'

'Why they are quite as wet as your feet; and I cannot bear to see your feet. Oh, please to let me manage them; I will do it very softly.'

'Oh, I don't think much of that,' I replied; 'I shall put some goose-grease to them. But how you are looking at me! I never saw anyone like you before. My name is John Ridd. What is your name?'

'Lorna Doone,' she answered, in a low voice, as if afraid of it, and hanging her head, so that I could see only her fore-head and eyelashes; 'if you please, my name is Lorna Doone; and I thought you must have known it.'

Then I stood up, and touched her hand, and tried to make her look at me; but she only turned away the more. Young and harmless as she was, her name alone made guilt of her. Nevertheless I could not help looking at her tenderly, and the more when her blushes turned into tears, and her tears to long, low sobs.

'Don't cry,' I said, 'whatever you do. I am sure you have never done any harm. I will give you all my fish, Lorna, and catch some more for mother; only don't be angry with me.'

'Do you know what they would do to us, if they found you here with me?'

'Beat us, I dare say, very hard, or me at least. They could never beat you.'

'No. They would kill us both outright, and bury us here by the water; and the water often tells me that I must come to that.'

'But what should they kill me for?'

'Because you have found the way up here, and they never could believe it. Now, please to go; oh please to go. They will kill us both in a moment. Yes, I like you very much' – for I was teasing her to say it – 'very much indeed, and I will call you John Ridd, if you like; only please to go, John. And when your feet are well, you know, you can come and tell me how they are.'

'But I tell you, Lorna, I like you very much indeed, nearly as much as Annie, and a great deal more than Lizzie. And I never saw anyone like you; and I must come back again tomorrow, and so must you, to see me; and I will bring you such a maun of things – there are apples still, and a thrush I caught with only one leg broken, and our dog has just had puppies' –

'Oh dear, they won't let me have a dog. There is not a dog in the valley. They say they are such noisy things' –

'Only put your hand in mine, – what little things they are, Lorna! – and I will bring you the loveliest dog; I will show you just how long he is.'

'Hush!' A shout came down the valley; and all my heart was trembling, like water after sunset, and Lorna's face was altered from pleasant play to terror. She shrank to me, and looked up at me, with such a power of weakness, that I at once made up my mind, to save her, or to die with her. The little girl took courage from me, and put her cheek quite close to mine.

'I will tell you what to do. They are only looking for me. You see that hole, that hole there?'

She pointed to a little niche in the rock, which verged the meadow, about fifty yards away from us. In the fading of the twilight I could just descry it.

'Yes, I see it; but they will see me crossing the grass to get there.'

'Look! look!' She could hardly speak. 'There is a way out from the top of it; they would kill me if I told it. Oh, here they come; I can see them.'

The little maid turned as white as the snow which hung on the other side of the water, not bearing any fire-arms, but then at me, and she cried, 'Oh dear! oh dear!' And then she began to sob aloud, being so young and unready. But I drew her behind the withy-bushes, and close down to the water, where it was quiet, and shelving deep, ere it came to the lip of the chasm. Here they could not see either of us from the upper valley, and might have sought a long time for us, even when they came quite near, if the trees had been clad with their summer clothes. Luckily I had picked up my fish, and taken my three-pronged fork away.

Crouching in that hollow nest, as children get together in ever so little compass, I saw a dozen fierce men come down, on the other side of the water, not bearing any fire-arms, but looking lax and jovial, as if they were come from riding and a dinner taken hungrily. 'Queen, queen!' they were shouting, here and there, and now and then: 'where the pest is our little queen gone?'

'They always call me "queen", and I am to be queen by and by,' Lorna whispered to me, with her soft cheek on my rough one, and her little heart beating against me: 'oh, they are crossing by the timber there, and then they are sure to see us.'

'Stop,' said I; 'now I see what to do. I must get into the water, and you must go to sleep.'

'To be sure, yes, away in the meadow there. But how bitter cold it will be for you!'

She saw in a moment the way to do it, sooner than I could tell her; and there was no time to lose.

'Now mind you never come again,' she whispered over her shoulder, as she crept away with a childish twist, hiding her white front from me; 'only I shall come sometimes – oh, here they are, Madonna!'

Daring scarce to peep, I crept into the water, and lay down bodily in it, with my head between two blocks of stone, and some flood-drift combing over me. For all this time, they were shouting, and swearing, and keeping such a hallabaloo, that the rocks all round the valley rang; and my heart quaked, so (what with this and the cold) that the water began to gurgle round me, and lap upon the pebbles.

Neither in truth did I try to stop it, being now so desperate, between the fear and the wretchedness; till I caught a glimpse of the little maid, whose beauty and whose kindliness had made me yearn to be with her. And then I knew that for her sake I was bound to be brave, and hide myself. She was lying beneath a rock, thirty or forty yards from me, feigning to be fast asleep, with her dress spread beautifully, and her hair drawn over her.

Presently one of the great rough men came round a corner upon her; and there he stopped, and gazed awhile at her fairness and her innocence. Then he caught her up in his arms, and kissed her so that I heard him; and if I had only brought my gun, I would have tried to shoot him.

'Here our queen is! Here's the queen, here's the captain's daughter!' he shouted to his comrades; 'fast asleep, by God, and hearty! Now I have first claim to her; and no one else shall touch the child. Back to the bottle, all of you!'

He set her dainty little form upon his great square shoulder, and her narrow feet in one broad hand; and so in triumph marched away, with the purple velvet of her skirt ruffling in his long black beard, and the silken length of her hair fetched out, like a cloud by the wind, behind her.

Going up that darkened glen, little Lorna, riding still the largest and most fierce of them, turned and put up a hand to me; and I put up a hand to her, in the thick of the mist and the willows.

I crept into a bush for warmth, and rubbed my shivering legs on bark, and longed for mother's fagot. Then, as daylight sank below the forget-me-not of stars, with a sorrow to be quit, I knew that now must be my time to get away, if there were any.

Therefore, wringing my sodden breeches, I managed to crawl from the bank to the niche in the cliff, which Lorna had shown me.

Through the dusk, I had trouble to see the mouth, at even five landyards of distance; nevertheless I entered well, and held on by some dead fern-stems, and did hope that no one would shoot me. Then hearing a noise in front of me, and like a coward not knowing where, but afraid to turn round or think of it, I felt myself going down some deep passage, into a pit of darkness. It was no good to catch the sides, for the whole thing seemed to go with me. Then, without knowing how, I was leaning over a night of water.

This water was of black radiance, as are certain diamonds, spanned across with vaults of rock, and carrying no image, neither showing marge nor end, but centred (as it might be) with a bottomless indrawal.

But suddenly a robin sang (as they will do after dark, towards spring) in the brown fern and ivy behind me. I took it for our little Annie's voice (for she could call any robin), and gathering quick warm comfort, sprang up the steep way towards the starlight. Climbing back, as the stones glid down, I heard the cold greedy wave go lapping, like a blind black dog, into the distance of arches, and hollow depths of darkness.

I can assure you, and tell no lie, that I scrambled back to the mouth of that pit, as if the evil one had been after me. And sorely I repented now of all my boyish folly, or madness it might well be termed, in venturing, with none to help, and nothing to compel me, into that accursed valley.

Therefore I began to search with the utmost care and diligence, although my teeth were chattering, and all my bones beginning to ache, with the chilliness and the wetness. Before very long the moon appeared, over the edge of the mountain, and among the trees at the top of it; and then I espied rough steps, and rocky, made as if with a sledge-hammer, narrow, steep, and far asunder, scooped here and there in the side of the entrance, and then round a bulge of the cliff, like the marks upon a great brown loaf, where a hungry child has picked at it. And higher up, where the light of the moon shone broader upon the precipice, there seemed to be a rude broken track, like the shadow of a crooked stick thrown upon a house-wall.

I set foot in the lowest stirrup (as I might almost call it), and clung to the rock with my nails, and worked to make a jump into the second stirrup. And I compassed that too, with the aid of my stick. But the third step-hole was the hardest of all, and the rock swelled out on me over my breast, and there seemed to be no attempting it, until I espied a good stout rope hanging in a groove of shadow, and just managed to reach the end of it.

How I clomb up, and across the clearing, and found my way home through the Bagworthy forest, is more than I can remember now, for I took all the rest of it then as a dream, by reason of perfect weariness.

I deserved a good beating that night, after making such a fool of myself, and grinding good fustian to pieces. But nobody could get out of me, where I had spent all the day and evening; although they worried me never so much, and longed to shake me to pieces.

A Man Justly Popular

IT happened upon a November evening (when I was about fifteen years old, and out-growing my strength very rapidly, my sister Annie being turned thirteen, and a deal of rain having fallen, and all the troughs in the yard being flooded) that the brook was coming down in a great brown flood, as if the banks never belonged to it. The foaming of it, and the noise, and the cresting of the corners, and the up and down, like a wave of the sea, were enough to frighten any duck, though bred upon stormy waters, which our ducks never had been.

There is always a hurdle, nine feet long, and four and a half in depth, swung by a chain at either end from an oak laid across the channel. But now our old drake was jammed between two bars of this hurdle, by the joint of his shoulder, speaking aloud as he rose and fell, with his top-knot full of water, unable to comprehend it, with his tail washed far away from him, but often compelled to be silent, being ducked very harshly against his will by the choking fall-to of the hurdle. And then there was scarcely the screw of his tail to be seen until he swung up again, and left small doubt by the way he spluttered, and failed to quack, and hung down his poor crest, but that drown he must in another minute, and frogs triumph over his body.

Annie was crying, and wringing her hands, and I was about to rush into the water, although I liked not the look of it, but hoped to hold on by the hurdle, when a man on horseback came suddenly round the corner of the great ash-hedge on the other side of the stream, and his horse's feet were in the water.

'Ho, there,' he cried; 'get thee back, boy. The flood will

carry thee down like a straw. I will do it for thee, and no trouble.'

With that he leaned forward, and spoke to his mare – she was just of the tint of a strawberry, a young thing, very beautiful – and she arched up her neck, as misliking the job; yet, trusting him, would attempt it. She entered the flood, with her dainty fore-legs sloped further and further in front of her, and her delicate ears pricked forward, and the size of her great eyes increasing; but he kept her straight in the turbid rush, by the pressure of his knee on her. Then she looked back, and wondered at him, as the force of the torrent grew stronger, but he bade her go on; and on she went, and it foamed up over her shoulders; and she tossed up her lip and scorned it, for now her courage was waking. Then as the rush of it swept her away, and she struck with her fore-feet down the stream, he leaned from his saddle, in a manner which I never could have thought possible, and caught up the old drake with his left hand, and set him between his holsters, and smiled at his faint quack of gratitude. In a moment all three were carried down-stream, and the rider lay flat on his horse, and tossed the hurdle clear from him, and made for the bend of smooth water.

They landed, some thirty or forty yards lower, in the midst of our kitchen-garden, where the winter-cabbage was; but though Annie and I crept in through the hedge, and were full of our thanks, and admiring him, he would answer us never a word, until he had spoken in full to the mare, as if explaining the whole to her. She answered him kindly with her soft eyes, and sniffed at him very lovingly, and they understood one another.

Having taken all this trouble, the gentleman turned round to us, with a pleasant smile on his face, as if he were lightly amused with himself; and we came up and looked at him. He was rather short, but very strongly built and springy, as his gait at every step showed plainly, although his legs were bowed with much riding, and he looked as if he lived on horseback. To a boy like me he seemed very old, being over twenty, and well-found in beard; but he was not more than four-and-twenty, fresh and ruddy-looking, with a short nose, and keen blue eyes, and a merry waggish jerk about him, as if the world were not in earnest. Yet he had a sharp, stern way, like the crack of a pistol, if anything misliked him; and we knew (for children see such things) that it was safer to tickle than tackle him.

'Well, young uns, what be gaping at?' He gave pretty Annie a chuck on the chin, and took me all in without winking. 'I am thy mother's cousin, boy, and am going up to house. Tom Faggus is my name, as everybody knows; and this is my young mare, Winnie.'

What a fool I must have been not to know it at once! Tom Faggus, the great highwayman, and his young blood-mare, the strawberry! Already her fame was noised abroad, nearly as much as her master's, especially as there were rumours that she was not a mare after all, but a witch.

He stopped to sup that night with us, and having changed his wet things first, he seemed to be in fair appetite, and praised Annie's cooking mightily, with a relishing noise like a smack of his lips, and a rubbing of his hands together, whenever he could spare them.

He had gotten John Fry's best small-clothes on, for he said he was not good enough to go into my father's (which mother kept to look at), nor man enough to fill them. But John was over-proud to have it in his power to say, that such a famous man had ever dwelt in any clothes of his; and afterwards he made show of them. For Mr Faggus' glory, then, though not so great as now it is, was spreading very fast indeed all about our neighbourhood, and even as far as Bridgewater.

Tom Faggus was a jovial soul, if ever there has been one;

not making bones of little things, nor caring to seek evil. There was about him such a love of genuine human nature, that if a traveller said a good thing, he would give him back his purse again. It is true that he took people's money, more by force than fraud; and the law (being used to the other course) was bitterly moved against him, although he could quote precedent.

'Now let us go and see Winnie, Jack,' he said to me after supper; 'she must be grieving for me, and I never let her grieve long.'

I was too glad to go with him, and Annie came slyly after us.

'Hit me, Jack, and see what she will do. I will not let her hurt thee.' He was rubbing her ears, all the time he spoke, and she was leaning against him. Then I made believe to strike him, and in a moment she caught me by the waistband, and lifted me clean from the ground, and was casting me down to trample upon me, when he stopped her suddenly.

'What think you of that, boy? Have you horse, or dog, that would do that for you? Ay, and more than that she will do. If I were to whistle, by and by, in the tone that tells my danger, she would break this stable-door down, and rush into the room to me. Nothing will keep her from me, then, stone-wall, or church-tower. Ah, Winnie, Winnie, you little witch, we shall die together.'

Tom Faggus had much cause to be harsh with the world; and yet all acknowledged him very pleasant, when a man gave up his money. And often and often he paid the toll for the carriage coming after him, because he had emptied their pockets, and would not add inconvenience. By trade he had been a blacksmith, in the town of Northmolton in Devonshire, a rough rude place at the end of Exmoor; so that many people marvelled if such a man was bred there. Not only could he read and write, but he had solid substance, and made such a fame at the shoeing of horses, that the farriers of Barum were like to lose their custom. And indeed he won a golden Jacobus, for the best-shod nag in the north of Devon, and some say that he never was forgiven.

But whether it were that, or not, he fell into bitter trouble within a month of his victory. His trade was growing upon him, and his sweetheart ready to marry him, when suddenly, like a thunderbolt, a lawyer's writ fell upon him.

This was the beginning of a lawsuit with Sir Robert Bampfylde, a gentleman of the neighbourhood, who tried to oust him from his common, and drove his cattle, and harassed them. And by that suit of law poor Tom was ruined altogether, for Sir Robert could pay for much swearing; and then all his goods and his farm were sold up, and even his smithery taken, and his sweetheart married another.

All this was very sore upon Tom; and he took it to heart so grievously, that he said, as a better man might have said, being loose of mind and property, 'The world hath preyed on me, like a wolf. God help me now to prey on the world.'

And in sooth it did seem, for a while, as if Providence were with him; for he took rare toll on the highway, and his name was soon as good as gold anywhere this side of Bristowe.

One of his earliest meetings was with Sir Robert Bampfylde himself, who was riding along the Barum road, with only one serving-man after him. Tom Faggus put a pistol to his head, being then obliged to be violent, through want of reputation; while the serving-man pretended to be a long way round the corner. Then the baronet pulled out his purse, quite trembling in the hurry of his politeness. Tom took the purse, and his ring, and time-piece, and then handed them back with a very low bow, saying that it was against all usage for him to rob a robber. Then he turned to the unfaithful knave, and trounced him right well for his cowardice, and stripped him of all his property.

But now Mr Faggus kept only one horse, lest the Government should steal them; and that one was the young mare Winnie. When I have added that Faggus as yet had never been guilty of bloodshed (for his eyes, and the click of his pistol at first, and now his high reputation made all his wishes respected), and that he never robbed a poor man, neither insulted a woman, but was very good to the Church, and of hot patriotic opinions, and full of jest and jollity, I have said as much as is fair for him, and shown why he was so popular. Everybody cursed the Doones, who lived apart disdainfully. But all good people liked Mr Faggus – when he had not robbed them – and many a poor sick man or woman blessed him for other people's money; and all the hostlers, stable-boys, and tapsters entirely worshipped him.

Master Huckaback Comes In

MR REUBEN HUCKABACK, whom many good folk in Dulverton will remember long after my time, was my mother's uncle. He owned the very best shop in the town, and did a fine trade in soft ware, especially when the packhorses came safely in at Christmas-time. And we being now his only kindred, except indeed his grand-daughter, little Ruth Huckaback, mother beheld it a Christian duty to keep as well as could be with him, both for love of a nice old man, and for the sake of her children.

Now this old gentleman must needs come away that time to spend the New Year-tide with us; not that he wanted to do it (for he hated country life), but because of my mother's pressing.

It had been settled between us, that we should expect him soon after noon, on the last day of December. For the Doones being lazy and fond of bed, as the manner is of dishonest folk, the surest way to escape them was to travel before they were up and about, to wit, in the forenoon of the day. But herein we reckoned without our host: for being in high festivity, as became good Papists, the robbers were too lazy, it seems, to take the trouble of going to bed; and forth they rode on the Old Year-morning, not with any view to business, but purely in search of mischief.

We had put off our dinner till one o'clock (which to me was a sad foregoing), and there was to be a brave supper at six of the clock, upon New Year's-eve; and the singers to come with their lanthorns, and do it outside the parlour-window, and then have hot cup till their heads should go round, after making away with the victuals. And Nicholas Snowe was to come in the evening, with his three tall comely daughters.

Now when I came in, before one o'clock, after seeing to the cattle – for the day was thicker than ever, and we must keep the cattle close at home, if we wished to see any more of them – I fully expected to find Uncle Ben sitting in the fireplace.

But 'Oh Johnny, Johnny,' my mother cried, running out of the grand show-parlour, 'I am so glad you are come at last. There is something sadly amiss, Johnny.'

'Well, mother dear, I am very sorry. But let us have our dinner. You know we promised not to wait for him after one o'clock; and you only make us hungry. Everything will be spoiled, mother, and what a pity to think of! After that I will go to seek for him in the thick of the fog, like a needle in a hayband.'

So we made a very good dinner indeed, though wishing that he could have some of it, and wondering how much to leave for him; and then, as no sound of his horse had been heard, I set out with my gun to look for him.

I had little fear, being no more a school-boy now, but a youth well acquaint with Exmoor. My carbine was loaded and freshly primed, and I knew myself to be even now a match in strength for any two men of the size around our neighbourhood, except in the Glen Doone. 'Girt Jan Ridd', I was called already, and folk grew feared to wrestle with me; though I was tired of hearing about it, and often longed to be smaller.

The soft white mist came thicker around me, as the evening fell; and the peat-ricks here and there, and the furze-hucks of the summer-time, were all out of shape in the twist of it. And presently, while I was thinking 'What a fool I am!' arose as if from below my feet, a long lamenting lonesome sound, as of an evil spirit not knowing what to do with it. For the moment I stood like a root, without either hand or foot to help me; and the hair of my head began to crawl, lifting my hat, as a snail lifts his house; and my heart, like a shuttle, went to and fro. But finding no harm to come of it, neither visible form approaching, I wiped my forehead and hoped for the best, and resolved to run every step of the way, till I drew our big bolt behind me.

Yet here I was disappointed, for no sooner was I come to the crossways by the black pool in the hole, but I heard through the patter of my own feet a rough low sound, very close in the fog, as of a hobbled sheep a-coughing. I listened, and feared, and yet listened again, though I wanted not to hear it.

'Lord have mercy upon me! O Lord, upon my soul have mercy! An' if I cheated Sam Hicks last week, Lord knowest how well he deserved it, and lied in every stocking's mouth – oh Lord, where be I a-going?'

These words, with many jogs between them, came to me through the darkness, and then a long groan, and a choking. I made towards the sound, as nigh as ever I could guess, and presently was met, point-blank, by the head of a mountain-pony. Upon its back lay a man, bound down, with his feet on the neck and his head to the tail, and his arms falling down like stirrups. The wild little nag was scared of its life by the unaccustomed burden, and had been tossing and rolling hard, in desire to get ease of it.

'Good and worthy sir,' I said to the man who was riding so roughly; 'fear nothing: no harm shall come to thee.'

'Help, good friend, whoever thou art,' he gasped, but could not look at me, because his neck was jerked so; 'God hath sent thee; and not to rob me, because it is done already.'

'What, Uncle Ben!' I cried, 'Uncle Ben here in this plight! What, Mr Reuben Huckaback!'

'An honest hosier and draper, serge and long-cloth warehouseman' – he groaned from rib to rib – 'at the sign of the Gartered Kitten, in the loyal town of Dulverton. For God's sake, let me down, good fellow, from this accursed hurdle-chine; and a groat of good money will I pay thee, safe in my house to Dulverton; but take notice that the horse is mine, no less than the nag they robbed from me.'

'What, Uncle Ben, dost thou not know me, thy dutiful nephew, John Ridd?'

Not to make a long story of it, I cut the thongs that bound him, and set him astride on the little horse; but he was too weak to stay so. Therefore I mounted him on my back, turning the horse into horse-steps; and leading the pony by the cords, which I fastened around his nose, set out for Plover's Barrows.

My mother made a dreadful stir, to see Uncle Ben in such a sorry plight as this; so I left him to her care and Annie's; and soon they fed him rarely, while I went out to look to the comfort of the captured pony. And in truth he was worth the catching, and served us very well afterwards; though Uncle Ben was inclined to claim him for his business at Dulverton where they have carts, and that like. 'But,' I said, 'you shall have him, sir, and welcome, if you will only ride him home, as first I found you riding him.' And with that he dropped it.

A very strange old man he was, short in his manner, though long of body, glad to do the contrary thing to what any one expected of him, and always looking sharply at people as if he feared to be cheated.

Of course, the Doones, and nobody else, had robbed good Uncle Reuben; and then they grew sportive, and took his horse, an especially sober nag, and bound the master upon the wild one, for a little change as they told him. For two or three hours they had fine enjoyment, chasing him through the fog, and making much sport of his groanings; and then waxing hungry they went their way, and left him to opportunity.

On the following day Master Huckaback declared that he would stay with us only one day more, upon a certain condition.

'Upon what condition, Uncle Ben? I grieve that you find it so lonely. We will have Farmer Nicholas up again, and the singers, and' –

'The fashionable milkmaids. I thank you, let me be. The wenches are too loud for me. But my condition is this, Jack – that you shall guide me tomorrow, without a word to any one, to a place where I may well descry the dwelling of these scoundrel Doones, and learn the best way to get at them, when the time shall come. Can you do this for me? I will pay you well, boy.'

I promised very readily to do my best to serve him; but vowed I would take no money for it, not being so poor as that came to. Accordingly, on the day following, with Uncle Reuben mounted on my ancient Peggy, I made foot for the westward, directly after breakfast. Uncle Ben refused to go unless I would take a loaded gun; and indeed it was always wise to do so in those days of turbulence. I could see that he was half-amiss with his mind about the business, and not so full of security as an elderly man should keep himself. Therefore, out I spake and said –

'Uncle Reuben, have no fear. I know every inch of the ground, sir; and there is no danger nigh us.'

'Fear, boy! Who ever thought of fear? 'Tis the last thing would come across me. Pretty things they primroses.'

At once I thought of Lorna Doone, the little maid of so many years back, and how my fancy went with her. Could Lorna ever think of me? Was I not a lout gone by, only fit for loach-sticking? Had I ever seen a face fit to think of near her? The sudden flash, the quickness, the bright desire to know one's heart, and not withhold her own from it, the soft withdrawal of rich eyes, the longing to love somebody, anybody, anything not imbrued with wickedness –

My uncle interrupted me, misliking so much silence now, with the naked woods falling over us. For we were come to Bagworthy forest, the blackest and the loneliest place of all that keep the sun out. I kept quite close to Peggy's head, and Peggy kept quite close to me, and pricked her ears at everything. However, we saw nothing there, except a few old owls and hawks, and a magpie sitting all alone, until we came to the bank of the hill, where the pony could not climb it. Uncle Ben was very loth to get off, because the pony seemed good company, and he thought he could gallop away on her, if the worst came to the worst; but I persuaded him that now he must go to the end of it. Therefore we made Peggy fast, in a place where we could find her; and speaking cheerfully, as if there was nothing to be afraid of, he took his staff, and I my gun, to climb the thick ascent.

There was now no path of any kind; which added to our courage all it lessened of our comfort, because it proved that the robbers were not in the habit of passing there. And we knew that we could not go astray, so long as we breasted the hill before us; inasmuch as it formed the rampart, or side-fence of Glen Doone. At last, though very loth to do it, I was forced to leave my gun behind, because I required one hand to drag myself up the difficulty, and one to help Uncle

Reuben. And so at last we gained the top, and looked out from the edge of the forest, where the ground was very stony, and like the crest of a quarry; and no more trees between us and the brink of a cliff below, three hundred yards below it might be, all strong slope and gliddery. And now for the first time I was amazed at the appearance of the Doones' stronghold, and understood its nature.

The chine of highland, whereon we stood, curved to the right and left of us, keeping about the same elevation, and crowned with trees and brushwood. At about half a mile in front of us, but looking as if we could throw a stone to strike any man upon it, another crest, just like our own, bowed around to meet it; but failed, by reason of two narrow clefts, of which we could only see the brink. One of these clefts was the Doone-gate, with a portcullis of rock above it; and the other was the chasm, by which I had once made entrance. Betwixt them, where the hills fell back, as in a perfect oval, traversed by the winding water, lay a bright green valley, rimmed with sheer black rock, and seeming to have sunken bodily from the bleak rough heights above. It looked as if no frost could enter, neither winds go ruffling: only spring, and hope, and comfort, breathe to one another.

But for all that, Uncle Reuben was none the worse nor better. He looked down into Glen Doone first, and sniffed as if he were smelling it, like a sample of goods from a wholesale house; and then he looked at the hills over yonder, and then he stared at me.

'See what a pack of fools they be? See you not, how this great Doone valley may be taken in half-an-hour?'

'Yes, to be sure I do, uncle; if they like to give it up, I mean.'

'Three culverins on yonder hill, and three on the top of this one – and we have them under a pestle. Ah, I have seen the wars, my lad, from Keinton up to Naseby; and I might have been a General now, if they had taken my advice' –

But I was not attending to him, being drawn away on a sudden by a sight which never struck the sharp eyes of our General. For I had long ago descried that little opening in the cliff, through which I made my exit, as before related, on the other side of the valley. No bigger than a rabbit-hole it seemed from where we stood; and yet of all the scene before me, that had the most attraction. Now gazing at it, with full thought of all that it had cost me, I saw a little figure come, and pause, and pass into it. Something very light and white, nimble, smooth, and elegant, gone almost before I knew that any one had been there. And yet my heart came to my ribs, and all my blood was in my face, and pride within me fought with shame, and vanity with self-contempt; for though seven years were gone, and I from boyhood come to manhood, and she must have forgotten me, and I had half-forgotten; at that moment, once for all, I felt that I was face to face with fate, weal or woe, in Lorna Doone.

John is Bewitched

THE next day, Master Reuben Huckaback being gone, my spirit began to burn, and pant, for something to go on with; and nothing showed a braver hope of movement, and adventure, than a lonely visit to Glen Doone, by way of the perilous passage discovered in my boyhood. Therefore I waited for nothing more than the slow arrival of new small-clothes, made by a good tailor at Porlock, for it seemed a pure duty to look my best; and when they were come and approved, I started, regardless of the expense, and forgetting (like a fool) how badly they would take the water.

What with urging of the tailor, and my own misgivings, the time was now come round again to the high-day of St Valentine, when all our maids were full of lovers, and all the lads looked foolish. And none of them more sheepish, or more innocent, than I myself, albeit twenty-one years old, and not afraid of men much, but terrified of women, at least, if they were comely. And what of all things scared me most was the thought of my own size, and knowledge of my strength, which came, like knots, upon me daily. This time, not being now so much afraid, I struck across the thicket land between the meeting waters, and came upon the Bagworthy stream near the great black whirlpool. Nothing amazed me so much as to find how shallow the stream now looked to me, although the pool was still as black, and greedy, as it used to be. And still the great rocky slide was dark, and difficult to climb; though the water, which once had taken my knees was satisfied now with my ankles. After some labour, I reached the top; and halted to look about me well, before trusting to broad daylight.

The winter had been a very mild one; and now the spring was toward, so that bank and bush were touched with it. The valley into which I gazed was fair with early promise having shelter from the wind, and taking all the sunshine.

All the time, I kept myself in a black niche of the rock, where the fall of the water began, till presently I ventured to look forth, where a bush was; and then I beheld the loveliest sight – one glimpse of which was enough to make me kneel in the coldest water.

By the side of the stream, she was coming to me, even among the primroses, as if she loved them all. I could not see what her face was, my heart so awoke and trembled; only that her hair was flowing from a wreath of white violets, and the grace of her coming was like the appearance of the first wind-flower. The pale gleam over the western cliffs threw a shadow of light behind her, as if the sun were lingering. Never do I see that light from the closing of the west, even in these my aged days, without thinking of her. Ah me, if it comes to that, what do I see of earth or heaven, without thinking of her?

Scarcely knowing what I did, as if a rope were drawing me, I came from the dark mouth of the chasm; and stood, afraid to look at her.

She was turning to fly, not knowing me, and frightened, perhaps, at my stature; when I fell on the grass (as I fell before her seven years agone that day), and I just said, 'Lorna Doone!'

She knew me at once, from my manner and ways, and a smile broke through her trembling, as sunshine comes through willow leaves; and being so clever she saw, of course, that she needed not to fear me.

'Oh, indeed,' she cried, with a feint of anger (because she had shown her cowardice, and yet in her heart she was laughing); 'oh, if you please, who are you, sir, and how do you know my name?'

'I am John Ridd,' I answered; 'the boy who gave you those beautiful fish, when you were only a little thing, seven years ago today.'

'Yes, the poor boy who was frightened so, and obliged to hide here in the water.'

'And do you remember how kind you were, and saved my life by your quickness, and went away riding upon a great man's shoulder, as if you had never seen me, and yet looked back through the willow-trees?'

'Oh, yes, I remember everything; because it was so rare to see any, except, – I mean, because I happen to remember. But I think, Master Ridd, you cannot know what the dangers of this place are, and the nature of the people.'

'Yes, I know enough of that; and I am frightened greatly, all the time when I do not look at you.'

She was too young to answer me, in the style some maidens would have used; the manner, I mean, which now we call from a foreign word 'coquettish'.

'Mistress Lorna, I will depart' – mark you, I thought that a powerful word – 'in fear of causing disquiet. If any rogue shot me, it would grieve you; I make bold to say it. Try to think of me, now and then; and I will bring you some new-laid eggs, for our young blue hen is beginning.'

'I thank you heartily,' said Lorna; 'but you need not come to see me. You can put them in my little bower, where I am almost always – I mean whither daily I repair; to think and to be away from them.'

'Only show me where it is. Thrice a day, I will come and stop – '

'Nay, Master Ridd, I would never show thee – never, because of peril – only that so happens it, thou hast found the way already.'

And she smiled, with a light that made me care to cry out for no other way, only the way to her dear heart. But only to myself I cried for anything at all, having enough of man in me, to be bashful with young maidens. So I touched her white hand softly, and resolved to yield her all my goods, although my mother was living, and then grew angry with myself (for a mile or more of walking) to think she would condescend so; and then, for the rest of the homeward road, was mad with every man in the world, who would dare to think of looking at her.

After this, one thing (more than all the rest) worried and perplexed me. This was, that I could not settle, turn and twist it as I might, how soon I ought to go again upon a visit to Glen Doone. For I liked not at all the falseness of it (albeit against murderers), the creeping out of sight, and hiding, and feeling as a spy might. And even more than this, I feared how Lorna might regard it; whether I might seem to her a prone and blunt intruder, a country youth not skilled in manners, as among the quality, even when they rob us. For I was not sure myself, but that it might be very bad manners, to go again too early without an invitation. However, I could not bring myself to consult any one upon this point, at least in our own neighbourhood, nor even to speak of it near home.

Now the wisest person in all our parts was reckoned to be a certain wise woman, well known all over Exmoor by the name of 'Mother Melldrum'. She came of an ancient family, but neither of Devon nor Somerset. Nevertheless she was quite at home with our proper modes of divination; and knowing that we liked them best – as each man does his own religion – she would always practise them for the people of the country.

Although well nigh the end of March, the wind blew wild and piercing, as I went on foot, that afternoon, to Mother Melldrum's dwelling. It was safer not to take a horse, lest (if anything vexed her) she should put a spell upon him.

The sun was low on the edge of the hills, by the time I entered the valley, for I could not leave home till the cattle were tended, and the distance was seven miles or more. The shadows of rocks fell far and deep, and the sound of the sea came up, and went the length of the valley, and there it lapped on a butt of rocks, and murmured like a shell.

Taking things one with another, and feeling all the lonesomeness and having no stick with me, I was much inclined to go briskly back, and come at a better season. And when I beheld a tall grey shape, of something or another, moving at the lower end of the valley, where the shade was, it gave me such a stroke of fear, I would have gone home, and then been angry at my want of courage, but that on the very turn and bending of my footsteps, the woman in the distance lifted up her staff to me; so that I was bound to stop.

The fearful woman was coming near, and more near to me; and I was glad to sit down on a rock, because my knees were shaking so.

But when she was come so nigh to me that I could descry her features, there was something in her countenance that made me not dislike her. She looked as if she had been visited by a many troubles, and had felt them one by one; yet held enough of kindly nature still to grieve for others. Long white hair, on either side, was falling down below her chin; and through her wrinkles, clear bright eyes seemed to spread themselves upon me.

'Thou art not come to me,' she said, looking through my simple face, as if it were Bristol pebbles, 'to be struck for sciatica, nor to be blessed for shingles. Give me forth thy hand, John Ridd; and tell why thou art come to me.'

But I was so much amazed, at her knowing my name and all about me, that I feared to place my hand in her power, or even my tongue by speaking.

'Have no fear of me, my son; I have no gift to harm thee; and if I had, it should be idle. Now, if thou hast any wit, tell me why I love thee.'

'I never had any wit, mother,' I answered, in our Devonshire way; 'and never set eyes on thee before, to the furthest of my knowledge.'

'And yet I know thee as well, John, as if thou wert my grandson. Remember you the old Oare oak, and the bog at the head of Exe, and the child who would have died there, but for thy strength and courage, and most of all thy kindness? That was my grand-daughter, John; and all I have on earth to love.'

Now that she came to speak of it, with the place and that, so clearly, I remembered all about it (a thing that happened last August), and thought how stupid I must have been, not to learn more of the little maid, who had fallen into the black pit, with a basketful of whortleberries, and who might have been gulfed, if her little dog had not spied me in the distance. I carried her on my back to mother; and then we dressed her all anew, and took her where she ordered us; but she did not tell us who she was, nor anything more than her Christian name, and that she was eight years old, and fond of fried batatas. And we did not seek to ask her more; as our manner is with visitors.

But thinking of this little story, and seeing how she looked at me, I lost my fear of Mother Melldrum, and began to like her; partly because I had helped her grandchild, and partly that if she were so wise, no need would have been for me to save the little maid from drowning. Therefore I stood up and said, though scarcely yet established in my power against hers –

'Good mother, the shoe she lost was in the mire, and not with us. And we could not match it, although we gave her a pair of sister Lizzie's.'

'My son, what care I for her shoe? How simple thou art, and foolish; according to the thoughts of some. Now tell me, for thou canst not lie, what has brought thee to me.'

'I am come to know,' I said, looking at a rock the while, to keep my voice from shaking, 'when I may go to see Lorna Doone.'

No more could I say, though my mind was charged to ask fifty other questions. But although I looked away, it was plain that I had asked enough. I felt that the wise woman gazed at me in wrath, as well as sorrow; and then I grew angry that any one should seem to make light of Lorna.

'John Ridd,' said the woman, observing this (for now I faced her bravely), 'of whom art thou speaking? Is it a comely daughter of the men who slew your father?'

'I cannot tell, mother. How should I know? And what is that to thee?'

'It is something to thy mother, John; and something to thyself, I trow; and nothing worse could befall thee.'

I waited for her to speak again; because she had spoken so sadly, that it took my breath away.

'John Ridd, if thou hast any value for thy body or thy soul, thy mother, or thy father's name, have nought to do with any Doone.'

She gazed at me in earnest so, and raised her voice in saying it, until the whole valley, curving like a great bell, echoed 'Doone', that it seemed to me my heart was gone, for every one and everything. If it were God's will for me to have no more of Lorna, let a sign come out of the rocks, and I would try to believe it. But no sign came; and I turned on the woman, and longed that she had been a man.

'You poor dame, with bones and blades, pails of water, and door-keys, what know you about the destiny of a maiden such as Lorna? Chill-blain you may treat, and bone-shave, ringworm, and the scaldings; even scabby sheep may limp the better for your strikings. John the Baptist, and his cousins, with the wool and hyssop, are for mares, and ailing dogs, and fowls that have the jaundice. Look at me now, Mother Melldrum, am I like a fool?'

'That thou art, my son. Alas that it were any other!'

Lorna Begins Her Story

BUT when the weather changed in earnest, and the frost was gone, and the south-west wind blew softly, and the lambs were at play with the daisies, it was more than I could do to keep from thought of Lorna. And although my heart was leaping high, with the prospect of some adventure, and the fear of meeting Lorna, I could not but be gladdened by the softness of the weather, and the welcome way of everything.

And, in good sooth, I had to spring ere ever I got to the top of the rift leading into Doone-glade. For the stream was rushing down in strength, and raving at every corner; a mort of rain having fallen last night, and no wind come to wipe it. However, I reached the head ere dark, with more difficulty than danger; and sat in a place, which comforted my back and legs desirably.

Hereupon I grew so happy, at being on dry land again, and come to look for Lorna, with pretty trees around me, that what did I do but fall asleep with the holly-stick in front of me, and my best coat sunk in a bed of moss, among wetness and wood-sorrel. Mayhap I had not done so, nor yet enjoyed the spring so much, if so be I had not taken three-parts of a gallon of cider, at home at Plover's Barrows, because of the lowness, and the sinking, ever since I met Mother Melldrum.

Suddenly my sleep was broken by a shade cast over me; between me and the low sunlight, Lorna Doone was standing.

'Master Ridd, are you mad?' she said, and took my hand to move me.

'Not mad, but half asleep,' I answered, feigning not to notice her, that so she might keep hold of me.

'Come away, come away, if you care for life. The patrol will be here directly. Be quick, Master Ridd, let me hide thee.'

'I will not stir a step,' said I, though being in the greatest fright that might be well imagined; 'unless you call me "John".'

'Well, John, then – Master John Ridd; be quick, if you have any to care for you.'

'I have many that care for me,' I said, just to let her know; 'and I will follow you, Mistress Lorna; albeit without any hurry, unless there be peril to more than me.'

Without another word, she led me into her little bower, where the inlet through the rock was. I spoke before of a certain deep and perilous pit, in which I was like to drown myself, through hurry and fright of boyhood. And even then I wondered greatly, and was vexed with Lorna, for sending me in that heedless manner into such an entrance. But now it was clear, that she had been right, and the fault mine own entirely; for the entrance to the pit was only to be found by seeking it. Inside the niche of native stone, the plainest thing of all to see, at any rate by daylight, was the stairway hewn from rock, and leading up the mountain, by means of which I had escaped, as before related. To the right side of this was the mouth of the pit, still looking very formidable; though Lorna laughed at my fear of it, for she drew her water thence. But on the left was a narrow crevice, very difficult to espy, and having a sweep of grey ivy laid over it. A man here coming from the brightness of the outer air, with eyes dazed by the twilight, would never think of seeing this, and following it to its meaning.

Lorna raised the screen for me, but I had much ado to pass, on account of bulk and stature. However, I got through at last, and broke into the pleasant room, the lone retreat of Lorna.

The chamber was of unhewn rock, round, as near as might be, eighteen or twenty feet across, and gay with rich variety of fern, and moss, and lichen. Overhead there was no ceiling but the sky itself, flaked with little clouds of April whitely wandering over it. The floor was made of soft, low grass, mixed with moss and primroses; and in a niche of shelter moved the delicate wood-sorrel.

'Where are the new-laid eggs, Master Ridd? Or hath blue hen ceased laying?'

I did not altogether like the way in which she said it, with a sort of a dialect, as if my speech could be laughed at.

'Here be some,' I answered, speaking as if in spite of her. 'I would have brought thee twice as many, but that I feared to crush them in the narrow ways, Mistress Lorna.'

And so I laid her out two dozen upon the moss of the rock ledge, unwinding the wisp of hay from each, as it came safe out of my pocket. Lorna looked with growing wonder, as I added one to one; and when I had placed them side by side, and bidden her now to tell them, to my amazement what did she do but burst into a flood of tears!

'What have I done?' I asked, with shame, scarce daring even to look at her, 'oh, what have I done to vex you so?'

'It is nothing done by you, Master Ridd,' she answered, very proudly, as if nought I did could matter; 'it is only something that comes upon me, with the scent of the pure true clover-hay. Moreover, you have been too kind; and I am not used to kindness.'

Some sort of awkwardness was on me, at her words and weeping, as if I would like to say something, but feared to make things worse perhaps than they were already. Therefore I abstained from speech, as I would in my own pain. And as it happened, this was the way to make her tell me more about it.

Lorna went a little way, as if she would not think of me, nor care for one so careless; and all my heart gave a sudden jump, to go like a mad thing after her; until she turned of her own accord, and with a little sigh came back to me. And then, without any let or hindrance, sitting over against me, now raising and now dropping fringe, over those sweet eyes that were the road-lights of her tongue, Lorna told me all about everything I wished to know, every little thing she knew, except indeed that point of points, how Master Ridd stood with her.

'There are but two in the world, who ever listen and try to help me; one of them is my grandfather, and the other is a man of wisdom, whom we call the Counsellor. My grandfather, Sir Ensor Doone, is very old and harsh of manner (except indeed to me); he seems to know what is right and wrong, but not to want to think of it. The Counsellor, on the other hand, though full of life and subtleties, treats my questions as of play, and not gravely worth his while to answer, unless he can make wit of them.

'I have no remembrance now of father, or of mother; although they say that my father was the eldest son of Sir Ensor Doone, and the bravest, and the best of them. And so they call me heiress to this little realm of violence; and in sorry sport sometimes, I am their Princess, or their Queen.

'Many people living here, as I am forced to do, would perhaps be very happy, and perhaps I ought to be so. We have a beauteous valley, the grass is so fresh, and the brook so bright and lively, and flowers of so many hues come after one another, that no one need be dull, if only left alone with them.

'Meantime, all around me is violence and robbery, coarse delight and savage pain, reckless joke and hopeless death. Is it any wonder, that I cannot sink with these, that I cannot so forget my soul, as to live the life of brutes, and die the death more horrible, because it dreams of waking? There is none to lead me forward, there is none to teach me right; young as I am, I live beneath a curse that lasts for ever.'

Here Lorna broke down for awhile, and cried so very piteously, that doubting of my knowledge, and my right or power to comfort, I did my best to hold my peace, and tried to look very cheerful. Then thinking that might be bad manners, I went to wipe her eyes for her.

'It does not happen many times, that I give way like this; more shame now to do so, when I ought to entertain you.

'We should not be so quiet here, and safe from interruption, but that I have begged one privilege, rather than commanded it. This was, that the lower end, just this narrowing of the valley, where it is most hard to come at, might be looked upon as mine, except for purposes of guard. Therefore none, beside the sentries, ever trespass on me here, unless it be my grandfather, or the Counsellor, or Carver.

'By your face, Master Ridd, I see that you have heard of Carver Doone. For strength, and courage, and resource, he bears the first repute among us, as might well be expected from the son of the Counsellor. But he differs from his father, in being very hot and savage, and quite free from argument.

'You must be tired of this story, but my life from day to day shows so little variance. Among the riders there is none whose safe return I watch for – I mean none more than other – and indeed there seems no risk; all are now so feared of us. Neither of the old men is there, whom I can revere or love (except alone my grandfather, whom I love with trembling); neither of the women any whom I like to deal with, unless it be a little maiden, whom I saved from starving.

'A little Cornish girl she is, and shaped in western manner; not so very much less in width, than if you take her lengthwise. Her father seems to have been a miner, a Cornishman (as she declares) of more than average excellence, and better than any two men to be found in Devonshire, or any four in Somerset. Very few things can have been beyond his power of performance; and yet he left his daughter to starve upon a peat-rick. She does not know how this was done, and looks upon it as a mystery, the meaning of which will some day be clear, and redound to her father's honour. His name was Simon Carfax, and he came as the captain of a gang, from one of the Cornish tin-mines. Gwenny Carfax, my young maid, well remembers how her father was brought up from Cornwall. Her mother had been buried, just a week or so before; and he was sad about it, and had been off his work, and was ready for another job. Then people came to him by night, and said that he must want a change, and everybody lost their wives, and work was the way to mend it. So what with grief, and over-thought, and the inside of a square bottle, Gwenny says they brought him off, to become a mighty captain, and choose the country round. The last she saw of him was this, that he went down a ladder somewhere on the wilds of Exmoor, leaving her with bread and cheese, and his travelling-hat to see to. And from that day to this, he never came above the ground again; so far as we can hear of.

'But Gwenny, holding to his hat, and having eaten the bread and cheese (when he came no more to help her), dwelt three days near the mouth of the hole; and then it was closed over, the while that she was sleeping. With weakness, and with want of food, she lost herself distressfully, and went away, for miles or more, and lay upon a peat-rick, to die before the ravens.

'I found this little stray thing lying, with her arms upon her, and not a sign of life, except the way that she was biting. Black root-stuff was in her mouth, and a piece of dirty sheep's wool, and at her feet an old egg-shell of some bird of the moorland. I brought her home with me, so far as this can be a home; and she made herself my sole attendant, without so much as asking me. She seems to have no kind of fear even of our roughest men; and yet she looks with reverence and awe upon the Counsellor. As for the wickedness, and theft, and revelry around her, she says it is no concern of hers, and they know their own business best. By this way of regarding men, she has won upon our riders; so that she is almost free from all control of place and season, and is allowed to pass where none even of the youths may go. Being so wide, and short, and flat, she has none to pay her compliments; and, were there any, she would scorn them, as not being Cornishmen. Sometimes she wanders far, by moonlight, on the moors, and up the rivers, to give her father (as she says) another chance of finding her; and she comes back, not a whit defeated, or discouraged, but confident that he is only waiting for the proper time.

'Herein she sets me good example of a patience and contentment, hard for me to imitate. Oftentimes, I am so vexed by things I cannot meddle with, yet cannot keep away from me, that I am at the point of flying from this dreadful valley, and risking all that can betide me, in the unknown outer world. If it were not for my grandfather, I would have done so long ago; but I cannot bear that he should die, with no gentle hand to comfort him; and I fear to think of the conflict, that must ensue for the government, if there be a disputed succession.

'Once indeed, I had the offer of escape, and kinsman's aid, and high place in the gay, bright world; and yet I was not tempted much, or, at least, dared not to trust it. And it ended very sadly, so dreadfully, that I even shrink from telling you about it; for that one terror changed my life, in a moment, at a blow, from childhood, and from thoughts of play, and commune with the flowers and trees, to sense of death and darkness and a heavy weight of earth.'

Lorna Ends Her Story

'It is scarce a twelvemonth yet, although it seems ten years agone. The fifteenth day of last July was very hot and sultry, long after the time of sundown; and I was paying heed to it, because of the old saying that if it rain then, rain will fall on forty days thereafter. I had been long by the waterside, at this lower end of the valley, plaiting a little crown of woodbine crocketed with sprigs of heath, – to please my grandfather, who likes to see me gay at supper-time.

'I made short cut through the ash-trees covert, which lies in the middle of our vale, with the water skirting, or cleaving it. You have never been up so far as that – at least to the best of my knowledge – but you see it, like a long grey spot, from the top of the cliffs above us. Here I was not likely to meet any of our people; because the young ones are afraid of some ancient tale about it, and the old ones have no love of trees, where gun-shots are uncertain.

'At a sudden turn of the narrow path, where it stooped again to the river, a man leaped out from behind a tree, and stopped me, and seized hold of me. I tried to shriek, but my voice was still; and I could only hear my heart.

'"Now, Cousin Lorna, my good cousin," he said, with ease, and calmness; "your voice is very sweet, no doubt, from all that I can see of you. But I pray you keep it still, unless you would give to dusty death your very best cousin, and trusty guardian, Alan Brandir of Loch Awe."

'"You my guardian!" I said, for the idea was too ludicrous; and ludicrous things always strike me first, through some fault of nature.

'"I have in truth that honour, madam," he answered with a sweeping bow; "unless I err in taking you for Mistress Lorna Doone."

'"You have not mistaken me. My name is Lorna Doone."

'"Then I am your faithful guardian, Alan Brandir of Loch Awe; called Lord Alan Brandir, son of a worthy peer of Scotland. Now will you confide in me?"

'"I confide in you!" I cried, looking at him with amazement; "why you are not older than I am!"

'"Yes I am, three years at least. You, my ward, are not sixteen. I, your worshipful guardian, am almost nineteen years of age!"

'Upon hearing this I looked at him, for that seemed then a venerable age; but the more I looked, the more I doubted, although he was dressed quite like a man. He led me, in a courtly manner, stepping at his tallest, to an open place beside the water where the light came in.

'"Now am I to your liking, cousin?" he asked, when I had gazed at him, until I was almost ashamed, except at such a stripling. "Does my Cousin Lorna judge kindly of her guardian, and her nearest kinsman? In a word, is our admiration mutual?"

'And as I gazed on this slight fair youth, clearly one of high birth and breeding (albeit over-boastful), a chill of fear crept over me; because he had no strength or substance, and would be no more than a pin-cushion, before the great swords of the Doones.

' "I pray be you not vexed with me," he went on in a softer voice; "for I have travelled far and sorely, for the sake of seeing you. I know right well among whom I am, and that their hospitality is more of the knife than the salt-stand. Nevertheless I am safe enough, for my foot is the fleetest in Scotland; and what are such hills as these to me? Tush! I have seen some border forays, among wilder spirits, and craftier men than these be. Once I mind some years agone, when I was quite a stripling lad," –

' "Worshipful guardian," I said, "there is no time now for history. If thou art in no haste, I am, and cannot stay here idling. Only tell me, how I am akin and under wardship to thee, and what purpose brings thee here."

' "In order, cousin – all things in order, even with fair ladies. First, I am thy uncle's son, my father is thy mother's brother, or at least thy grandmother's, – unless I am deceived in that which I have guessed, and no other man. But first, your leave, young Mistress Lorna; I cannot lay down legal maxims, without aid of smoke."

'He leaned against a willow-tree, and drawing from a gilded box a little dark thing like a stick, placed it between his lips, and then striking a flint on steel, made fire, and caught it upon touch-wood. With this he kindled the tip of the stick, until it glowed with a ring of red, and then he breathed forth curls of smoke, blue, and smelling on the air, like spice. I had never seen this done before, though acquainted with tobacco-pipes; and it made me laugh, until I thought of the peril that must follow it.

' "Cousin, have no fear," he said; "this makes me all the safer; they will take me for a glow worm, and thee for the flower it shines upon. But to return – of law I learned, as you may suppose, but little; although I have capacities. But the thing was far too dull for me. But heed not that; enough that being curious now, I followed up the quarry, and I am come to this at last – we, even we, the lords of Loch Awe, have an outlaw for our cousin; and I would we had more, if they be like you."

' "Sir," I answered, being amused by his manner, which was new to me (for the Doones are much in earnest), "surely you count it no disgrace, to be of kin to Sir Ensor Doone, and all his honest family!"

' "If it be so, it is in truth the very highest honour, and would heal ten holes in our escutcheon. What noble family, but springs from a captain among robbers? Trade alone can spoil our blood; robbery purifies it. The robbery of one age is the chivalry of the next. We may start anew, and vie with even the nobility of France, if we can once enrol but half the Doones upon our lineage."

' "I like not to hear you speak of the Doones, as if they were no more than that," I exclaimed, being now unreasonable; "but will you tell me, once for all, sir, how you are my guardian?"

' "That I will do. You are my ward, because you were my father's ward, under the Scottish law; and now my father being so deaf, I have succeeded to that right – at least in my own opinion – under which claim I am here, to neglect my trust no longer, but to lead you away from scenes and deeds, which (though of good repute and comely) are not the best for young gentlewomen. There, spoke I not like a guardian? After that can you mistrust me?"

'I turned aside, and thought a little. Although he seemed so light of mind, and gay in dress and manner, I could not doubt his honesty; and saw, beneath his jaunty air, true mettle, and ripe bravery. Moreover I felt (though not as now) that Doone Glen was no place for me, or any proud young maiden. But while I thought, the yellow lightning spread behind a bulk of clouds, three times ere the flash was done, far off, and void of thunder; and from the pile of cloud before it, cut as from black paper, and lit to depths of blackness by the blaze behind it, a form as of an aged man, sitting in a chair, loose-mantled, seemed to lift a hand, and warn.

'This minded me of my grandfather, and all the care I owed him. Moreover, now the storm was rising, and I began to grow afraid; for of all things awful to me, thunder is the dreadfulest.

' "I cannot go, I will not go with you, Lord Alan Brandir. You are not grave enough for me, you are not old enough for me. Nor would I leave my grandfather, without his full permission. I thank you much for coming, sir; but begone at once by the way you came; and pray how did you come, sir?"

' "Down the cliffs I came; and up them I must make way back again. Now adieu, fair cousin Lorna, I see you are in haste tonight; but I am right proud of my guardianship. Give me just one flower for token" – here he kissed his hand to me, and I threw him a truss of woodbine – "adieu, fair cousin, trust me well, I will soon be here again."

' "That thou never shalt, sir," cried a voice as loud as a culverin; and Carver Doone had Alan Brandir, as a spider hath a fly. The boy made a little shriek at first, with the sudden shock and the terror; then he looked, methought, ashamed of himself, and set his face to fight for it. Very bravely he strove, and struggled, to free one arm, and to grasp his sword; but as well might an infant buried alive attempt to lift his gravestone. Carver Doone, with his great arms wrapped around the slim gay body, smiled (as I saw by the flash from heaven) at the poor young face turned up to him; then (as a nurse bears off a child, who is loth to go to bed) he lifted the youth from his feet, and bore him away into the darkness.

'I was young then. I am older now: older by ten years, in thought, although it is not a twelvemonth since. If that black deed were done again, I could follow, and could combat it, could throw weak arms on the murderer, and strive to be murdered also. I am now at home with violence; and no dark death surprises me.

'But, being as I was that night, the horror overcame me. The crash of thunder overhead, the last despairing look, the death-piece framed with blaze of lightning – my young heart was so affrighted, that I could not gasp.

'Yet hearkening, as a coward does, through the wailing of the wind, and echo of far noises, I heard a sharp sound as of iron, and a fall of heavy wood. No unmanly shriek came with it, neither cry for mercy. Carver Doone knows what it was; and so did Alan Brandir.'

Here Lorna Doone could tell no more, being overcome with weeping. Only through her tears she whispered, as a thing too bad to tell, that she had seen that giant Carver, in a few days afterwards, smoking a little round brown stick, like those of her poor cousin. I could not press her any more with questions, or for clearness; although I longed very much to know, whether she had spoken of it, to her grandfather, or the Counsellor. But she was now in such condition, both of mind and body, from the force of her own fear multiplied by telling it, that I did nothing more than coax her, at a distance humbly; and so that she could see that some one was at least afraid of her. This so brought her round, that all her fear was now for me, and how to get me safely off, without mischance to any one.

But the worst of all was this, that in my great dismay and anguish to see Lorna weeping so, I promised not to cause her any further trouble from anxiety and fear of harm. And this being brought to practice, meant that I was not to show myself within the precincts of Glen Doone, for at least another month. Unless indeed (as I contrived to edge into the agreement) anything should happen to increase her present trouble and every day's uneasiness. In that case, she was to throw a dark mantle, or covering of some sort, over a large white stone, which hung within the entrance to her retreat – I mean the outer entrance – and which, though unseen from the valley itself, was conspicuous from the height where I had stood with Uncle Reuben.

A Royal Invitation

ONE day, when work was over, I had seen to the horses and just as I was saying to myself, that in five days more my month would be done, and myself free to seek Lorna, a man came riding up from the ford where the road goes through the Lynn stream. He stopped at our gate, and stood up from his saddle, and holloed, as if he were somebody; and all the time he was flourishing a white thing in the air, like the bands our parson weareth. So I crossed the court-yard to speak with him.

'Service of the King!' he saith; 'service of our lord the King! Come hither, thou great yokel, at risk of fine and imprisonment.

'Plover Barrows farm!' said he; 'God only knows how tired I be. Is there anywhere in this cursed county a cursed place called "Plover Barrows farm"? For last twenty mile at least they told me, 'twere only half-a-mile further, or only just round corner. Now tell me that, and I fain would thwack thee, if thou were not thrice my size.'

'Sir,' I replied, 'you shall not have the trouble. This is Plover's Barrows farm, and you are kindly welcome. Sheep's kidneys is for supper, and the ale got bright from the tapping. But why do you think ill of us? We like not to be cursed so.'

'Nay, I think no ill,' he said; 'sheep's kidneys is good, uncommon good, if they do them without burning. But I be so galled in the saddle ten days, and never a comely meal of it.

And when they hear "King's service" cried, they give me the worst of everything. All the way down from London, I had a rogue of a fellow in front of me, eating the fat of the land before me, and every one bowing down to him. He could go three miles to my one, though he never changed his horse. He might have robbed me at any minute, if I had been worth the trouble. A red mare he rideth, strong in the loins, and pointed quite small in the head. I shall live to see him hanged yet.'

All this time he was riding across the straw of our courtyard, getting his weary legs out of the leathers, and almost afraid to stand yet. A coarse-grained, hard-faced man he was, some forty years of age or so, and of middle height and stature. Across the holsters lay his cloak, made of some red skin, and shining from the sweating of the horse.

'But stay, almost I forgot my business. Hungry I am, and sore of body, from my heels right upward, and sorest in front of my doublet; yet may I not rest, nor bite barley-bread, until I have seen and touched John Ridd. God grant that he be not far away; I must eat my saddle, if it be so.'

'Have no fear, good sir,' I answered; 'you have seen and touched John Ridd. I am he, and not one likely to go beneath a bushel.'

'It would take a large bushel to hold thee, John Ridd. In the name of the King, His Majesty, Charles the Second, these presents!'

He touched me with the white thing which I had first seen him waving, and which I now beheld to be sheepskin, such as they call parchment. It was tied across with cord, and fastened down in every corner with unsightly dabs of wax. By order of the messenger (for I was over-frightened now to think of doing anything), I broke enough of seals to keep an Easter ghost from rising; and there I saw my name in large.

'Read, my son; read, thou great fool, if indeed thou canst read,' said the officer to encourage me; 'there is nothing to kill thee, boy, and my supper will be spoiling. Stare not at me so, thou fool; thou art big enough to eat me; read, read, read.'

'If you please, sir, what is your name?' I asked: though why I asked him I know not, except from fear of witchcraft.

'Jeremy Stickles is my name, lad, nothing more than a poor apparitor of the worshipful Court of King's Bench. And at this moment a starving one, and no supper for me, unless thou wilt read.'

Being compelled in this way, I read pretty nigh as follows; not that I give the whole of it, but only the gist and the emphasis: –

'To our good subject, John Ridd, etc.' – describing me ever so much better than I knew myself – 'by these presents, greeting. These are to require thee, in the name of our lord the King, to appear in person before the Right Worshipful the Justices of His Majesty's Bench at Westminster, laying aside all thine own business, and there to deliver such evidence as is within thy cognizance, touching certain matters whereby the peace of our said lord the King, and the well-being of this realm, is, are, or otherwise may be impeached, impugned, imperilled, or otherwise detrimented. As witness these presents.' And then there were four seals, and then a signature I could not make out, only that it began with a J, and ended with some other writing, done almost in a circle. Underneath was added in a different handwriting, 'Charges will be borne. The matter is full urgent.'

The messenger watched me, while I read so much as I could read of it; and he seemed well-pleased with my surprise, because he had expected it. Then, not knowing what else to do, I looked again at the cover, and on the top of it I saw, 'Ride, Ride, Ride! On His Gracious Majesty's business; spur and spare not.'

It may be supposed by all who know me, that I was taken hereupon with such a giddiness in my head, and noisiness in my ears, that I was forced to hold by the crook driven in below the thatch for holding of the hay-rakes. There was scarcely any sense left in me, only that the thing was come by power of Mother Melldrum, because I despised her warning, and had again sought Lorna.

And what would Lorna think of me? Here was the long month just expired, after worlds of waiting; there would be her lovely self, peeping softly down the glen, and fearing to encourage me; yet there would be nobody else, and what an insult to her! Now my only chance of seeing her, before I went, lay in watching from the cliff and espying her, or a signal from her.

This, however, I did in vain, until my eyes were weary, and often would delude themselves with hope of what they ached for. But though I lay hidden behind the trees upon the crest of the stony fall, and waited so quiet that the rabbits and squirrels played around me, and even the keen-eyed weasel took me for a trunk of wood – it was all as one; no cast of colour changed the white stone, whose whiteness now was hateful to me; nor did wreath or skirt of maiden break the loneliness of the vale.

The Judge Makes His Mark

A JOURNEY to London seemed to us, in those bygone days, as hazardous and dark an adventure as could be forced on any man. I mean, of course, a poor man; for to a great nobleman with ever so many outriders, attendants, and retainers, the risk was not so great, unless the highwaymen knew of their coming beforehand, and so combined against them. To a poor man, however, the risk was not so much from those gentlemen of the road, as from the more ignoble footpads, and the landlords of the lesser hostels, and the loose unguarded soldiers, over and above the pitfalls and the quagmires of the way; so that it was hard to settle, at the first out-going, whether a man were wise to pray more for his neck or for his head.

And indeed, we never could have made our journey without either fight or running, but for the free pass which dear Annie had procured from Master Faggus. (I had for some time suspected a love between them.) And when I let it be known, by some hap, that I was the own cousin of Tom Faggus, and honoured with his society, there was not a house upon the road but was proud to entertain me, in spite of my fellow-traveller bearing the red badge of the King.

'I will keep this close, my son Jack,' he said, having stripped it off with a carving-knife; 'your flag is the best to fly. The man who starved me on the way down, the same shall feed me fat going home.'

Therefore we pursued our way, in excellent condition, having thriven upon the credit of that very popular highwayman, and being surrounded with regrets that he had left the profession, and sometimes begged to intercede that he might help the road again. For all the landlords on the road declared that now small ale was drunk, nor much of spirits called for; because the farmers need not prime to meet only common riders, neither were these worth the while to get drunk with afterwards. Master Stickles himself undertook, as an officer of the King's Justices, to plead this case with Squire Faggus (as everybody called him now), and to induce him, for the general good, to return to his proper ministry.

The night was falling very thick by the time we were come to Tyburn, and here the King's officer decided that it would be wise to halt; because the way was unsafe by night across the fields to Charing village. I for my part was nothing loth, and preferred to see London by daylight.

And after all, it was not worth seeing, but a very hideous and dirty place, not at all like Exmoor. Some of the shops were very fine, and the signs above them finer still, so that I was never weary of standing still to look at them.

But this being the year of our Lord 1683, more than nine years and a half since the death of my father, and the beginning of this history, all London was in a great ferment, about a dispute between the Court of the King and the City. This seemed to occupy all the attention of the judges, and my case (which had appeared so urgent) was put off from time to time, while the Court and the City contended.

I had heard of the law's delays, but I never thought at my years to have such bitter experience of the evil; and it seemed to me that if the lawyers failed to do their duty, they ought to pay people for waiting upon them, instead of making them pay for it. But here I was, now in the second month, living at my own charges, in the house of a worthy furrier at the sign of the Seal and Squirrel, abutting upon the Strand road, which leads from Temple Bar to Charing. Here I did very well indeed, having a mattrass of good skin-dressings, and plenty to eat every day of my life, but the butter was something to cry 'but' thrice at (according to a conceit of our school days), and the milk must have come from cows driven to water. However, these evils were light compared with the heavy bill sent up to me, every Saturday afternoon.

At length, being quite at the end of my money, and seeing no other help for it, I determined to listen to clerks no more, but force my way up to the Justices, and insist upon being heard by them, or discharged from my recognisance. For so they had termed the bond or deed which I had been forced to execute, in the presence of a chief clerk or notary, the very day after I came to London. And the purport of it was, that on pain of a heavy fine or escheatment, I would hold myself ready and present, to give evidence when called upon. Having delivered me up to sign this, Jeremy Stickles was quit of me, and went upon other business; not but what he was kind and good to me, when his time and pursuits allowed of it.

And so it was that one day, according to special orders, I stood, face to face, and alone with Judge Jeffreys.

His lordship was busy with some letters, and did not look up for a minute or two, although he knew that I was there. Then he closed his letters, well-pleased with their import, and fixed his bold broad stare on me, as if I were an oyster opened, and he would know how fresh I was.

'May it please your worship,' I said, 'here I am according to order, awaiting your good pleasure.'

'Thou art made to weight, John, more than order. How much dost thou tip the scales to?'

'Only twelvescore pounds, my lord, when I be in wrestling trim. And sure I must have lost weight here, fretting so long in London.'

'Ha, ha! Much fret is there in thee! Hath His Majesty seen thee?'

'Yes, my lord, twice or even thrice; and he made some jest concerning me.'

'A very bad one, I doubt not. His humour is not so dainty as mine, but apt to be coarse and unmannerly. Now John, or Jack, by the look of thee, thou art more used to be called.'

'Yes, your worship, when I am with old Molly, and Betty Muxworthy.'

'Peace, thou forward varlet! There is a deal too much of thee. We shall have to try short commons with thee, and thou art a very long common. Ha, ha! where is that rogue Spank? Spank must hear that by-and-by. It is beyond thy great thick head, Jack.'

'Not so, my lord; I have been to school, and had very bad jokes made upon me.'

'Ha, ha! It hath hit thee hard. And faith, it would be hard to miss thee, even with harpoon. And thou lookest like to blubber, now. Capital, in faith! I have thee on every side,

Jack, and thy sides are manifold; many-folded at any rate. Thou shalt have double expenses, Jack, for the wit thou hast provoked in me.'

'Heavy goods lack heavy payment, is a proverb down our way, my lord.'

'Ah, I hurt thee, I hurt thee, Jack. The harpoon hath no tickle for thee. Now, Jack Whale, having hauled thee hard, we will proceed to examine thee.' Here all his manner was changed, and he looked with his heavy brows bent upon me, as if he had never laughed in his life, and would allow none else to do so.

'I am ready to answer, my lord,' I replied, 'if he asks me nought beyond my knowledge, or beyond my honour.'

'Hadst better answer me everything, lump. What hast thou to do with honour? Now is there in thy neighbourhood a certain nest of robbers, miscreants, and outlaws, whom all men fear to handle?'

'Yes, my lord. At least I believe some of them be robbers; and all of them are outlaws.'

'And what is your high sheriff about, that he doth not hang them all? Or send them up for me to hang, without more to-do about them?'

'I reckon that he is afraid, my lord; it is not safe to meddle with them. They are of good birth, and reckless; and their place is very strong.'

'Good birth! What was Lord Russell of, Lord Essex, and this Sidney? 'Tis the surest heirship to the block, to be the chip of an old one. What is the name of this pestilent race, and how many of them are there?'

'They are the Doones of Bagworthy forest, may it please your worship. And we reckon there be about forty of them, beside the women and children.'

'Forty Doones, all forty thieves; and women and children! Thunder of God! How long have they been there then?'

'They may have been there thirty years, my lord; and

indeed they may have been forty. Before the great war broke out they came, longer back than I can remember.'

'Ay, long before thou wast born, John. Good, thou speakest plainly. Woe betide a liar, whenso I get hold of him. Ye want me on the Western Circuit; by God, and ye shall have me, when London traitors are spun and swung. Riotous knaves in West England, drunken outlaws, you shall dance, if ever I play pipe for you. John Ridd, I will come to Oare Parish, and rout out the Oare of Babylon.'

'Although your worship is so learned,' I answered, seeing that now he was beginning to make things uneasy; 'your worship, though being Chief Justice, does little justice to us. We are downright good and loyal folk; and I have not seen, since here I came to this great town of London, any who may better us, or even come anigh us, in honesty, and goodness, and duty to our neighbours. For we are very quiet folk, not prating our own virtues' –

'Enough, good John, enough! Knowest thou not that modesty is the maidenhood of virtue, lost even by her own approval?

'Now hast thou ever seen a man, whose name is Thomas Faggus?'

'Yes, sir, many and many a time. He is my own worthy cousin; and I fear that he hath intentions' – here I stopped, having no right there to speak about our Annie.

'Tom Faggus is a good man,' he said; and his great square face had a smile which showed me he had met my cousin; 'Master Faggus hath made mistakes as to the title to property, as lawyers oftentimes may do; but take him all for all, he is a thoroughly straightforward man; presents his bill, and has it paid, and makes no charge for drawing it. Nevertheless, we must tax his costs, as of any other solicitor.'

'To be sure, to be sure, my lord!' was all that I could say, not understanding what all this meant.

'I fear he will come to the gallows,' said the Lord Chief

Justice, sinking his voice below the echoes; 'tell him this from me, Jack. He shall never be condemned before me; but I cannot be everywhere; and some of our Justices may keep short memory of his dinners. Tell him to change his name, turn parson, or do something else, to make it wrong to hang him. Parson is the best thing; he hath such command of features, and he might take his tithes on horseback. Now a few more things, John Ridd; and for the present I have done with thee.'

All my heart leaped up at this, to get away from London so: and yet I could hardly trust to it.

'Is there any sound round your way of disaffection to His Majesty, His most gracious Majesty?'

'No, my lord: no sign whatever. We pray for him in church perhaps; and we talk about him afterwards, hoping it may do him good, as it is intended. But after that we have nought to say, not knowing much about him – at least till I get home again.'

'That is as it should be, John. And the less you say the better. But I have heard of things in Taunton, and even nearer to you in Dulverton, and even nigher still upon Exmoor; things which are of the pillory kind, and even more of the gallows. I see that you know nought of them. Nevertheless, it will not be long before all England hears of them. Now, John, I have taken a liking to thee; for never man told me the truth, without fear or favour, more thoroughly and truly than thou hast done. Keep thou clear of this, my son. It will come to nothing; yet many shall swing high for it. Even I could not save thee, John Ridd, if thou wert mixed in this affair. I meant to use thee as my tool; but I see thou art too honest and simple. I will send a sharper down; but never let me find thee, John, either a tool for the other side, or a tube for my words to pass through.'

Here the Lord Justice gave me such a glare, that I wished myself well rid of him, though thankful for his warnings;

and seeing how he had made upon me a long abiding mark of fear, he smiled again in a jocular manner, and said, –

'Now, get thee gone, Jack. I shall remember thee; and I trow, thou wilt'st not for many a day forget me.'

John Has Hope of Lorna

MUCH as I longed to know more about Lorna, and though all my heart was yearning, I could not reconcile it yet with my duty to mother and Annie, to leave them the very day after my arrival home. For lo, before breakfast was out of our mouths, there came all the men of the farm, and their wives, and even the two crow-boys, dressed as if going to Barnstaple fair, to inquire how Master John was, and whether it was true that the King had made him one of his body-guard; and if so, what was to be done with the belt for the championship of the West-Counties' wrestling, which I had held now for a year or more, and none were ready to challenge it. Strange to say, this last point seemed the most important of all to them; and none asked who was to manage the farm, or answer for their wages; but all asked who was to wear the belt.

To this I replied, after shaking hands twice over all round with all of them, that I meant to wear the belt myself, for the honour of Oare parish, so long as ever God gave me strength, and health to meet all comers: for I had never been asked to be body-guard; and if asked I would never have done it. Some of them cried that the King must be mazed, not to keep me for his protection, in these violent times of Popery. I could have told them that the King was not in the least afraid of Papists, but on the contrary, very fond of them; however, I held my tongue, remembering what Judge Jeffreys bade me.

I knew that my first day's task on the farm would be strictly watched by every one, even by my gentle mother, to see what I had learned in London. But could I let still another day pass, for Lorna to think me faithless? So what did I do but take my chance; reckless whether any one heeded me or not, only craving Lorna's heed, and time for ten words to her.

And first I went, I know not why, to the crest of the broken highland, whence I had agreed to watch for any mark or signal. And sure enough at last I saw (when it was too late to see) that the white stone had been covered over with a cloth or mantle, – the sign that something had arisen to make Lorna want me. For a moment, I stood amazed at my evil fortune; that I should be too late, in the very thing of all things on which my heart was set!

Then nothing could stop me; it was not long, although to me it seemed an age, before I stood in the niche of rock at the head of the slippery watercourse, and gazed into the quiet glen, where my foolish heart was dwelling.

At last, a little figure came, looking very light and slender in the moving shadows. Who was I to crouch, or doubt, or look at her from a distance; what matter if they killed me now, if one tear came to bury me? Therefore I rushed out at once, as if shot-guns were unknown yet; not from any real courage, but from prisoned love burst forth.

I know not whether my own Lorna was afraid of what I looked, or what I might say to her, or of her own thoughts of me: all I know is that she looked frightened, when I hoped for gladness.

Therefore I went slowly towards her, taken back in my impulse, and said all I could come to say, with some distress in doing it.

'Mistress Lorna, I had hope that you were in need of me.'

'Oh, yes; but that was long ago; two months ago, or more, sir.' And saying this she looked away, as if it were over.

But I was now so dazed and frightened, that it took my breath away, and I could not answer, feeling sure that I was robbed, and some one else had won her. And I tried to turn away, without another word, and go.

But I could not help one stupid sob, though mad with myself for allowing it, but it came too sharp for pride to stay it, and it told a world of things. Lorna heard it, and ran to me, with her bright eyes full of wonder, pity, and great kindness, as if amazed that I had more than a simple liking for her. Then she held out both hands to me; and I took and looked at them.

'Master Ridd, I did not mean,' she whispered, very softly, 'I did not mean to vex you.'

'If you would be loth to vèx me, none else in this world can do it,' I answered out of my great love, but fearing yet to look at her, mine eyes not being strong enough.

'Come away from this bright place,' she answered, trembling in her turn; 'I am watched and spied of late. Come beneath the shadows, John.'

She led me to her own rich bower; and if in spring it were a sight, what was it in summer glory? But although my mind had notice of its fairness and its wonder, all that in my presence dwelt, all that in my heart was felt, was the maiden moving gently, and afraid to look at me.

For now the power of my love was abiding on her, new to her, unknown to her; not a thing to speak about, nor even to think clearly; only just to feel and wonder, with a pain of sweetness. She could look at me no more, neither could she look away, with a studied manner – only to let fall her eyes, and blush, and be put out with me, and still more with herself.

At last Lorna slowly raised her eyelids, with a gleam of dew below them, and looked at me doubtfully. Any look with so much in it never met my gaze before.

'Darling, do you love me?' was all that I could say to her.

'Yes, I like you very much,' she answered, with her eyes gone from me, and her dark hair falling over, so as not to show me things.

'But do you love me, Lorna, Lorna; do you love me more than all the world?'

'Not by any means,' said Lorna; 'no; I like you very much, when you do not talk so wildly; and I like to see you come as if you would fill our valley up, and I like to think that even Carver would be nothing in your hands – but as to liking you like that, what should make it likely? especially when I have made the signal, and for some two months or more, you have never even answered it! If you like me so ferociously, why do you leave me for other people to do just as they like with me?'

'To do as they like! Oh, Lorna, not to make you marry Carver?'

'Not yet, not yet. They are not half so impetuous as you are, John. I am only just seventeen, you know, and who is to think of marrying? But they wanted me to give my word, and be formally betrothed to him in the presence of my grandfather. There is a youth named Charleworth Doone, every one calls him "Charlie"; a headstrong and gay young man, very gallant in his looks and manner; and my uncle, the Counsellor, chose to fancy that Charlie looked at me too much, coming by my grandfather's cottage.

'Well, they wanted me to promise, and even to swear a solemn oath (a thing I have never done in my life) that I would wed my eldest cousin, this same Carver Doone, who is twice as old as I am, being thirty-five and upwards. That was why I gave the token that I wished to see you, Master Ridd. They pointed out how much it was for the peace of all the family, and for mine own benefit; but I would not listen for a moment, though the Counsellor was most eloquent, and my grandfather begged me to consider, and Carver smiled his pleasantest, which is a truly frightful thing. Then both he and his crafty father were for using force with me; but Sir Ensor would not hear of it; and they have put off that extreme, until he shall be past its knowledge, or, at least, beyond preventing it. And now I am watched, and spied, and followed. I could not be here speaking with you even in my own nook and refuge, but for the aid, and skill, and courage of dear little Gwenny Carfax. She is now my chief reliance, and through her alone I hope to baffle all my enemies, since others have forsaken me.'

In fewest words I told her, that my seeming negligence was nothing but my bitter loss and wretched absence far away; of which I had so vainly striven to give any tidings without danger to her. When she heard all this, and saw what I had brought from London (which was nothing less than a ring of pearls with a sapphire in the midst of them, as pretty as could well be found), she let the gentle tears flow fast, and came and sat close beside me.

'Oh, you crafty Master Ridd!' said Lorna, looking up at me, and blushing now a far brighter blush than when she spoke of Charlie; 'I thought that you were much too simple ever to do this sort of thing. No wonder you can catch the fish, as when first I saw you.'

'Have I caught you, little fish? Or must all my life be spent in hopeless angling for you?'

'Neither one, nor the other, John! You have not caught me yet altogether, though I like you dearly, John; and if you will only keep away, I shall like you more and more. As for hopeless angling, John – that all others shall have until I tell you otherwise.'

And then she drew my ring from off that snowy twig her finger, and held it out to me; and then, seeing how my face was falling, thrice she touched it with her lips, and sweetly gave it back to me. 'John, I dare not take it now; else I should be cheating you. I will try to love you dearly, even as you deserve and wish. Keep it for me just till then. Something tells me I shall earn it, in a very little time. Perhaps you will be sorry then, sorry when it is all too late, to be loved by such as I am.'

What could I do at her mournful tone, but kiss a thousand times the hand which she put up to warn me, and vow that I would rather die with one assurance of her love, than without it live for ever, with all beside that the world could give? Upon this she looked so lovely, with her dark eyelashes trembling, and her soft eyes full of light, and the colour of clear sunrise mounting on her cheeks and brow, that I was forced to turn away, being overcome with beauty.

'Dearest darling, love of my life,' I whispered through her clouds of hair, 'nought you say can vex me, dear, unless you say, "Begone, John Ridd; I love another more than you." '

'Then I shall never vex you, John. Never, I mean, by saying that. Now, John, Master John Ridd, it is high time for you to go home to your mother. I love your mother very much, from what you have told me about her, and I will not have her cheated.'

'If you truly love my mother,' said I, very craftily, 'the only way to show it is by truly loving me.'

Upon that, she laughed at me in the sweetest manner, and with such provoking ways, that I knew, as well as if she herself had told me, I knew quite well, while all my heart was burning hot within me, and mine eyes were shy of hers, and her eyes were shy of mine; for certain and for ever this I knew – as in a glory – that Lorna Doone had now begun, and would go on, to love me.

John Fry's Errand

Now many people wished to know that harvest-time, as indeed I myself did very greatly, what had brought Master Huckaback over from Dulverton, at that time of year, when the clothing business was most active on account of harvest wages, and when the new wheat was beginning to sample from the early parts up the country (for he meddled as well in corn-dealing) and when we could not attend to him properly, by reason of our occupation. And yet more surprising it seemed to me, that he should bring his granddaughter also, instead of the troops of dragoons, without which he had vowed he would never come here again.

He seemed in no hurry to take his departure, though his visit was so inconvenient to us, as himself indeed must have noticed: and presently Lizzie, who was the sharpest among us, said in my hearing that she believed he had purposely timed his visit so that he might have liberty to pursue his own object, whatsoever it were, without interruption from us.

For his mode was directly after breakfast to pray to the Lord a little (which used not to be his practice), and then to go forth upon Dolly, the which was our Annie's pony, very quiet and respectful, with a bag of good victuals hung behind him, and two great cavalry pistols in front. And he always wore his meanest clothes, as if expecting to be robbed, or to disarm the temptation thereto; and he never took his golden chronometer, neither his bag of money. So much the girls found out and told me (for I was never at home myself by day); and they very craftily spurred me on, having less noble ideas perhaps, to hit upon Uncle Reuben's track, and follow, and see what became of him. For he never returned until dark or more, just in time to be in before us, who were coming home from the harvest. And then Dolly always seemed very weary, and stained with a muck from beyond our parish. But I refused to follow him, not only for the loss of a day's work to myself, and at least half a day to the other men, but chiefly because I could not think that it would be upright and manly.

But when I came home one evening, late and almost weary, there was no Annie cooking my supper, nor Lizzie by the fire reading, nor even little Ruth Huckaback watching the shadows and pondering. Upon this, I went to the girls' room, not in the very best of tempers; and there I found all three of them eagerly listening to John Fry, who was telling some great adventure.

'What does all this nonsense mean?'

'Well,' says Annie, 'we might have put up with it, if it had not been for Uncle Reuben's taking Dolly, my own pet Dolly, away every morning, quite as if she belonged to him, and keeping her out until close upon dark, and then bringing her home in a frightful condition. And then when we came to consider it, Ruth was the cleverest of us all; for she said that surely we must have some man we could trust, about the farm, to go on a little errand; and then I remembered that old John Fry would do anything for money.'

'Not for money, plaize, miss,' said John Fry, taking a pull at the beer; 'but for the love o' your swate faice.'

'To be sure, John; with the King's behind it. And so Lizzie ran for John Fry at once, and gave him full directions, how he was to slip out of the barley in the confusion of the breakfast, so that none might miss him; and to run back to the black combe bottom, and there he would find the very same pony which Uncle Ben had been tied upon, and there is no faster upon the farm. And then, without waiting for any breakfast, unless he could eat it either running or trotting, he was to travel all up the black combe, by the track Uncle Reuben had taken; and up at the top to look forward carefully, and so to trace him without being seen.'

'Then let him begin again,' said I; 'things being gone so far, it is now my duty to know everything, for the sake of you girls and mother.'

When John, upon his forest pony, which he had much ado to hold (its mouth being like a bucket), was come to the top of the long black combe, two miles or more from Plover's Barrows, and winding to the southward, he stopped his little nag short of the crest, and got off, and looked ahead of him, from behind a tump of whortles. It was a long flat sweep of moorland over which he was gazing, with a few bogs here and there, and brushy places round them.

John Fry knew the place well enough, but he liked it none the more for that, neither did any of our people; and, indeed, all the neighbourhood of Thomshill and Larksborough, and most of all Black Barrow Down lay under grave imputation of having been enchanted with a very evil spell.

Therefore it was very bold in John (as I acknowledged) to venture across that moor alone, even with a fast pony under him, and some whiskey by his side. And he would never have done so, either for the sake of Annie's sweet face, or of the golden guinea, but the truth was that he could not resist his own great curiosity. For, carefully spying across the moor, from behind the tufts of whortles, at first he could discover nothing having life and motion, except three or four wild cattle roving in vain search for nourishment, and a diseased sheep banished hither, and some carrion crows keeping watch on her. But when John was taking his very last look, being only too glad to go home again, and acknowledge himself baffled, he thought he saw a figure moving in the furthest distance upon Black Barrow Down, scarcely a thing to be sure of yet, on account of the want of colour. But as he watched, the figure passed between him and a naked cliff, and appeared to be a man on horseback, making his way very carefully, in fear of bogs and serpents. For all about there it is adders' ground, and large black serpents dwell in the marshes, and can swim as well as crawl.

Therefore he only waited awhile, for fear of being discovered, till Master Huckaback turned to the left, and entered a little gully, whence he could not survey the moor. Then John remounted, and crossed the rough land and the stony places, and picked his way among the morasses, as fast as ever he dared to go; until, in about half an hour, he drew nigh the entrance of the gully. And now it behoved him to be most wary; for Uncle Ben might have stopped in there, either to rest his horse or having reached the end of his journey. And in either case, John had little doubt that he himself would be pistolled, and nothing more ever heard of him. Therefore he had made his pony come to the mouth of it sideways, and leaned over, and peered in around the rocky corner, while the little horse cropped at the briars.

But he soon perceived that the gully was empty, so far at least as its course was straight; and with that he hastened into it, though his heart was not working easily. When he had traced the winding hollow for half a mile or more, he saw that it forked, and one part led to the left up a steep red bank, and the other to the right, being narrow, and slightly tending downwards. Some yellow sand lay here and there between the starving grasses, and this he examined narrowly for a trace of Master Huckaback.

At last he saw that, beyond all doubt, the man he was pursuing had taken the course which led down hill; and down the hill he must follow him. And this John did with deep misgivings, and a hearty wish that he had never started upon so perilous an errand. For now he knew not where he was, and scarcely dared to ask himself, as the passage seemed darker and deeper, when suddenly he turned a corner, and saw a scene which stopped him.

For there was the Wizard's Slough itself, as black as death, and bubbling, with a few scant yellow reeds in a ring around it. Outside these, bright watergrass of the liveliest green was creeping, tempting any unwary foot to step, and plunge, and founder. And on the marge were blue campanula, sundew, and forget-me-not, such as no child could resist. On either side, the hill fell back, and the ground was broken with tufts of rush, and flag, and marestail, and a few rough alder-trees overclogged with water. And not a bird was seen, or heard, neither rail nor water-hen, wag-tail, nor reed-warbler.

Of this horrible quagmire, the worst upon all Exmoor, John had heard from his grandfather, and even from his mother, when they wanted to keep him quiet; but his father had feared to speak of it to him, being a man of piety, and up to the tricks of the evil one. This made John the more desirous to have a good look at it now, only with his girths well up, to turn away and flee at speed, if anything should happen. And now he proved how well it is to be wary and wide-awake, even in lonesome places. For at the other side of the Slough, and a few landyards beyond it, where the ground was less noisome, he had observed a felled tree lying over a great hole in the earth, with staves of wood, and slabs of stone, and some yellow gravel around it. And there was Dolly, as large as life, tied to a stump not far beyond, and flipping the flies away with her tail.

While John was trembling within himself, lest Dolly should get scent of his pony, and neigh and reveal their presence, although she could not see them, suddenly to his great amazement something white arose out of the hole, under the brown trunk of the tree. Seeing this his blood went back within him; yet was he not able to turn and flee, but rooted his face in among the loose stones, and kept his quivering shoulders back, and prayed to God to protect him. However, the white thing itself was not so very awful, being nothing more than a long-coned night-cap with a tassel on the top, such as criminals wear at hanging-time. But when John saw a man's face under it, and a man's neck and shoulders slowly rising out of the pit, he could not doubt that this was the place where the murderers come to life again, according to the Exmoor story. He knew that a man had been hanged last week, and that this was the ninth day after it.

Therefore he could bear no more, thoroughly brave as he had been; neither did he wait to see what became of the gallows-man; but climbed on his horse with what speed he might, and rode away at full gallop.

This story told by John Fry that night, and my conviction of its truth, made me very uneasy, especially as following upon the warning of Judge Jeffreys, and the hints received from Jeremy Stickles, as well as sundry tales and rumours, and signs of secret understanding, seen and heard on market-days, and at places of entertainment. We knew for certain that at Taunton, Bridgewater, and even Dulverton, there was much disaffection towards the King, and regret for the days of the Puritans. Albeit I had told the truth, and the pure and simple truth, when, upon my examination, I had assured his lordship, that to the best of my knowledge there was nothing of the sort with us.

But now I was beginning to doubt whether I might not have been mistaken; especially when we heard, as we did, of arms being landed at Lynmouth, in the dead of night, and of the tramp of men having reached some one's ears, from a hill where a famous echo was. For it must be plain to any conspirator (without the example of the Doones) that for the secret muster of men, and the stowing of unlawful arms, and communication by beacon lights, scarcely a fitter place could be found than the wilds of Exmoor, with deep ravines running far inland from an unwatched and mostly sheltered sea.

But even supposing it probable that something against King Charles the Second (or rather against his Roman advisers, and especially his brother) were now in preparation amongst us, was it likely that Master Huckaback, a wealthy man, and a careful one, known moreover to the Lord Chief Justice, would have anything to do with it?

And how was it likely to be, as to the Doones themselves? So far as they had any religion at all, by birth they were Roman Catholics. On the other hand, they were not likely to entertain much affection for the son of the man who had banished them, and confiscated their property. And it was not at all impossible that desperate men, such as they were, having nothing to lose, but estates to recover, and not being held by religion much, should cast away all regard for the birth from which they had been cast out, and make common cause with a Protestant rising, for the chance of revenge and replacement.

Before I could quite make up my mind how to act in this difficulty, and how to get at the rights of it (for I would not spy after Uncle Reuben, though I felt no great fear of the Wizard's Slough, and none of the man with white night-cap), a difference came again upon it, and a change of chances. For Uncle Ben went away, as suddenly as he first had come to us, neither giving reason for his departure, nor claiming the pony.

The Crowning Moment

ALTHOUGH I had been under interdict for two months from my darling – 'One for your sake, one for mine,' she had whispered – lighter heart was not on Exmoor than I bore for most of that time. For she was safe; I knew that daily by a mode of signals, well-contrived between us now, on the strength of our experience. But when the harvest was done, and the thatching of the ricks made sure against south-western tempests, and all the reapers gone, I began to burn in spirit for the sight of Lorna.

Therefore unashamed of grief, but much abashed with joy, was I, that October morning, when I saw my Lorna coming, purer than the morning dew, than the sun more bright and clear.

Suddenly at sight of me, for I leaped forth at once, in fear of seeming to watch her unawares, the bloom upon her cheeks was deepened, and the radiance of her eyes; and she came to meet me gladly. I knew that the crowning moment of my life was coming – that Lorna would own her love for me.

'I have loved you long and long,' I spoke in a low soft voice; 'when you were a little child, as a boy I worshipped you: then when I saw you a comely girl, as a stripling I adored you: now that you are a full-grown maiden, all the rest I do, and more, – I love you, more than tongue can tell, or heart can hold in silence. I have waited long and long; and though I am so far below you, I can wait no longer; but must have my answer.'

'You have been very faithful, John,' she murmured to the fern and moss; 'I suppose I must reward you.'

'That will not do for me,' I said; 'I will not have reluctant liking, nor assent for pity's sake; which only means endurance. I must have all love, or none; I must have your heart of hearts; even as you have mine, Lorna.'

While I spoke, she glanced up shyly through her fluttering lashes, to prolong my doubt one moment, for her own delicious pride. Then she opened wide upon me all the glorious depth and softness of her loving eyes, and flung both arms around my neck, and answered with her heart on mine –

'Darling, you have won it all. I shall never be my own again. I am yours, my own one, for ever and for ever.'

And then I slipped my little ring upon the wedding finger; and this time Lorna kept it, and looked with fondness on its beauty, and clung to me with a flood of tears.

'There now, none shall make you weep,' I said, drawing her closer to me. 'Darling, you shall sigh no more, but live in peace and happiness, with me to guard and cherish you: and who shall dare to vex you?' But she drew a long sad sigh, and looked at the ground with the great tears rolling, and pressed one hand upon the trouble of her pure young breast.

'It can never, never be,' she murmured to herself alone: 'Who am I, to dream of it? Something in my heart tells me, it can be so never, never.'

Running Distracted

I HURRIED home with deep exulting, yet some sad misgivings, for Lorna had made me promise now to tell my mother everything. But although by our mother's reluctant consent a large part of the obstacles between Annie and Tom Faggus had now been removed, on the other hand Lorna and myself gained little, except as regarded comfort of mind, and some ease to the conscience. Moreover, our chance of frequent meetings and delightful converse was much impaired, at least for the present; because mother made me promise never to risk my life by needless visits. And upon this point, that is to say, the necessity of the visit, she was well content, as she said, to leave me to my own good sense and honour.

After this, for another month, nothing worthy of notice happened, except perhaps that I found it needful, according to the strictest good sense and honour, to visit Lorna, immediately after my discourse with mother, and to tell her all about it. My beauty gave me one sweet kiss with all her heart.

'And now,' she continued, 'you bound me, John, with a very beautiful ring to you, and when I dare not wear it, I carry it always on my heart. But I will bind you to me, you dearest, with the very poorest and plainest thing that ever you set eyes on. Look at it, what a queer old thing! There are some ancient marks upon it, very grotesque and wonderful; it looks like a cat in a tree almost; but never mind what it looks like. This old ring must have been a giant's; therefore it will fit you perhaps, you enormous John. It has been on the front of my old glass necklace (which my grandfather found them taking away, and very soon made them give back again) ever since I can remember; and long before that, as some woman told me. Now you seem very greatly amazed; pray what thinks my lord of it?'

'Mistress Lorna, this is not the ring of any giant. It is nothing more nor less than a very ancient thumb-ring. I will accept it, my own one love; and it shall go to my grave with me.' And so it shall, unless there be villains who would dare to rob the dead.

I asked her where the glass necklace was, from which the ring was fastened, and which she had worn in her childhood, and she answered that she hardly knew, but remembered that her grandfather had begged her to give it up to him, when she was ten years old or so, and had promised to keep it for her, until she could take care of it; at the same time giving her back the ring, and fastening it from her pretty neck, and telling her to be proud of it. And so she always had been, and now from her sweet breast she took it, and it became John Ridd's delight.

All this I told my mother truly, according to my promise; and she was greatly pleased with Lorna for having been so good to me, and for speaking so very sensibly; and then she looked at the great gold ring, but could by no means interpret. Only she was quite certain, as indeed I myself was, that it must have belonged to an ancient race of great consideration, and high rank, in their time.

And before I got used to my ring, or people could think

that it belonged to me (plain and ungarnished though it was), and before I went to see Lorna again, we all had something else to think of, not so pleasant, and even more puzzling.

This was the arrival of Master Jeremy Stickles, who had been a good friend to me in London, and had earned my mother's gratitude, so far as ever he chose to have it. And he seemed inclined to have it all; for he made our farm-house his headquarters, and kept us quite at his beck and call, going out at any time of the evening, and coming back at any time of the morning, and always expecting us to be ready, whether with horse, or man, or maidens, or fire, or provisions. We knew that he was employed somehow upon the service of the King, and had at different stations certain troopers and orderlies, quite at his disposal; also we knew that he never went out, nor even slept in his bedroom, without heavy fire-arms well loaded, and a sharp sword nigh his hand; and that he held a great commission, under royal signet, requiring all good subjects, all officers of whatever degree, and especially justices of the peace, to aid him to the utmost, with person, beast, and chattel, or to answer it at their peril.

'John,' he said, 'you have some right to know the meaning of all this, being trusted as you were by the Lord Chief Justice. But he found you scarcely supple enough, neither gifted with due brains. There be some people fit to plot, and others to be plotted against, and others to unravel plots, which is the highest gift of all. Therefore His Majesty's advisers have chosen me for this high task, and they could not have chosen a better man. Now, heard you much in London town about the Duke of Monmouth?'

'Not so very much,' I answered; 'not half so much as in Devonshire.'

'Things are changed since you were in town. There is much disaffection everywhere, and it must grow to an outbreak. The King hath many troops in London, and meaneth to bring more from Tangier; but he cannot command these country places; and the trained bands cannot help him much, even if they would. In ten words (without trying thy poor brain too much), I am here to watch the gathering of a secret plot, not so much against the King as against the due succession. Now hearken to one who wishes thee well, and plainly sees the end of it, – stick thou to the winning side, and have nought to do with the other one.'

But now my own affairs were thrown into such disorder, that I could think of nothing else, and had the greatest difficulty in hiding my uneasiness. For suddenly, without any warning, or a word of message, all my Lorna's signals ceased. The first time I stood on the wooded crest, and found no change from yesterday, I could hardly believe my eyes, or thought at least that it must be some great mistake on the part of my love. But though I waited at every hour of day and far into the night, no light footstep came to meet me, no sweet voice was in the air; all was lonely, drear, and drenched with sodden desolation. It seemed as if my love was dead, and the winds were at her funeral.

Once I sought far up the valley, where I had never been before, even beyond the copse, where Lorna had found and lost her brave young cousin. The last outlying cot was a gloomy, low, square house, without any light in the windows, roughly built of wood and stone, as I saw when I drew nearer. Suspecting it to be Carver's dwelling, I was led by curiosity, and perhaps by jealousy, to have a closer look at it. I went warily, being now almost among this nest of cockatrices. Then I took a careful survey of the dwelling, and its windows, and its door, and aspect, as if I had been a robber meaning to make privy entrance. It was well for me that I did this, as you will find hereafter.

Before I took myself home that night, I had resolved to penetrate Glen Doone from the upper end, and learn all about my Lorna. Not but what I might have entered from my unsuspected channel, as so often I had done; but that I saw fearful need for knowing something more than that. Here was every sort of trouble gathering upon me; here was Jeremy Stickles stealing upon every one in the dark; here was Uncle Reuben plotting, Satan only could tell what; here was a white night-capped man coming bodily from the grave; here was my own sister Annie committed to a highway-man, and mother in distraction; most of all, – here, there, and where, – was my Lorna, stolen, dungeoned, perhaps outraged. If I left my Lorna so; if I let those black-soul'd villains work their pleasure on my love – then let maidens cease from men, and rest their faith in tabby-cats.

A Very Desperate Venture

THE journey was a great deal longer to fetch around the Southern hills, and enter by the Doone-gate, than to cross the lower land, and steal in by the water-slide. However, I durst not take a horse (for fear of the Doones, who might be abroad upon their usual business), but started betimes in the evening, so as not to hurry, or waste any strength upon the way. And thus I came to the robbers' highway, walking circumspectly, scanning the sky-line of every hill, and searching the folds of every valley, for any moving figure.

And then I was, or seemed to be, particularly unlucky; for as I drew near the very entrance, lightly of foot, and warily, the moon (which had often been my friend) like an enemy broke upon me, topping the eastward ridge of rock, and filling all the open spaces with the play of wavering light. I shrank back into the shadowy quarter, on the right side of the road; and gloomily employed myself to watch the triple entrance, on which the moonlight fell askew.

All across and before the three rude and beetling archways, hung a felled oak overhead, black, and thick, and threatening. This, as I heard before, could be let fall in a moment, so as to crush a score of men, and bar the approach of horses. Behind this tree, the rocky mouth was spanned, as by a gallery, with brushwood and piled timber, all upon a ledge of stone, where thirty men might lurk unseen, and fire at any invader. From that rampart it would be impossible to dislodge them, because the rock fell sheer below them twenty feet, or it may be more; while overhead it towered three hundred, and so jutted over that nothing could be cast upon them; even if a man could climb the height.

Now I could see those three rough arches, jagged, black, and terrible; and I knew that only one of them could lead me to the valley; neither gave the river now any further guidance; but dived underground with a sullen roar, where it met the cross-bar of the mountain. I had no means at all of judging which was the right way of the three, and knew that the other two would lead to almost certain death, in the ruggedness and darkness. But it struck me that, in times of peace, the middle way was the likeliest; and the others diverging right and left in their further parts might be made to slide into it (not far from the entrance), at the pleasure of the warders.

Therefore, without more hesitation, I plunged into the middle way, holding a long ash staff before me, shodden at the end with iron. Presently I was in black darkness, groping along the wall, and feeling a deal more fear than I wished to feel; especially when upon looking back I could no longer see the light, which I had forsaken. Then I stumbled over something hard, and sharp, and very cold, moreover so grievous to my legs, that it needed my very best doctrine and humour to forbear from swearing, in the manner they use in London. But when I arose, and felt it, and knew it to be a culverin, I was somewhat reassured thereby, inasmuch as it was not likely that they would plant this engine, except in the real and true entrance.

Therefore I went on again, more painfully and wearily, and presently found it to be good that I had received that knock, and borne it with such patience; for otherwise I might have blundered full upon the sentries, and been shot without more ado. As it was, I had barely time to draw back, as I turned a corner upon them; and if their lanthorn had been in its place, they could scarce have failed to descry me, unless indeed I had seen the gleam before I turned the corner.

There seemed to be only two of them, of size indeed and stature as all the Doones must be, but I need not have feared to encounter them both, had they been unarmed, as I was. It was plain, however, that each had a long and heavy carbine, not in his hands (as it should have been), but standing close beside him. So I kept well back at the corner, and laid one cheek to the rock face, and kept my outer eye round the jut, in the wariest mode I could compass, watching my opportunity.

The two villains looked very happy – which villains have no right to be, but often are, meseemeth – they were sitting in a niche of rock, with the lanthorn in the corner, quaffing something from glass measures, and playing some trivial game. Presently Charlie, or Charleworth Doone, the younger and taller man, reached forth his hand to seize the money, which he swore he had won that time. Upon this, the other jerked his arm, vowing that he had no right to it; whereupon Charlie flung at his face the contents of the glass he was sipping, but missed him and hit the candle, which spluttered with a flare of blue flame (from the strength perhaps of the spirit) and then went out completely. At this, one swore, and the other laughed; and before they had settled what to do, I was past them and round the corner.

And then, like a giddy fool as I was, I needs must give

them a startler – the whoop of an owl, done so exactly, as John Fry had taught me, and echoed by the roof so fearfully, that one of them dropped the tinder box, and the other caught up his gun and cocked it, at least as I judged by the sounds they made. However, as the luck of the matter went, it proved for my advantage; for I heard one say to the other, –

'Curse it, Charlie, what was that? It scared me so, I have dropped my box; my flint is gone, and everything. Will the brimstone catch from your pipe, my lad?'

'My pipe is out, Phelps, ever so long. Damn it, I am not afraid of an owl, man. Give me the lanthorn, and stay here. I'm not half done with you yet, my friend.'

And so after some rude jests, and laughter, and a few more oaths, I heard Charlie coming towards me, with a loose and not too sober footfall. Therefore I followed him, without any especial caution; and soon I had the pleasure of seeing his form against the moonlit sky. Down a steep and winding path, with a handrail at the corners, Master Charlie tripped along – and indeed there was much tripping, and he must have been an active fellow to recover as he did – and after him walked I, much hoping (for his own poor sake) that he might not turn, and espy me.

So he led me very kindly to the top of the meadow land, where the stream from underground broke forth, seething quietly with a little hiss of bubbles. Hence I had fair view and outline of the robbers' township, spread with bushes here and there, but not heavily overshadowed.

I knew that the Captain's house was first, both from what Lorna had said of it, and from my mother's description, and now again from seeing Charlie halt there for a certain time, and whistle on his fingers, and hurry on, fearing consequences. The tune that he whistled was strange to me, and lingered in my ears, as having something very new and striking, and fantastic in it. And I repeated it softly to myself, while I marked the position of the houses.

Master Charlie went down the village, and I followed him carefully, keeping as much as possible in the shadowy places, and watching the windows of every house, lest any light should be burning. As I passed Sir Ensor's house, my heart leaped up, for I spied a window, higher than the rest above the ground, and with a faint light moving. This could hardly fail to be the room wherein my darling lay; for here that impudent young fellow had gazed while he was whistling. And here my courage grew tenfold, and my spirit feared no evil – for lo, if Lorna had been surrendered to that scoundrel, Carver, she would not have been at her grandfather's house, but in Carver's accursed dwelling.

My heart was in my mouth, as they say, when I stood in the shade by Lorna's window, and whispered her name gently. The Doones had been their own builders, for no one should know their ins and outs; and of course their work was clumsy. As for their windows, they stole them mostly from the houses round about. But though the window was not very close, I might have whispered long enough, before she would have answered me; frightened as she was, no doubt, by many a rude overture. And I durst not speak aloud, because I saw another watchman posted on the western cliff, and commanding all the valley. And now this man (having no companion for drinking or for gambling) espied me against the wall of the house, and advanced to the brink, and challenged me.

'Who are you there? Answer! One, two, three; and I fire at thee.'

The nozzle of his gun was pointed full upon me, as I could see, with the moonlight striking on the barrel; he was not more than fifty yards off, and now he began to reckon. Being almost desperate about it, I began to whistle, wondering how far I should get before I lost my windpipe: and as luck would have it, my lips fell into that strange tune I had practised last; the one I had heard from Charlie. My mouth would scarcely frame the notes, being parched with terror; but to my surprise, the man fell back, dropped his gun, and saluted. Oh sweetest of all sweet melodies!

That tune was Carver Doone's passport (as I heard long afterwards), which Charleworth Doone had imitated, for decoy of Lorna. The sentinel took me for that vile Carver; who was like enough to be prowling there, for private talk with Lorna; but not very likely to shout forth his name if it might be avoided. The watchman, perceiving the danger perhaps of intruding on Carver's privacy, not only retired along the cliff, but withdrew himself to good distance.

Meanwhile he had done me the kindest service; for Lorna came to the window at once, to see what the cause of the shout was, and drew back the curtain timidly. Then she opened the rough lattice; and then she watched the cliff and trees; and then she sighed very sadly.

'Oh, Lorna, don't you know me?' I whispered.

'John!' she cried, yet with sense enough not to speak aloud: 'oh, you must be mad, John.'

'As mad as a March hare,' said I, 'without any news of my darling. You knew I would come: of course you did.'

'Well, I thought, perhaps – you know: now, John, you need not eat my hand. Do you see they have put iron bars across?'

'To be sure. Do you think I should be contented, even with this lovely hand, but for these vile iron bars? I will have them out before I go. Now tell me,' I said; 'what means all this? Why are you so pent up here? Why have you given me no token? Has your grandfather turned against you? Are you in any danger?'

'My poor grandfather is very ill: I fear that he will not live long. The Counsellor and his son are now the masters of the valley; and I dare not venture forth, for fear of anything they might do to me. When I went forth, to signal for you, Carver tried to seize me; but I was too quick for him. Little

Gwenny is not allowed to leave the valley now; so that I could send no message. I have been so wretched, dear, lest you should think me false to you. The tyrants now make sure of me. You must watch this house, both night and day, if you wish to save me. There is nothing they would shrink from, if my poor grandfather – I hear the old nurse moving. Grandfather is sure to send for me. Keep back from the window.'

However, it was only Gwenny Carfax, Lorna's little handmaid: my darling brought her to the window, and presented her to me, almost laughing through her grief.

'Oh, I am so glad, John; Gwenny, I am so glad you came. I have wanted long to introduce you to my "young man", as you call him. It is rather dark, but you can see him. I wish you to know him again, Gwenny.'

'Whoy!' cried Gwenny, with great amazement, standing on tiptoe to look out, and staring as if she were weighing me: 'her be bigger nor any Doone! I shall knoo thee again, young man; nor fear of that. Now, missis, gae on coortin', and I will gae outside and watch for 'ee.' Though expressed not over delicately, this proposal arose, no doubt, from Gwenny's sense of delicacy; and I was very thankful to her for taking her departure.

'She is the best little thing in the world,' said Lorna, softly laughing; 'and the queerest, and the truest. Nothing will bribe her against me. Now go, do go, good John; kind, dear, darling John; if you love me, go.'

'How can I go, without settling anything?' I asked, very sensibly. 'How shall I know of your danger now? Hit upon something; you are so quick. Anything you can think of; and then I will go, and not frighten you.'

'I have been thinking long of something,' Lorna answered rapidly, 'you see that tree with the seven rooks' nests, bright against the cliffs there? Can you count them, from above, do you think? From a place where you will be safe, dear' –

'No doubt, I can; or if I cannot, it will not take me long to find a spot whence I can do it.'

'Gwenny can climb like any cat. If you see but six rooks' nests, I am in peril, and want you. If you see but five, I am carried off by Carver.'

'Good God!' said I, at the mere idea, in a tone which frightened Lorna.

'Fear not, John,' she whispered sadly, and my blood grew cold at it: 'I have means to stop him; or at least to save myself. If you can come within one day of that man's getting hold of me, you will find me quite unharmed. After that you will find me dead, or alive, according to circumstances, but in no case such that you need blush to look at me.'

Her dear sweet face was full of pride, as even in the gloom I saw. I only said, 'God bless you, darling!' and she said the same to me, in a very low sad voice.

A weight of care was off my mind; though much of trouble hung there still. One thing was quite certain – if Lorna could not have John Ridd, no one else should have her.

A Good Turn for Jeremy

ONE afternoon I had been working very hard in the copse of young ash with my bill-hook and shearing-knife, at the western corner of our farm, which was nearest to Glen Doone, and where I could easily run to a height commanding a view of the seven rooks' nests.

It was time to go home to supper now, and I felt very friendly towards it, having been hard at work for some hours, with only the voice of the little rill, and some hares, and a pheasant, for company. The sun was gone down behind the black wood on the further cliffs of Bagworthy, and the russet of the tufts and spear-beds was becoming grey, while the greyness of the sapling ash grew brown against the sky; the hollow curves of the little stream became black beneath the grasses and the fairy fans innumerable.

Therefore I wiped my bill-hook and shearing-knife very carefully, for I hate to leave tools dirty; and was doubting whether I should try for another glance at the seven rooks' nests, or whether it would be too dark for it. It was now a quarter of an hour mayhap, since I had made any chopping noise, because I had been assorting my spars, and tying them in bundles, instead of plying the bill-hook; and the gentle tinkle of the stream was louder than my doings. To this, no doubt, I owe my life, which then (without my dreaming it) was in no little jeopardy.

For, just as I was twisting the bine of my very last faggot, before tucking the cleft tongue under, there came three men outside the hedge, where the western light was yellow; and by it I could see that all three of them carried fire-arms. These men were not walking carelessly, but following down the hedge-trough, as if to stalk some enemy: and for a moment it struck me cold, to think it was I they were looking for. With the swiftness of terror, I concluded that my visits to Glen Doone were known, and now my life was the forfeit. I had no time to fly, but with a sort of instinct, threw myself flat in among the thick fern, and held my breath, and lay still as a log. Then the three men came to the gap in the hedge, where I had been in and out so often; and stood up, and looked in over.

'Somebody been at work here –' it was the deep voice of Carver Doone; 'jump up, Charlie, and look about; we must have no witnesses.'

'Give me a hand behind,' said Charlie, the same handsome young Doone I had seen that night; 'this bank is too devilish steep for me.'

'Nonsense, man!' cried the third; 'only a hind cutting faggots; and of course he hath gone home long ago. Blind man's holiday, as we call it. I can see all over the place; and there is not even a rabbit there.'

At that I drew my breath again, and thanked God I had gotten my coat on.

'He is right,' said Charlie, who was standing up high (on a root perhaps), 'there is nobody there now, captain; and lucky for the poor devil that he keepeth workman's hours. Even nis chopper is gone, I see.'

'No dog, no man, is the rule about here, when it comes to coppice work,' continued the other; 'there is not a man would dare work there, without a dog to scare the pixies.'

'There is a big youngfellow upon this farm,' Carver Doone muttered sulkily, 'with whom I have an account to settle, if ever I come across him. He hath a cursed spite to us, because we shot his father. He was going to bring the lumpers upon us, only he was afeared, last winter. And he hath been in London lately, for some traitorous job, I doubt. But come, let us onward. No lingering, or the viper will be in the bush from us. Body and soul, if he give us the slip, both of you shall answer it.'

'No fear, captain, and no hurry,' Charlie answered gallantly; 'would I were as sure of living a twelvemonth, as he is of dying within the hour! Extreme unction for him in my bullet patch. Remember, I claim to be his confessor, because hc hath insulted me.'

The words of Carver Doone had filled me with such anger, knowing what I did about him, and his pretence to Lorna, and their threats against some unknown person so aroused my pity, that much of my prudence was forgotten, or at least the better part of courage, which loves danger at long distance. And so I followed them down the fence, as gently as a rabbit goes; only I was inside it, and they on the outside;

but yet so near, that I heard the branches rustle as they pushed them.

I heard them, for I durst not look; and could scarce keep still, for trembling – I heard them trampling outside the gap; uncertain which track they should follow.

'We shall see him better in there,' said Carver, in his horrible gruff voice, like the creaking of the gallows chain; 'sit there behind holly hedge, lads, while he cometh down yonder hill; and then our good evening to him; one at his body, and two at his head; and good aim, lest we baulk the devil.'

'I tell you, captain, that will not do,' said Charlie, almost whispering: 'you are very proud of your skill, we know, and can hit a lark if you see it: but he may not come until after dark, and we cannot be too nigh to him. This holly hedge is too far away. He crosses down here from Slocombslade, not from Tibbacot, I tell you; but along that track to the left there, and so by the foreland to Glenthorne, where his boat is in the cove. Do you think I have tracked him so many evenings, without knowing his line to a hair? Will you fool away all my trouble?'

'Come then, lad; we will follow thy lead. Thy life for his, if we fail of it.'

I heard them stumbling down the hill, which was steep and rocky in that part; and peering through the hedge, I saw them enter a covert, by the side of the track which Master Stickles followed, almost every evening, when he left our house upon business. And then I knew who it was they were come on purpose to murder – a thing which I might have guessed long before, but for terror and cold stupidity.

It was no time to dwell upon that, only to try, if might be, to prevent the crime they were bound upon, to stop the king's messenger from travelling any further, if only I could catch him.

And this was exactly what I did; and a terrible run I had

for it, fearing at every step to hear the echo of shots in the valley, and dropping down the scrubby rocks with tearing and violent scratching. Then I crossed Bagworthy stream, not far below Doone-valley, and breasted the hill towards Slocombslade, with my heart very heavily panting. Why Jeremy chose to ride this way, instead of the more direct one (which would have been over Oare-hill), was more than I could account for: but I had nothing to do with that; all I wanted was to save his life.

And this I did by about a minute; and (which was the hardest thing of all) with a great-horse pistol at my head, as I seized upon his bridle.

'Jeremy, Jerry,' was all I could say, being so fearfully short of breath; for I had crossed the ground quicker than any horse could.

'Spoken just in time, John Ridd!' cried Master Stickles, still however pointing the pistol at me: 'I might have known thee by thy size. John. What art doing here?'

'Come to save your life. For God's sake, go no further. Three men in the covert there, with long guns, waiting for thee.'

'Ha! I have been watched of late. That is why I pointed at thee, John. Back round this corner, and get thy breath, and tell me all about it. I never saw a man so hurried. I could beat thee now, John.'

Jeremy Stickles was a man of courage, and presence of mind, and much resource: otherwise he would not have been appointed for this business; nevertheless he trembled greatly, when he heard what I had to tell him.

'We will let them cool their heels, John Ridd,' said Jeremy, after thinking a little. 'I cannot fetch my musketeers either from Glenthorne or Lynmouth, in time to seize the fellows. And three desperate Doones, well-armed, are too many for you and me. One result this attempt will have, it will make us attack them sooner than we had intended. And one more it will have, good John, it will make me thy friend for ever. Mayhap, in the troubles coming, it will help thee not a little to have done me this good turn.'

Upon that he shook me by the hand, with a pressure such as we feel not often; and having learned from me how to pass quite beyond view of his enemies, he rode on to his duty, whatever it might be.

A Troubled State

STICKLES took me aside the next day, and opened all his business to me, whether I would or not.

Disaffection to the King, or rather dislike to his brother, James, and fear of Roman ascendancy, had existed now for several years, and of late were spreading rapidly. There was at the time I speak of, a great surge in England, not rolling yet, but seething: and one which a thousand Chief Justices, and a million Jeremy Stickles, should never be able to stop or turn, by stringing up men in front of it; any more than a rope of onions can repulse a volcano. But the worst of it was, that this great movement took a wrong channel at first; not only missing legitimate line, but roaring out that the back ditchway was the true and established course of it.

All the towns of Somersetshire and half the towns of Devonshire were full of pushing eager people, ready to swallow anything, or to make others swallow it. Taunton, Bridgewater, Minehead, and Dulverton took the lead of the other towns in utterance of their discontent, and threats of what they meant to do, if ever a Papist dared to climb the Protestant throne of England. On the other hand, the Tory leaders were not as yet under apprehension of an immediate outbreak, for the struggle was not very likely to begin in earnest, during the life of the present King; unless he should (as some people hoped) be so far emboldened as to make public profession of the faith which he held (if any). So the Tory policy was to watch their opponents, being well apprised of all their schemes and intended movements, to wait for some bold overt act, and then to strike severely. And as a Tory watchman – or spy, as the Whigs would call him – Jeremy Stickles was now among us; and his duty was threefold.

First, and most ostensibly, to see to the levying of poundage in the little haven of Lynmouth, and further up the coast, which was now becoming a place of resort for the folk whom we call smugglers.

Second, his duty was (though only the Doones had discovered it) to watch those outlaws narrowly, and report of their manners, doings, reputation and politics, whether true to the King and the Pope, or otherwise.

Jeremy Stickles' third business was entirely political; to learn the temper of our people and the gentle families, to watch the movements of the trained bands (which could not always be trusted), to discover any collecting of arms and drilling of men among us, to prevent any importation of gunpowder, of which there had been some rumour; in a word, to observe and forestall the enemy.

Now in providing for this last-mentioned service, the Government had made a great mistake, doubtless through their anxiety to escape any public attention. For all the disposable force at their emissary's command amounted to no more than a score of musketeers, and these so divided along the coast as scarcely to suffice for the duty of sentinels. He held a commission, it is true, for the employment of the train-bands, but upon the understanding that he was not to call upon them (except as a last resource) for any political object; although he might use them against the Doones as private criminals, if found needful; and supposing that he could get them.

'So you see, John,' he said, in conclusion, 'I have more work than tools to do it with. I am heartily sorry I ever accepted such a mixed and meagre commission. The only thing that I can do, with any chance of success, is to rout out these vile Doone fellows, and burn their houses over their heads. Now what think you of that, John Ridd?'

'Destroy the town of the Doones,' I said, 'and all the Doones inside it! Surely, Jeremy, you would never think of such a cruel act as that!'

'A cruel act, John! It would be a mercy for at least three counties. No doubt you folk, who live so near, are well accustomed to them, and would miss your liveliness in coming home after nightfall, and the joy of finding your sheep and cattle right, when you not expected it. But after awhile you might get used to the dulness of being safe in your beds, and not losing your sisters and sweethearts. Surely, on the whole, it is as pleasant not to be robbed as to be robbed?'

He laughed in a very unseemly manner; while I descried nothing to laugh about. I was thinking, of course, and thinking more than all the rest, about the troubles that might ensue to my own beloved Lorna. If an attack of Glen Doone were made by savage soldiers and rude train-bands, what might happen, or what might not, to my darling? Therefore, when Jeremy Stickles again placed the matter before me, commending my strength and courage, and skill, and finished by saying that I would be worth at least four common men to him, I cut him short as follows: –

'Master Stickles, once for all, I will have nought to do with it. The reason why is no odds of thine, nor in any way disloyal. Only in thy plans remember, that I will not strike a blow, neither give any counsel, neither guard any prisoners.'

'Good, my lord: so be it. But one thing I tell thee in earnest. We will have thy double-dealing uncle, Huckaback of Dulverton, and march him first to assault Doone Castle, sure as my name is Stickles. I hear that he hath often vowed to storm the valley himself, if only he could find a dozen musketeers to back him. Now, we will give him chance to do it, and prove his loyalty to the King, which lies under some suspicion of late.'

All this made me very uncomfortable, for many and many reasons, the chief and foremost being of course my anxiety about Lorna. If the attack succeeded, what was to become of her? Who would rescue her from the brutal soldiers, even supposing that she escaped from the hands of her own people, during the danger and ferocity?

In another way, I was vexed moreover – for after all we must consider the opinions of our neighbours – namely, that I knew quite well how everybody for ten miles round (for my fame must have been at least that wide, after all my wrestling), would lift up hands and cry out thus – 'Black shame on John Ridd, if he lets them go without him!'

Among all these troubles, there was however, or seemed to be, one comfort. Tom Faggus returned from London very proudly and very happily, with a royal pardon in black and white, which everybody admired the more, because no one could read a word of it. The Squire himself acknowledged cheerfully that he could sooner take fifty purses than read a single line of it. Some people indeed went so far as to say that the parchment was made from a sheep Tom had stolen, and that was why it prevaricated so, in giving him a character.

Two Fools Together

AND now a thing came to pass which tested my adoration pretty sharply, inasmuch as I would far liefer have faced Carver Doone and his father, nay even the roaring lion himself, with his hoofs and flaming nostrils, than have met, in cold blood, Sir Ensor Doone, the founder of all the colony, and the fear of the very fiercest.

But that I was forced to do at this time, and in the manner following. When I went up one morning to look for my seven rooks' nests, behold there were but six to be seen; for the top-most of them all was gone, and the most conspicuous. I looked again; yes, there could be no doubt about it; the signal was made for me to come, because my love was in danger. For me to enter the valley now, during the broad daylight, could have brought no comfort, but only harm to the maiden, and certain death to myself.

So I waited till it grew towards dark, and was just beginning to prepare for my circuit around the hills, when I saw a short figure approaching from a thickly-wooded hollow on the left side of my hiding-place. It proved, to my great delight, to be the little maid Gwenny Carfax. She started a moment, at seeing me, but more with surprise than fear; and then she laid both her hands upon mine, as if she had known me for twenty years.

'Young man,' she said, 'you must come with me. I was gwain' all the way to fetch thee. Old man be dying; and her can't die, or at least her won't, without first considering thee.'

'Considering me!' I cried: 'what can Sir Ensor Doone want with considering me? Has Mistress Lorna told him?'

'All concerning thee, and thy doings; when she knowed old man were so near his end. That vexed he was about thy low blood, a' thought her would come to life again, on purpose for to bate 'ee. But after all, there can't be scarcely such bad luck as that. Now, if her strook thee, thou must take it; there be no denaying of 'un. Fire I have seen afore, hot and red, and raging; but I never seen cold fire afore, and it maketh me burn and shiver.'

And in truth, it made me both burn and shiver, to know that I must either go straight to the presence of Sir Ensor

Doone, or give up Lorna, once for all, and rightly be despised by her.

Therefore, with great misgiving of myself, I followed Gwenny; who led me along very rapidly, with her short broad form gliding down the hollow, from which she had first appeared. Soon we were at the top of Doone valley. In the chilly dusk air it looked most untempting, especially during that state of mind under which I was labouring. As we crossed towards the Captain's house, we met a couple of great Doones lounging by the waterside. Gwenny said something to them, and although they stared very hard at me, they let me pass without hindrance. It is not too much to say that, when the little maid opened Sir Ensor's door, my heart thumped, quite as much with terror as with hope of Lorna's presence.

Lorna led me into a cold dark room, rough and very gloomy, although with two candles burning. I took little heed of the things in it, though I marked that the window was open. That which I heeded was an old man, very stern and comely, with death upon his countenance; yet not lying in his bed, but set upright in a chair, with a loose red cloak thrown over him. Upon this his white hair fell, and his pale fingers lay in a ghastly fashion, without a sign of life or movement, or of the power that kept him up; all rigid, calm, and relentless. Only in his great black eyes, fixed upon me solemnly, all the power of his body dwelt, all the life of his soul was burning.

'Ah,' said the old man, and his voice seemed to come from a cavern of skeletons; 'are you that great John Ridd?'

'John Ridd is my name, your honour,' was all that I could answer; 'and I hope your worship is better.'

'Child, have you sense enough to know what you have been doing?'

'Yes, I know right well,' I answered, 'that I have set mine eyes far above my rank.'

'Are you ignorant that Lorna Doone is born of the oldest families remaining in North Europe?'

'I was ignorant of that, your worship; yet I knew of her high descent from the Doones of Bagworthy.'

The old man's eyes, like fire, probed me whether I was jesting; then perceiving how grave I was, and thinking that I could not laugh (as many people suppose of me), he took on himself to make good the deficiency with a very bitter smile.

'And know you of your own low descent, from the Ridds, of Oare?'

'Sir,' I answered, being as yet unaccustomed to this style of speech, 'the Ridds, of Oare, have been honest men, twice as long as the Doones have been rogues.'

'I would not answer for that, John,' Sir Ensor replied, very quietly, when I expected fury. 'If it be so, thy family is the very oldest in Europe. Now hearken to me, boy, or clown, or honest fool, or whatever thou art; hearken to an old man's words, who has not many hours to live. There is nothing in this world to fear, nothing to revere or trust, nothing even to hope for; least of all, is there ought to love. Therefore I deprive you of nothing, but add to your comfort, and (if there be such a thing) to your happiness, when I forbid you ever to see that foolish child again. Though I have little confidence in man's honour, I have some reliance in woman's pride. You will pledge your word in Lorna's presence, never to see or to seek her again; never even to think of her more. Now call her, for I am weary.'

He kept his great eyes fixed upon me with their icy fire (as if he scorned both life and death), and on his haughty lips some slight amusement at my trouble, and then he raised one hand (as if I were a poor dumb creature), and pointed to the door. Although my heart rebelled and kindled at his proud disdain, I could not disobey him freely; but made a low salute, and went straightway in search of Lorna.

She was crying softly at a little window, and listening to

the river's grief. To my arm she made no answer, neither to my seeking eyes; but to my heart, once for all, she spoke with her own upon it. Not a word, nor sound between us; not even a kiss was interchanged; but man, or maid, who has ever loved hath learned our understanding.

Therefore it came to pass, that we saw fit to enter Sir Ensor's room, in the following manner. All one side of her hair came down, in a way to be remembered, upon the left and fairest part of my favourite otter-skin waistcoat; and her head as well would have lain there doubtless, but for the danger of walking so. I, for my part, was too far gone to lag behind in the matter: but carried my love bravely, fearing neither death nor hell, while she abode beside me.

Old Sir Ensor looked much astonished. For forty years he had been obeyed and feared by all around him.

'Ye two fools!' he said at last, with a depth of contempt which no words may utter: 'ye two fools!'

'May it please your worship,' I answered softly; 'may be we are not such fools as we look. But though we be, we are well content, so long as we may be two fools together.'

'Why, John,' said the old man, with a spark, as of smiling in his eyes; 'thou art not altogether the clumsy yokel, and the clod, I took thee for.'

'Oh no, grandfather; oh dear grandfather,' cried Lorna, with such zeal and flashing, that her hands went forward; 'nobody knows what John Ridd is, because he is so modest. I mean, nobody except me, dear.' And here she turned to me again, and rose upon tiptoe, and kissed me.

'I have seen a little of the world,' said the old man, while I was half ashamed, although so proud of Lorna; 'but this is beyond all I have seen, and nearly all I have heard of. It is more fit for southern climates, than for the fogs of Exmoor.'

'It is fit for all the world, your worship; with your honour's good leave, and will,' I answered in humility, being still ashamed of it; 'when it happens so to people, there is nothing that can stop it, sir.'

Now Sir Ensor Doone was leaning back upon his brown chair-rail, and as I spoke he coughed a little; and he sighed a good deal more; and perhaps his dying heart desired to open time again, with such a lift of warmth and hope as he descried in our eyes, and arms.

'Fools you are; be fools for ever,' said Sir Ensor Doone at last; while we feared to break his thoughts, but let each other know our own, with little ways of pressure: 'it is the best thing I can wish you; boy and girl, be boy and girl, until you have grandchildren.'

Partly in bitterness he spoke, and partly in pure weariness and then he turned so as not to see us; and his white hair fell, like a shroud, around him.

I will not deceive any one, by saying that Sir Ensor Doone gave (in so many words) his consent to my resolve about Lorna. This he never did, except by his speech last written down; from which, as he mentioned grandchildren, a lawyer might have argued it. Not but what he may have meant to bestow on us his blessing; only that he died next day, without taking the trouble to do it.

He called indeed for his box of snuff, which was a very high thing to take; and which he never took without being in very good humour, at least for him. And though it would not go up his nostrils, through the failure of his breath, he was pleased to have it there, and not to think of dying.

He never asked for any one to come near him, not even a priest, nor a monk or friar; but seemed to be going his own way, peaceful, and well contented. Only the chief of the women said, that from his face she believed and knew, that he liked to have me at one side of his bed, and Lorna upon the other. An hour or two ere the old man died, when only we two were with him, he looked at us both very dimly and softly, as if he wished to do something for us, but had left it now too late. Lorna hoped that he wanted to bless us; but he only frowned at that, and let his hand drop downward, and crooked one knotted finger.

'He wants something out of the bed, dear,' Lorna whispered to me; 'see what it is, upon your side, there.'

I followed the bent of his poor shrunken hand, and sought among the pilings; and there I felt something hard and sharp, and drew it forth and gave it to him. It flashed, like the spray of a fountain upon us, in the dark winter of the room. He could not take it in his hand, but let it hang, as daisies do; only making Lorna see that he meant her to have it.

'Why, it is my glass necklace!' Lorna cried, in great surprise; 'my necklace he always promised me; and from which you have got the ring, John. May I have it now, dear grandfather?'

Then she gave to me the trinket, for the sake of safety; and I stowed it in my breast. He seemed to me to follow this, and to be well content with it.

Before Sir Ensor Doone was buried, the greatest frost of the century had set in, with its iron hand, and step of stone, on everything. The strong men broke three good pickaxes, ere they got through the hard brown sod, chequed with flakes of frosty white, where old Sir Ensor was to lie upon his back, awaiting the darkness of the Judgment-day.

Not a tear was shed upon him, except from the sweetest of all sweet eyes; not a sigh pursued him home. Except in hot anger, his life had been very cold, and bitter, and distant; and now a week had exhausted all the sorrow of those around him, a grief flowing less from affection than fear.

After all was over, I strode across the moors very sadly; trying to keep the cold away, by virtue of quick movement. Not a flake of snow had fallen yet; all the earth was caked and hard, with a dry brown crust upon it; all the sky was banked with darkness, hard, austere, and frowning. It was freezing hard and sharp, with a piercing wind to back it; and I had observed that the holy water froze upon Sir Ensor's coffin.

The Great Winter

IN the bitter morning, I arose knowing I must bring in snug every sheep, horse and cow, with plenty to eat. An odd white light was on the rafters, such as I never had seen before; while all the length of the room was grisly, like the heart of a mouldy oat-rick. Half the lattice was quite blocked up, as if plastered with grey lime; and little fringes, like ferns, came through, where the joining of the lead was.

With some trouble, and great care, lest the ancient frame should yield, I spread the lattice open; and saw at once that not a moment must be lost, to save our stock. All the earth was flat with snow, all the air was thick with snow; more than this no man could see, for all the world was snowing.

I shut the window, and dressed in haste; and then set forth to find John Fry, Jem Slocombe, and Bill Dadds. But this was easier thought than done; for when I opened the court-yard door, I was taken up to my knees at once, and the power of the drifting cloud prevented sight of anything. It must have snowed most wonderfully to have made that depth of covering in about eight hours. For one of Master Stickles' men, who had been out all the night, said that no snow began to fall until nearly midnight.

All this time it was snowing harder than it ever had snowed before, so far as a man might guess at it; and the leaden depth of the sky came down, like a mine turned upside down on us. Not that the flakes were so very large; for I have seen much larger flakes in a shower of March, while sowing peas; but that there was no room between them, neither any relaxing, nor any change of direction. Yet after a deal of floundering, some laughter and a little swearing, we came all safe to the lower meadow, where most of our flock was hurdled.

But behold, there was no flock at all! None, I mean, to be seen anywhere; only at one corner of the field, by the eastern end, where the snow drove in, a great white billow, as high as a barn and as broad as a house. This great drift was rolling and curling beneath the violent blast, tufting and combing with rustling swirls, and carved (as in patterns of cornice) where the grooving chisel of the wind swept round.

But although, for people who had no sheep, the sight was a very fine one, yet for us, with our flock beneath it, this great mount had but little charm. We four men set to in earnest, digging with all our might and main, shovelling away at the great white pile, and fetching it into the meadow. Each man made for himself a cave, scooping at the soft cold flux, which slid upon him at every stroke, and throwing it out behind him, in piles of castled fancy. At last we drove our tunnels in (for we worked indeed for the lives of us), and all converging towards the middle, held our tools and listened.

Further in, and close under the bank, where they had huddled themselves for warmth, we found the poor sheep packed as closely as if they were in a great pie. It was strange to observe how their vapour, and breath, and the moisture exuding from their wool had scooped, as it were, a coved room for them, lined with a ribbing of deep yellow snow. Two or three of the weaklier hoggets were dead, from want of air, and from pressure; but more than three-score were as lively as ever; though cramped and stiff for a little while.

Then of the outer sheep (all now snowed and frizzled like a lawyer's wig) I took the two finest and heaviest, and with one beneath my right arm, and the other beneath my left, I went straight home to the upper sheppey, and set them inside, and fastened them. Sixty-and-six I took home in that way, two at a time on each journey; and the work grew harder and harder each time, as the drifts of the snow were deepening. No other man should meddle with them: I was resolved to try my strength against the strength of the elements; and try it I did, ay and proved it. A certain fierce delight burned in me, as the struggle grew harder; but rather would I die than yield; and at last I finished it. People talk of it to this day: but none can tell what the labour was, who have not felt that snow and wind.

Of the sheep upon the mountain, and the sheep upon the western farm, and the cattle on the upper burrows, scarcely one in ten was saved; do what we would for them. And this was not through any neglect but from the pure impossibility of finding them at all. That great snow never ceased a moment for three days and nights; and then when all the earth was filled, and the topmost hedges were unseen, and the trees broke down with weight (wherever the wind had not lightened them), a brilliant sun broke forth and showed the loss of all our customs.

That night, such a frost ensued as we had never dreamed of, neither read in ancient books, or histories of Frobisher. The kettle by the fire froze, and the crock upon the hearth-cheeks; many men were killed, and cattle rigid in their head-ropes. Then I heard that fearful sound, which never I had heard before, neither since have heard (except during that same winter), the sharp yet solemn sound of trees, burst open by the frost-blow.

We were losing half our stock, do all we could to shelter them. Even the horses in the stables (mustered altogether, for the sake of breath and steaming) had long icicles from their muzzles, almost every morning. But of all things the very gravest, to my apprehension, was the impossibility of hearing, or having any token, of or from my loved one. Not that those three days alone of snow (tremendous as it was) could have blocked the country so; but that the sky had never ceased, for more than two days at a time, for full three weeks thereafter, to pour fresh piles of fleecy mantle; neither had the wind relaxed a single day from shaking them. As a rule, it snowed all day, cleared up at night, and froze intensely, with the stars as bright as jewels, earth spread out in lustrous twilight, and the sounds in the air as sharp and crackling as artillery; then in the morning snow again, before the sun could come to help.

I believe it was on Epiphany morning, or somewhere about that period, when Lizzie ran into the kitchen to me, where I was thawing my goose-grease, and having caught me, by way of wonder (for generally I was out shovelling, long before my 'young lady' had her nightcap off), she positively kissed me, for the sake of warming her lips perhaps, or because she had something proud to say.

'You great fool, John,' said my lady, as Annie and I used to call her, on account of her airs and graces; 'what a pity you never read, John!'

'Much use, I should think, in reading!' I answered, though pleased with her condescension; 'read, I suppose, with roof coming in, and only this chimney left sticking out of the snow!'

'The very time to read, John,' said Lizzie, looking grander; 'our worst troubles are the need, whence knowledge can deliver us. Now, will you listen to what I have read about climates ten times worse than this; and where none but clever men can live?'

So when I had done my morning's work, I listened to her patiently; and it was out of my power to think that all she said was foolish. She told me that in the 'Arctic Regions', as they call some places a long way north, where the Great Bear lies all across the heavens, and no sun is up, for whole months at a time, that here they always had such winters as we were having now. Nevertheless the people there (although the snow was fifty feet deep, and all their breath fell behind them frozen, like a log of wood dropped from their shoulders), yet they managed to get along, by a little cleverness. Through the sparkle of the whiteness, and the ups and downs of cold, any man might get along with a boat on either foot, to prevent his sinking. She told me how these boats were made; very strong and very light, of ribs with skin across them; five feet long, and one foot wide; and turned up at each end, even as a canoe is.

Then she told me another thing equally useful to me; although I would not let her see how much I thought about it. And this concerned the use of sledges, and their power of gliding, and the lightness of their following; all of which I could see at once, through knowledge of our own farm-sleds; which we employ in lieu of wheels, used in flatter districts. When I had heard all this from her, a mere chit of a girl as she was, unfit to make a snowball even, or to fry snow-pancakes, I looked down on her with amazement, and began to wish a little that I had given more time to books.

Therefore I fell to at once, upon that hint from Lizzie, and being used to thatching-work, and the making of traps, and so on, before very long I built myself a pair of strong and light snow-shoes, framed with ash and ribbed of withy, with half-tanned calf-skin stretched across, and an inner sole to support my feet. At first I could not walk at all, but floundered about most piteously, catching one shoe in the other, and both of them in the snow-drifts, to the great amusement of the maidens, who were come to look at me. But after a while I grew more expert, with a fixed resolve not to notice pain or stiffness; and sure enough, before dark next day, I could get along pretty freely. The astonishment of poor John Fry, Bill Dadds, and Jem Slocombe, when they saw me coming down the hill upon them, in the twilight, where they were clearing the furze rick and trussing it for cattle, was more than I can tell you; because they did not let me see it, but ran away with one accord, and floundered into a snow-drift. They believed, and so did every one else (especially when I grew able to glide along pretty rapidly), that I had stolen Mother Melldrum's sieves, on which she was said to fly over the foreland at midnight every Saturday.

And 'tis certain that poor Lizzie had not dreamed what my first application of her lesson would be.

Not Too Soon

WHEN I started on my road across the hills and valleys (which now were pretty much alike), the utmost I could hope to do was to gain the crest of hills, and look into the Doone Glen. Hence I might at least descry whether Lorna still was safe, by the six nests still remaining, and the view of the Captain's house. When I was come to the open country, far beyond the sheltered homestead, and in the full brunt of the wind, the keen blast of the cold broke on me, and the mighty breadth of snow.

At last I got to my spy-hill (as I had begun to call it), although I never should have known it, but for what it looked on. And even to know this last again required all the eyes of love, soever sharp and vigilant. For all the beautiful Glen Doone (shaped from out the mountains, as if on purpose for the Doones, and looking in the summer-time like a sharp-cut vase of green) now was besnowed half up the sides, and at either end so, that it was more like the white basins wherein we boil plum-pudding.

Seeing no Doones now about, and doubting if any guns would go off, in this state of the weather, and knowing that no man could catch me up (except with shoes like mine), I even resolved to slide the cliffs, and bravely go to Lorna.

It helped me much in this resolve, that the snow came on again, thick enough to blind a man who had not spent his time among it, as I had done now for days and days. I set my back and elbows well against a snow-drift, hanging far adown the cliff, and saying some of the Lord's Prayer, threw myself on Providence. Before there was time to think or dream, I landed very beautifully upon a ridge of run-up snow in a quiet corner. Having set myself aright, and being in good spirits, I made boldly across the valley (where the snow was furrowed hard), being now afraid of nobody.

The house was partly drifted up, though not so much as ours was; and I crossed the little stream almost without knowing that it was under me. At first, being pretty safe against interference from the other huts, by virtue of the blinding snow, and the difficulty of walking, I examined all the windows; but these were coated so with ice, like ferns and flowers and dazzling stars, that no one could so much as guess what might be inside of them.

I was forced, much against my will, to venture to the door and knock, in a hesitating manner, not being sure but what my answer might be the mouth of a carbine. However, it was not so, for I heard a pattering of feet and a whispering going on, and then a trembling voice through the keyhole, asking, 'Who's there?'

'Only me, John Ridd,' I answered; upon which Gwenny let me in, and barred the door again like lightning.

'What is the meaning of all this, Gwenny?' I asked, as I slipped about on the floor, for I could not stand there firmly with my great snow-shoes on.

'Maning enough, and bad maning too,' the Cornish girl made answer. 'Us be shut in here, and starving, and durstn't let any body in upon us. I wish thou wer't good to ate, young man: I could manage the most of thee.'

I was so frightened by her eyes, full of wolfish hunger, that I could only say, 'Good God!' having never seen the like before. Then drew I forth a large piece of bread, which I had brought in case of accidents, and placed it in her hands. She leaped at it, as a starving dog leaps at sight of his supper, and she set her teeth in it, and then withheld it from her lips, with something very like an oath at her own vile greediness; and then away round the corner with it, no doubt for her young mistress. I meanwhile was occupied, to the best of my ability, in taking my snow-shoes off, yet wondering much within myself, why Lorna did not come to me.

But presently I knew the cause; for Gwenny called me, and I ran, and found my darling quite unable to say so much as, 'John, how are you?' Between the hunger, and the cold, and the excitement of my coming, she had fainted away, and lay back on a chair, as white as the snow around us. I ran to coax my Lorna back to sense, and hope, and joy, and love.

'I never expected to see you again. I had made up my mind to die, John; and to die without your knowing it.'

As I repelled this fearful thought in a manner highly fortifying, the tender hue flowed back again into her famished cheeks and lips, and a softer brilliance glistened from the depth of her dark eyes.

'After all, Mistress Lorna,' I said, pretending to be gay, for a smile might do her good; 'you do not love me as Gwenny does; for she even wanted to eat me.'

'And shall, afore I have done, young man,' Gwenny answered laughing; 'you come in here with they red chakes, and make us think o' sirloin.'

'I have something here such as you never tasted the like of, being in such appetite. Look here, Lorna; smell it first. I have had it ever since Twelfth-day, and kept it all the time for you. Annie made it. That is enough to warrant it good cooking.'

And then I showed my great mince-pie in a bag of tissue paper, and I told them how the mince-meat was made of golden pippins finely shred, with the undercut of the sirloin, and spice and fruit accordingly and far beyond my knowledge. But Lorna would not touch a morsel, until she had thanked God for it, and given me the kindest kiss, and put a piece in Gwenny's mouth.

Then I begged to know the meaning of this state of things.

'The meaning is sad enough,' said Lorna; 'and I see no way out of it. We are both to be starved until I let them do what they like with me.'

'That is to say, until you choose to marry Carver Doone, and be slowly killed by him.'

'Slowly! No, John, quickly. I hate him with such bitterness, that less than a week would kill me.'

'Not a doubt of that,' said Gwenny: 'Oh, she hates him nicely, then: but not half so much as I do.'

I told them both that this state of things could be endured no longer; on which point they agreed with me, but saw no means to help it.

Then I spoke, with a strange tingle upon both sides of my heart, knowing that this undertaking was a serious one for all, and might burn our farm down, –

'If I warrant to take you safe, and without much fright or hardship, Lorna, will you come with me?'

'To be sure I will, dear,' said my beauty with a smile, and a glance to follow it; 'I have small alternative, to starve, or go with you, John.'

'Gwenny, have you courage for it? Will you come with your young mistress?'

'Will I stay behind!' cried Gwenny, in a voice that settled it. And so we began to arrange about it; and I was much excited. It was useless now to leave it longer: if it could be done at all, it could not be too quickly done. It was the Counsellor who had ordered, after all other schemes had failed, that his niece should have no food until she would obey him. He had strictly watched the house, taking turns with Carver, to ensure that none came nigh it bearing food or comfort. But this evening, they had thought it needless to remain on guard; and it would have been impossible, because themselves were busy, offering high festival to all the valley, in right of their own commandership.

And then I saw, far down the stream (or rather down the bed of it, for there was no stream visible), a little form of fire arising, red, and dark, and flickering. Presently it caught on something, and went upward boldly; and then it struck into many forks, and then it fell, and rose again.

'Do you know what all that is, John? The Doones are firing Dunkery beacon, to celebrate their new captain.'

'But how could they bring it here, through the snow? If they have sledges, I can do nothing.'

'They brought it before the snow began. The moment poor grandfather was gone, even before his funeral, the young men, having none to check them, began at once upon it. Ah, now look! The tar is kindled.'

I looked upon this very gravely, knowing that this heavy outrage to the feelings of the neighbourhood would cause more stir than a hundred sheep stolen, or a score of houses sacked. Not of course that the beacon was of the smallest use to any one, neither stopped anybody from stealing: yet I knew that we valued it, and were proud, and spoke of it as a mighty institution.

In this I saw great obstacle to what I wished to manage. For when this pyramid should be kindled thoroughly, and pouring light and blazes round, would not all the valley be like a white room full of candles? Thinking thus, I was half inclined to abide my time for another night; and then my second thoughts convinced me that I would be a fool in this. For lo, what an opportunity! All the Doones would be drunk of course, in about three hours' time, and getting more and more in drink, as the night went on. As for the fire, it must sink in about three hours or more, and only cast uncertain shadows friendly to my purpose. And then the outlaws must cower round it, as the cold increased on them, helping the weight of the liquor; and in their jollity any noise would be cheered as a false alarm. Most of all, and which decided once for all my action, – when these wild and reckless villains should be hot with ardent spirits, what was door, or wall, to stand betwixt them and my Lorna?

This thought quickened me so much that I touched my darling reverently, and told her in a few short words how I hoped to manage it.

'Sweetest, in two hours' time, I shall be again with you. Keep the bar up, and have Gwenny ready to answer any one. You are safe while they are dining, dear, and drinking healths, and all that stuff! and before they have done with that, I shall be again with you. Have everything you care to take in a very little compass; and Gwenny must have no baggage. I shall knock loud, and then wait a little; and then knock twice, very softly.'

With this, I folded her in my arms; and she looked frightened at me; not having perceived her danger: and then I told Gwenny over again what I had told her mistress: but she only nodded her head and said, 'Young man, go and teach thy grandmother.'

Brought Home at Last

WHEN, on my way home, I came to my old ascent, where I had often scaled the cliff and made across the mountains, it struck me that I would just have a look at my first and painful entrance, to wit, the water-slide. I never for a moment imagined that this could help me now; for I never had dared to descend it, even in the finest weather; still I had a curiosity to know what my old friend was like, with so much snow upon him. But, to my very great surprise, there was scarcely any snow there at all, though plenty curling high over head from the cliff, like bolsters over it.

All my water-slide was now less a slide than path of ice; furrowed where the waters ran over fluted ridges; seamed where wind had tossed and combed them, even while congealing; and crossed with little steps wherever the freezing torrent lingered. And here and there the ice was fibred with the trail of sludge-weed, slanting from the side, and matted, so as to make resting-place.

Lo, it was easy track and channel, as if for the very purpose made, down which I could guide my sledge, with Lorna sitting in it. There were only two things to be feared; one lest the rolls of snow above should fall in and bury us; the other lest we should rush too fast, and so be carried headlong into the black whirlpool at the bottom, the middle of which was still unfrozen, and looking more horrible by the contrast. Against this danger I made provision, by fixing a stout bar across; but of the other we must take our chance, and trust ourselves to Providence.

I hastened home at my utmost speed, and told my mother for God's sake to keep the house up till my return, and to have plenty of fire blazing and plenty of water boiling, and food enough hot for a dozen people, and the best bed aired with the warming-pan. Dear mother smiled softly at my excitement, though her own was not much less, I am sure, and enhanced by sore anxiety.

After this I took some brandy, both within and about me; the former, because I had sharp work to do; and the latter in fear of whatever might happen, in such great cold, to my comrades. Then I went to the upper linhay, and took our new light pony-sledd, which had been made almost as much for pleasure as for business; though God only knows how our girls could have found any pleasure in bumping along so. On the snow, however, it ran as sweetly as if it had been made for it.

I girded my own body with a dozen turns of hayrope, twisting both the ends in under at the bottom of my breast, and winding the hay on the skew a little, that the hempen thong might not slip between, and so cut me in the drawing. I put a good piece of spare rope in the sledd, and the cross-seat with the back to it, which was stuffed with our own wool, as well as two or three fur coats.

With that I drew my traces hard, and set my ashen staff into the snow, and struck out with my best foot foremost (the best one at snow-shoes, I mean), and the sledd came after me as lightly as en elf might follow. I went on at a very tidy speed; being only too thankful that the snow had ceased, and no wind as yet arisen. And from the ring of low white vapour girding all the verge of sky, and from the rosy blue above, as well as from the moon itself and the light behind it, having learned the signs of frost from its bitter twinges, I knew that we should have a night as keen as ever England felt.

Daring not to risk my sledd by any fall from the valley-cliffs, I dragged it very carefully up the steep incline of ice, through the narrow chasm, and so to the very brink and verge where first I had seen my Lorna, in the fishing-days of boyhood. As then I had a trident fork, for sticking of the loaches, so now I had a strong ash stake to lay across from rock to rock, and break the speed of descending. With this I moored the sledd quite safe, at the very lip of the chasm, where all was now substantial ice, green and black in the moonlight; and then I set off up the valley, skirting along one side of it.

I crossed to the door of Lorna's house, and made the sign, and listened, after taking my snow-shoes off.

But no one came, as I expected, neither could I espy a

light. And I seemed to hear a faint low sound, like the moaning of the snow-wind. Then I knocked again more loudly, with a knocking at my heart; and receiving no answer, set all my power at once against the door. In a moment it flew inwards, and I glided along the passage with my feet still slippery. There in Lorna's room I saw, by the moonlight flowing in, a sight which drove me beyond sense.

Lorna was behind a chair, crouching in the corner, with her hands up, and a crucifix, or something that looked like it. In the middle of the room lay Gwenny Carfax, stupid, yet with one hand clutching the ankle of a struggling man. Another man stood above my Lorna, trying to draw the chair away. In a moment I had him round the waist, and he went out of the window with a mighty crash of glass; luckily for him that window had no bars like some of them. Then I took the other man by the neck; and he could not plead for mercy. I bore him out of the house as lightly as I would bear a baby, yet squeezing his throat a little more than I fain would do to an infant. I cast him, like a skittle, from me into a snowdrift, which closed over him. Then I looked for the other fellow, tossed through Lorna's window; and found him lying stunned and bleeding, neither able to groan yet. Charleworth Doone, if his gushing blood did not much mislead me.

It was no time to linger now: I fastened my shoes in a moment, and caught up my own darling with her head upon my shoulder, where she whispered faintly; and telling Gwenny to follow me, or else I would come back for her, if she could not walk the snow, I ran the whole distance to my sledd, caring not who might follow me. Then by the time I had set up Lorna, sturdy Gwenny came along, having trudged in the track of my snow-shoes, although with two bags on her back. I set her in beside her mistress, to support her, and keep warm; and then with one look back at the glen, which had been so long my home of heart, I hung behind the sledd, and launched it down the steep and dangerous way.

Though the cliffs were black above us, and the road unseen in front, and a great white grave of snow might at a single word come down, Lorna was as calm and happy as an infant in its bed. She knew that I was with her; and when I told her not to speak, she touched my hand in silence. Gwenny was in a much greater fright, having never seen such a thing before, neither knowing what it is to yield to pure love's confidence. I could hardly keep her quiet, without making a noise myself. But with my staff from rock to rock, and my weight thrown backward, I broke the sledd's too rapid way.

Unpursued, yet looking back as if some one must be after us, we skirted round the black whirling pool, and gained the meadows beyond it. Lorna was now so far oppressed with all the troubles of the evening, and the joy that followed them, as well as by the piercing cold and difficulty of breathing, that she lay quite motionless, like fairest wax in the moonlight – when we stole a glance at her, beneath the dark folds of the cloak; and I thought that she was falling into the heavy snow-sleep, whence there is no awaking.

Therefore I drew my traces tight, and set my whole strength to the business. And so in about an hour's time, in spite of many hindrances, we came home to the old courtyard, and all the dogs saluted us. My heart was quivering, and my cheeks as hot as the Doones' bonfire, with wondering both what Lorna would think of our farm-yard, and what my mother would think of her. Upon the former subject my anxiety was wasted, for Lorna neither saw a thing, nor even opened her heavy eyes.

They carried her into the house, and because I thought I was not wanted among so many women, and should only get the worst of it, and perhaps do harm to my darling, I went and brought Gwenny in, and gave her a potful of bacon and peas, and an iron spoon to eat it with, which she did right heartily.

Then I asked her how she could have been such a fool as to let those two vile fellows enter the house where Lorna was; and she accounted for it so naturally, that I could only blame myself. For my agreement had been to give one loud knock (if you happen to remember) and after that two little knocks. Well, these two drunken rogues had come; and one, being very drunk indeed, had given a great thump; and then nothing more to do with it; and the other, being three-quarters drunk, had followed his leader (as one might say) but feebly, and making two of it. Whereupon up jumped Lorna, and declared that her John was there.

Then there came a message for me, that my love was sensible, and was seeking all around for me. In the settle was my Lorna, propped with pillows round her, and her clear hands spread sometimes to the blazing fire-place. In her eyes no knowledge was of anything around her, only both her lovely hands were entreating something, to spare her or to love her; and the lines of supplication quivered in her sad white face.

'All go away except my mother,' I said very quietly, but so that I would be obeyed; and everybody knew it. Then mother came to me alone; and she said, 'The frost is in her brain: I have heard of this before, John.' 'Mother, I will have it out,' was all that I could answer her; 'leave her to me altogether: only you sit there and watch.' For I felt that Lorna knew me, and no other soul but me; and that if not interfered with, she would soon come home to me. And presently the glance that watched me, as at a distance and in doubt, began to flutter and to brighten, and the small entreating hands found their way, as if by instinct, to my great protecting palms; and trembled there, and rested there.

For a little while we lingered thus, neither wishing to move away, neither caring to look beyond the presence of the other; both alike so full of hope, and comfort, and true happiness; if only the world would let us be. And then a little sob disturbed us, and mother tried to make believe that she was only coughing. But Lorna, guessing who she was, jumped up so very rashly that she almost set her frock on fire from the great ash-log; and away she ran to the old oak chair, where mother was by the clock-case pretending to be knitting, and she took the work from mother's hands, and laid them both upon her head, kneeling humbly, and looking up.

'God bless you, my fair mistress!' said mother, bending nearer, and then as Lorna's gaze prevailed, 'God bless you, my sweet child!'

The Squire Weighs the Evidence

JEREMY STICKLES was gone south, ere ever the frost set in, for the purpose of mustering forces to attack the Doone Glen. But now this weather had put a stop to every kind of movement; for even if men could have borne the cold, they could scarcely be brought to face the perils of the snow-drifts. And to tell the truth, I cared not how long this weather lasted, so long as we had enough to eat, and could keep ourselves from freezing. Not only that I did not want Master Stickles back again, to make more disturbances; but also that the Doones could not come prowling after Lorna, while the snow lay piled between us, with the surface soft and dry. Of course, they would very soon discover where their lawful queen was, although the track of sledd and snow-shoes had been quite obliterated by another shower, before the revellers could have grown half as drunk as they intended. And it gave me no little pleasure to think how mad that Carver must be with me, for robbing him of the lovely bride whom he was starving into matrimony. However, I was not pleased at all with the prospect of the consequences; but set all hands on to thresh the corn, ere the Doones could come and burn the ricks.

But now, about the tenth of March, the fog, which had hung about (even in full sunshine), vanished, and the shrouded hills shone forth with brightness manifold. And now the sky at length began to come to its true manner, which we had not seen for months, the fickle sky which suits our England, though abused by foreign folk.

And soon the dappled softening sky gave some earnest of its mood; for a brisk south wind arose, and the blessed rain came driving; cold indeed, yet most refreshing to the skin, all parched with snow, and the eyeballs so long dazzled. So when the first of the rain began, and the old familiar softness spread upon the window glass, we all ran out, and filled our eyes, and filled our hearts, with gazing.

But then a heavy gale of wind arose, with violent rain from the south-west, which lasted almost without a pause, for three nights and two days. At first, the rain made no impression on the bulk of snow, but ran from every sloping surface, and froze on every flat one, through the coldness of the earth; and so it became impossible for any man to keep his legs, without the help of a shodden staff. After a good while, however, the air growing very much warmer, this state of things began to change, and a worse one to succeed it; for now the snow came thundering down from roof, and rock, and ivied tree, and floods began to roar and foam in every trough and gulley. Indeed, the strangest sight of all to me was in the bed of streams, and brooks, and especially of the Lynn river. It was worth going miles to behold such a thing, for a man might never have the chance again.

It was now high time to work very hard; both to make up for the farm-work lost during the months of frost and snow, and also to be ready for a great and vicious attack from the

Doones, who would burn us in our beds, at the earliest opportunity.

Then, in spite of the floods, and the sloughs being out, and the state of the roads most perilous, Squire Faggus came at last, riding his famous strawberry mare. There was a great ado between him and Annie, as you may well suppose, after some four months of parting.

Tom Faggus had very good news to tell, and he told it with such force of expression as made us laugh very heartily. He had taken up his purchase from old Sir Roger Bassett of a nice bit of land, to the south of the moors, and in the parish of Molland. This farm of Squire Faggus (as he truly now had a right to be called) was of the very finest pasture, when it got good store of rain. And Tom, who had ridden the Devonshire roads with many a reeking jacket, knew right well that he might trust the climate for that matter. Tom saw at once what it was fit for – the breeding of fine cattle.

Then he pressed us both on another point, the time for his marriage to Annie: and mother looked at me to say when, and I looked back at mother. However, knowing something of the world, and unable to make any further objections, by reason of his prosperity, I said that we must even do as the fashionable people did, and allow the maid herself to settle, when she would leave home and all.

We had quite a high dinner of fashion that day, with Betty Muxworthy waiting, and Gwenny Carfax at the gravy, and when the young maidens were gone – and only mother, and Tom, and I remained at the white deal table, with brandy, and schnapps, and hot water jugs – Squire Faggus said quite suddenly, and perhaps on purpose to take us aback, in case of our hiding anything –

'What do you know of the history of that beautiful maiden, good mother?'

'Not half so much as my son does,' mother answered, with

a soft smile at me: 'and when John does not choose to tell a thing, wild horses will not pull it out of him.'

'That is not at all like me, mother,' I replied rather sadly; 'you know almost every word about Lorna, quite as well as I do.'

'Almost every word, I believe, John; for you never tell a falsehood. But the few unknown may be of all the most important to me.'

To this I made no answer, for fear of going beyond the truth, or else of making mischief. Tom Faggus told us that he was sure he had seen my Lorna's face before, many and many years ago, when she was quite a little child, but he could not remember where it was, or anything more about it at present; though he would try to do so afterwards. He could not be mistaken, he said, for he had noticed her eyes especially; and had never seen such eyes before, neither again, until this day. I asked him if he had ever ventured into the Doone-valley; but he shook his head, and replied that he valued his life a deal too much for that. Then we put it to him, whether anything might assist his memory; but he said that he knew not of aught to do so, unless it were another glass of schnapps.

This being provided, he grew very wise, and told us clearly and candidly that we were both very foolish. For he said that we were keeping Lorna, at the risk not only of our stock, and the house above our heads, but also of our precious lives; and after all was she worth it, although so very beautiful? Upon which I told him, with indignation, that her beauty was the least part of her goodness, and that I would thank him for his opinion, when I had requested it.

'Bravo, our John Ridd!' he answered: 'fools will be fools till the end of the chapter: and I might be as big a one, if I were in thy shoes, John. Nevertheless, in the name of God, don't let that helpless child go about, with a thing worth half the county on her.'

'She is worth all the county herself,' said I, 'and all England put together: but she has nothing worth half a rick of hay upon her; for the ring I gave her cost only' – and here I stopped, for mother was looking, and I never would tell her how much it had cost me; though she had tried fifty times to find out.

'Tush, the ring!' Tom Faggus cried, with a contempt that moved me; 'I would never have stopped a man for that. But the necklace, you great oaf, the necklace is worth all your farm put together, and your Uncle Ben's fortune to the back of it; ay, and all the town of Dulverton.'

'What,' said I, 'that common glass thing, which she has had from her childhood!'

'Glass indeed! They are the finest brilliants ever I set eyes on: and I have handled a good many. Trust me, good mother, and simple John, for knowing brilliants, when I see them. I would have stopped an eight-horse coach, with four carabined outriders, for such a booty as that.'

My mother went herself to fetch Lorna, that the trinket might be examined. On the shapely curve of her neck it hung, like dewdrops upon a white hyacinth; and I was vexed that Tom should have the chance to see it there. But even as if she had read my thoughts, or outrun them with her own, Lorna turned away, and softly took the jewels from the place which so much adorned them. And as she turned away, they sparkled through the rich dark waves of hair. Then she laid the glittering circlet in my mother's hands; and Tom Faggus took it eagerly, and bore it to the window.

'Don't you go out of sight,' I said; 'you cannot resist such things as those, if they be what you think them.'

'Jack, I shall have to trounce thee yet. I am now a man of honour, and entitled to the duello. What will you take for it, Mistress Lorna? Do you think it is worth five pounds, now?'

'Oh no! I never had so much money as that in all my life.

It is very bright and very pretty; but it cannot be worth five pounds, I am sure.'

'What a chance for a bargain! Oh, if it were not for Annie, I could make my fortune.'

'But, sir, I would not sell it to you, not for twenty times five pounds. My grandfather was so kind about it; and I think it belonged to my mother.'

'There are twenty-five rose diamonds in it, and twenty-five large brilliants that cannot be matched in London. How say you, Mistress Lorna, to a hundred thousand pounds?'

Then Tom Faggus delivered all around a dissertation on precious stones, and his sentiments about those in his hand. He said that the work was very ancient, but undoubtedly very good; the cutting of every line was true, and every angle was in its place. He said that the necklace was made, he would answer for it, in Amsterdam, two or three hundred years ago, long before London jewellers had begun to meddle with diamonds; and on the gold clasp he found some letters, done in some inverted way, the meaning of which was beyond him; also a bearing of some kind, which he believed was a mountain-cat.

I knew what Lorna was thinking of; she was thinking all the time that her necklace had been taken by the Doones with violence upon some great robbery; and that Squire Faggus knew it, though he would not show his knowledge. We said no more about the necklace, for a long time afterwards; neither did my darling wear it, now that she knew its value, but did not know its history.

Every Man Must Defend Himself

SCARCELY had Tom left us, and Annie's tears not dry yet (for she always made a point of crying upon his departure), when in came Master Jeremy Stickles, splashed with mud from head to foot, and not in the very best of humours, though happy to get back again.

'Curse those fellows!' he cried, with a stamp which sent the water hissing from his boot among the embers; 'a pretty plight you may call this, for His Majesty's Commissioner to return to his headquarters in!

'Well, this is better than being chased over the moors for one's life, John. All the way from Landacre Bridge, I have ridden a race for my precious life, at the peril of my limbs and neck. Three great Doones galloping after me, and a good job for me that they were so big, or they must have overtaken me. Just go and see to my horse, John, that's an excellent lad.'

It was only right in Jeremy Stickles, and of the simplest common sense, that he would not tell, before our girls, what the result of his journey was. But he led me aside in the course of the evening, and told me all about it; saying that I knew, as well as he did, that it was not woman's business.

He complained that the weather had been against him bitterly, closing all the roads around him; even as it had done with us. It had taken him eight days, he said, to get from Exeter to Plymouth; whither he found that most of the troops had been drafted off from Exeter. When all were told, there was but a battalion of one of the King's horse regiments, and two companies of foot soldiers; and their commanders had orders, later than the date of Jeremy's commission, on no account to quit the southern coast and march inland. Therefore, although they would gladly have come for a brush with the celebrated Doones, it was more than they durst attempt, in the face of their instructions.

To the justices of the county Master Stickles now was forced to address himself, although he would rather have had one trooper than a score from the very best trained bands. For these trained bands had afforded very good soldiers, in the time of the civil wars, and for some years afterwards; but now their discipline was gone; and the younger generation had seen no real fighting. Each would have his own opinion, and would want to argue it; and if this were not allowed, he went about his duty in such a temper as to prove that his own way was the best.

Neither was this the worst of it; for Jeremy made no doubt but what (if he could only get the militia to turn out in force) he might manage, with the help of his own men, to force the stronghold of the enemy; but the truth was that the officers, knowing how hard it would be to collect their men at that time of the year, and in that state of the weather, began with one accord to make every possible excuse.

And so it came to pass that the King's Commissioner returned, without any army whatever; but with promise of two hundred men when the roads should be more passable. And meanwhile, what were we to do, abandoned as we were to the mercies of the Doones, with only our own hands to help us? He agreed with me, that we could not hope to escape an attack from the outlaws, and the more especially now that they knew himself to be returned to us. Furthermore, he recommended that all the entrances to the house should at once be strengthened, and a watch must be maintained at night; and he thought it wiser that I should go (late as it was) to Lynmouth, if a horse could pass the valley, and fetch every one of his mounted troopers, who might now be quartered there.

Knowing how fiercely the floods were out, I resolved to

travel the higher road, by Cosgate and through Countisbury; therefore I swam my horse through the Lynn, at the ford below our house (where sometimes you may step across), and thence galloped up and along the hills. But when I descended the hill towards Lynmouth, I feared that my journey was all in vain.

For the East Lynn (which is our river) was ramping and roaring frightfully, lashing whole trunks of trees on the rocks, and rending them, and grinding them. And into it rushed, from the opposite side, a torrent even madder; upsetting what it came to aid; shattering wave with boiling billow, and scattering wrath with fury. It was certain death to attempt the passage; and the little wooden footbridge had been carried away long ago. And the men I was seeking must have their dwelling on the other side of this deluge, for on my side there was not a single house.

I followed the bank of the flood to the beach, some two or three hundred yards below; and there had the luck to see Will Watcombe on the opposite side, caulking an old boat. Though I could not make him hear a word, from the deafening roar of the torrent, I got him to understand at last that I wanted to cross over. Upon this he fetched another man, and the two of them launched a boat; and paddling well out to sea, fetched round the mouth of the frantic river. The other man proved to be Stickles' chief mate; and so he went back, and fetched his comrades, bringing their weapons, but leaving their horses behind. As it happened there were but six of them; however to have even these was a help; and I started again at full speed for my home; for the men must follow afoot, and cross our river high up on the moorland.

It was lucky that I came home so soon; for I found the house in a great commotion, and all the women trembling. When I asked what the matter was, Lorna, who seemed the most self-possessed, answered that it was all her fault, for she alone had frightened them. She had gone out to the garden towards dusk, when she descried two glittering eyes glaring at her steadfastly, from the elder bush beyond the stream. The elder was soothing its wrinkled leaves, being at least two months behind time; and among them this calm cruel face appeared; and she knew it was the face of Carver Doone.

The maiden lost all presence of mind hereat, and could only gaze, as if bewitched. Then Carver Doone, with his deadly smile, gloating upon her horror, lifted his long gun, and pointed full at Lorna's heart. In vain she strove to turn away; fright had stricken her stiff as stone.

With no sign of pity in his face, no quiver of relenting, but a well-pleased grin at all the charming palsy of his victim, Carver Doone lowered, inch by inch, the muzzle of his gun. When it pointed to the ground, between her delicate arched insteps, he pulled the trigger, and the bullet flung the mould all over her. It was a refinement of bullying, for which I swore to God that night, upon my knees, in secret, that I would smite down Carver Doone; or else he should smite me down.

My darling fell away on a bank of grass, and wept at her own cowardice. And while she leaned there, quite unable yet to save herself, Carver came to the brink of the flood, which alone was between them, and he stroked his jet-black beard.

'I have spared you this time,' he said, in his deep, calm voice, 'only because it suits my plans; and I never yield to temper. But unless you come back tomorrow, pure, and with all you took away, and teach me to destroy that fool, who has destroyed himself for you, your death is here, your death is here, where it has long been waiting.'

Although his gun was empty, he struck the breech of it with his finger; and then he turned away, not deigning even once to look back again; and Lorna saw his giant figure striding across the meadow-land, as if the Ridds were nobodies, and he the proper owner.

Now, we expected a sharp attack that night after the words of Carver, which seemed to be meant to mislead us.

But before the maidens went to bed, Lorna made a remark which seemed to me a very clever one, and then I wondered how on earth it had never occurred to me before.

'What I believe is this, John. You know how high the rivers are, higher than ever they were before, and twice as high, you have told me. I believe that Glen Doone is flooded, and all the houses under water.'

'You little witch,' I answered; 'what a fool I must be not to think of it! Of course it is; it must be. The torrent from all the Bagworthy forest, and all the valleys above it, and the great drifts in the glen itself, never could have outlet down my famous waterslide. The valley must be under twenty feet at least. Well, if ever there was a fool, I am he, for not having thought of it. Consider three months of snow, snow, snow, and a fortnight of rain on the top of it, and all to be drained in a few days away! And great barricades of ice still in the rivers blocking them up, and ponding them.'

'Although I am sorry to think of all the poor women flooded out of their houses, and sheltering in the snowdrifts, there is one good of it: they cannot send many men against us, with all this trouble upon them.'

'You are right,' I replied; 'how clever you are! and that is why there were only three to cut off Master Stickles. And now we shall beat them, I make no doubt, even if they come at all. And I defy them to fire the house: the thatch is too wet for burning.'

A Rude Encounter

I HAD little fear, after what Lorna had told me, as to the result of the combat. It was not likely that the Doones could bring more than eight or ten men against us, while their homes were in such danger; and to meet these we had eight good men, including Jeremy, and myself, all well-armed and resolute, besides our three farm-servants, and the parish-clerk, and the shoemaker. These five could not be trusted much for any valiant conduct, although they spoke very confidently over their cans of cider. Neither were their weapons fitted for much execution, unless it were at close quarters, which they would be likely to avoid. Bill Dadds had a sickle, Jem Slocombe a flail, the cobbler had borrowed the constable's staff (for the constable would not attend, because there was no warrant), and the parish clerk had brought his pitch-pipe, which was enough to break any man's head. But John Fry, of course, had his blunderbuss, loaded with tin-tacks and marbles, and more likely to kill the man who discharged it than any other person.

Now it was my great desire, and my chiefest hope, to come across Carver Doone that night, and settle the score between us; not by any shot in the dark, but by a conflict man to man. As yet, since I came to full-grown power, I had never met any one whom I could not play tee-totum with; but now at last I had found a man whose strength was not to be laughed at. I could guess it in his face, I could tell it in his arms, I could see it in his stride and gait, which more than all the rest betray the substance of a man. And being so well used to wrestling, and to judge antagonists, I felt that here (if anywhere) I had found my match.

Therefore I was not content to abide within the house, or go the rounds with the troopers; but betook myself to the rickyard, knowing that the Doones were likely to begin their onset there. For they had a pleasant custom, when they visited farmhouses, of lighting themselves towards picking up anything they wanted, or stabbing the inhabitants, by first creating a blaze in the rickyard.

Perhaps I was wrong in heeding the ricks, at such a time as that; especially as only the clover was of much importance. But it seemed to me like a sort of triumph that they should even be able to boast of having fired our mow-yard. Therefore I stood in a nick of the clover, whence we had cut some trusses, with my club in hand, and gun close by.

The robbers rode into our yard as coolly as if they had been invited, having lifted the gate from the hinges first, on account of its being fastened. Then they actually opened our stable-doors, and turned our honest horses out, and put their own rogues in the place of them. At this my breath was quite taken away; for we think so much of our horses. By this time I could see our troopers, waiting in the shadow of the house, round the corner from where the Doones were, and expecting the order to fire. But Jeremy Stickles very wisely kept them in readiness, until the enemy should advance upon them.

'Two of you lazy fellows go,' it was the deep voice of Carver Doone, 'and make us a light to cut their throats by. Only one thing, once again. If any man touches Lorna, I will stab him where he stands. She belongs to me. There are two other young damsels here, whom you may take away if you please. And the mother, I hear, is still comely. Now for our rights. We have borne too long the insolence of these yokels. Kill every man, and every child, and burn the cursed place down.'

As he spoke thus blasphemously, I set my gun against his breast; the aim was sure as death itself. If I only drew the trigger (which went very lightly) Carver Doone would breathe no more. And yet – will you believe me? – I could not pull the trigger. Would to God that I had done so! Instead I dropped my carbine, and grasped again my club, which seemed a more straightforward implement.

Presently two young men came towards me, bearing brands of resined hemp, kindled from Carver's lamp. The foremost of them set his torch to the rick within a yard of me, the smoke concealing me from him. I struck him with a back-handed blow on the elbow, as he bent it; and I heard the bone of his arm break, as clearly as ever I heard a twig snap. With a roar of pain he fell on the ground, and his torch dropped there, and singed him. The other man stood amazed at this, not having yet gained sight of me; till I caught his firebrand from his hand, and struck it into his countenance. With that he leaped at me; but I caught him, in a manner learned from early wrestling, and snapped his collar-bone, as I laid him upon the top of his comrade.

Suddenly a blaze of fire lit up the house, and brown smoke hung around it. Six of our men had let go at the Doones, by Jeremy Stickles' order, as the villains came swaggering down in the moonlight, ready for rape or murder. Two of them fell, and the rest hung back, to think at their leisure what this was. They were not used to this sort of thing: it was neither just nor courteous.

Being unable any longer to contain myself, I came across the yard, expecting whether they would shoot at me. However, no one shot at me; and I went up to Carver Doone, whom I knew by his size in the moonlight, and I took him by the beard, and said, 'Do you call yourself a man?'

For a moment, he was so astonished that he could not answer. None had ever dared, I suppose, to look at him in that way; and he saw that he had met his equal, or perhaps his master. And then he tried a pistol at me; but I was too quick for him.

'Now, Carver Doone, take warning,' I said to him, very soberly; 'you have shown yourself a fool, by your contempt of me. I may not be your match in craft; but I am in manhood. You are a despicable villain. Lie low in your native muck.'

And with that word, I laid him flat upon his back in our strawyard, by a trick of the inner heel, which he could not have resisted (though his strength had been twice as great as mine), unless he were a wrestler. Seeing him down, the others ran, though one of them made a shot at me, and some of them got their horses, before our men came up; and some went away without them. And among these last was Captain Carver, who arose, while I was feeling myself (for I had a little wound), and strode away with a train of curses, enough to poison the light of the moon.

We gained six very good horses, by this attempted rapine, as well as two young prisoners, whom I had smitten by the clover-rick. Two dead Doones were left behind, and buried in the churchyard, without any service over them.

One thing was quite certain, that the Doones had never before received so rude a shock, and so violent a blow to their supremacy, since first they had built up their power, and become the Lords of Exmoor. I knew that Carver Doone would gnash those mighty teeth of his, and curse the men around him, for the blunder (which was in truth his own) of over confidence and carelessness. And at the same time, all the rest would feel that such a thing had never happened, while old Sir Ensor was alive; and that it was caused by nothing short of gross mismanagement.

Without waiting for any warrant, only saying something about '*captus in flagrante delicto*' – if that be the way to spell it – Stickles sent our prisoners off, bound and looking miserable, to the jail at Taunton. Before any surgeon could arrive, they were off with a well-armed escort. That day we were reinforced so strongly from the stations along the coast, even as far as Minehead, that we not only feared no further attack, but even talked of assaulting Glen Doone, without waiting for the train-bands. However, it was resolved to wait, and keep a watch upon the valley, and let the floods go down again.

A Visit from the Counsellor

Now when I arrived home one evening, as I came in, soon after dark, my sister Eliza met me at the corner of the cheese-room.

'Do you know a man of about Gwenny's shape, nearly as broad as he is long, but about six times the size of Gwenny, and with a length of snow-white hair, and a thickness also; as the copses were last winter. He never can comb it, that is quite certain, with any comb yet invented.'

'Then go you and offer your services. There are few things you cannot scarify. I know the man from your description, although I have never seen him. Now where is my Lorna?'

'Your Lorna is with Annie, having a good cry, I believe; and Annie too glad to second her. She knows that this great man is here and knows that he wants to see her. But she begged to defer the interview, until dear John's return.'

I was almost sure that the man who was come must be the Counsellor himself; of whom I felt much keener fear than of his son Carver. And knowing that his visit boded ill to me and Lorna, I went and sought my dear; and led her with a heavy heart, from the maiden's room to mother's, to meet our dreadful visitor.

I ventured to show myself, in the flesh, before him; although he feigned not to see me: but he advanced with zeal to Lorna; holding out both hands at once.

'My darling child, my dearest niece; how wonderfully well you look! Mistress Ridd, I give you credit. This is the country of good things. I never would have believed our

Queen could have looked so Royal. Surely of all virtues, hospitality is the finest, and the most romantic. Dearest Lorna, kiss your uncle; it is quite a privilege.'

'Perhaps it is to you, sir,' said Lorna, who could never quite check her sense of oddity; 'but I fear that you have smoked tobacco, which spoils reciprocity.'

'You are right, my child. How keen your scent is. It is always so with us. Your grandfather was noted for his olfactory powers. Ah, a great loss, dear Mrs Ridd, a terrible loss to this neighbourhood! But to return to our muttons – a figure which you will appreciate – I may now be regarded, I think, as this young lady's legal guardian; although I have not had the honour of being formally appointed such. Her father was the eldest son of Sir Ensor Doone; and I happened to be the second son. As Lorna's guardian, I give my full and ready consent to her marriage with your son, madam.'

'O how good of you, sir, how kind! Well, I always did say, that the learnedest people were, almost always, the best and kindest, and the most simple-hearted.'

'Madam, that is a great sentiment. What a goodly couple they will be! and if we can add him to our strength' –

'Oh no, sir, oh no!' cried mother: 'you really must not think of it. He has always been brought up so honest' –

'Hem! that makes a difference. A decided disqualification for domestic life among the Doones. But, surely, he might get over those prejudices, madam?'

'Oh no, sir! he never can: he never can indeed. When he was only that high, sir, he could not steal even an apple, when some wicked boys tried to mislead him.'

'Ah,' replied the Counsellor, shaking his white head gravely; 'then I greatly fear that his case is quite incurable. I have known such cases; violent prejudice, bred entirely of education, and anti-economical to the last degree.

'But while we talk of the heart, what is my niece Lorna doing, that she does not come and thank me, for my perhaps too prompt concession to her youthful fancies? Ah, if I had wanted thanks, I should have been more stubborn.'

Lorna, being challenged thus, came up and looked at her uncle, with her noble eyes fixed full upon his, which beneath his white eyebrows glistened, like dormer windows piled with snow.

'Well, uncle, I should be very grateful, if I thought that you did so from love of me; or if I did not know that you have something yet concealed from me.'

'And my consent,' said the Counsellor, 'is the more meritorious, the more liberal, frank, and candid, in the face of an existing fact, and a very clearly established one.'

'What fact do you mean, sir? Is it one that I ought to know?'

'In my opinion it is, good niece. It forms, to my mind, so fine a basis for the invariable harmony of the matrimonial state. To be brief, you two young people (ah, what a gift is youth! one can never be too thankful for it) you will have the rare advantage of commencing married life, with a subject of common interest to discuss, whenever you weary of – well, say of one another; if you can now, by any means, conceive such a possibility. And perfect justice meted out: mutual good-will resulting, from the sense of reciprocity.'

'I do not understand you, sir. Why can you not say what you mean, at once?'

'My dear child, I prolong your suspense. However, if you must have my strong realities, here they are. Your father slew dear John's father, and dear John's father slew yours.'

Having said thus much, the Counsellor leaned back upon his chair, and shaded his calm white-bearded eyes from the rays of our tallow candles. He was a man who liked to look, rather than to be looked at. But Lorna came to me for aid; and I went up to Lorna; and mother looked at both of us.

'Now, Sir Counsellor Doone,' I said, with Lorna squeezing both my hands, I never yet knew how (considering that she was walking all the time, or something like it); 'you know right well, Sir Counsellor, that Sir Ensor Doone gave approval.' I cannot tell what made me think of this: but so it came upon me.

'Approval to what, good rustic John? To the slaughter so reciprocal?'

'No, sir, not to that; even if it ever happened; which I do not believe. But to the love betwixt me and Lorna; which your story shall not break, without more evidence than your word. And even so, shall never break; if Lorna thinks as I do.'

'How say you then, John Ridd,' he cried, stretching out one hand, like Elijah; 'is this a thing of the sort you love? Is this what you are used to?'

'So please your worship,' I answered; 'no kind of violence can surprise us, since first came Doones upon Exmoor. Up to that time none heard of harm; except of taking a purse, may be, or cutting a strange sheep's throat. And the poor folk who did this were hanged, with some benefit of clergy. But ever since the Doones came first, we are used to anything.'

'Thou varlet,' cried the Counsellor, with the colour of his eyes quite changed with the sparkles of his fury; 'is this the way we are to deal with such a low-bred clod as thou? To question the doings of our people, and to talk of clergy! What, dream you not that we could have clergy, and of the right sort too, if only we cared to have them? Tush! Am I to spend my time, arguing with a plough-tail Bob?'

'You think,' answered Lorna very softly, 'that this is a happy basis for our future concord. I do not quite think that, my uncle; neither do I quite believe that a word of it is true. In our happy valley, nine-tenths of what is said is false; and you were always wont to argue, that true and false are but a blind turned upon a pivot. Without any failure of respect for your character, good uncle, I decline politely to believe a word of what you have told me. And even if it were proved to me, all I can say is this, if my John will have me, I am his for ever.'

'You old villain,' cried my mother, shaking her fist at the Counsellor. 'What is the good of the Quality; if this is all that comes of it? Out of the way! You know the words that make the deadly mischief; but not the ways that heal them.'

'That is the worst of them,' said the old man, when I had led him into our kitchen, with an apology at every step, and given him hot schnapps and water, and a cigarro of brave Tom Faggus: 'you never can say much, sir, in the way of reasoning (however gently meant and put) but what these women will fly out. It is wiser to put a wild bird in a cage, and expect him to sit and look at you, and chirp without a feather rumpled, than it is to expect a woman to answer reason reasonably.' Saying this, he looked at his puff of smoke as if it contained more reason.

'Now of this business, John,' he said, after getting to the bottom of the second glass, and having a trifle or so to eat, and praising our chimney-corner; 'taking you on the whole, you know, you are wonderfully good people: and instead of giving me up to the soldiers, as you might have done, you are doing your best to make me drunk.

'My son, I meant to come down upon you tonight; but you have turned the tables upon me through your simple way of taking me, as a man to be believed; combined with the comfort of this place, and the choice of tobacco, and cordials. I have not enjoyed an evening so much: God bless me if I know when!'

The Way to Make the Cream Rise

THAT night the reverend Counsellor, not being in such state of mind as ought to go alone, kindly took our best old bedstead. I set him up, both straight and heavy, so that he need but close both eyes, and keep his mouth just open; and in the morning, he was thankful for all that he could remember.

I, for my part, scarcely knew whether he really had begun to feel good-will towards us, and to see that nothing else could be of any use to him; or whether he was merely acting, so as to deceive us. And it had struck me, several times, that he had made a great deal more of the spirit he had taken than the quantity would warrant, with a man so wise and solid. Neither did I quite understand a little story which Lorna told me, how that in the night awaking, she had heard, or seemed to hear, a sound of feeling in her room; as if there had been some one groping carefully among the things within her drawers, or wardrobe-closet. But the noise had ceased at once, she said, when she sat up in bed and listened; and knowing how many mice we had, she took courage, and fell asleep again.

After breakfast, the Counsellor (who looked no whit the worse for schnapps, but even more grave and venerable) followed our Annie into the dairy, to see how we managed the clotted cream, of which he had eaten a basinful.

'Have you ever heard,' asked the Counsellor, who enjoyed this talk with Annie, 'that if you pass across the top, without breaking the surface, a string of beads, or polished glass, or any thing of that kind, the cream will set three times as solid, and in thrice the quantity?'

'No, sir; I have never heard that,' said Annie, staring with all her simple eyes; 'what a thing it is to read books, and grow learned! But it is very easy to try it: I will get my coral necklace; it will not be witchcraft, will it, sir?'

'Certainly not,' the old man replied. 'But coral will not do, my child, neither will anything coloured. The beads must be of plain common glass; but the brighter they are the better.'

'Then I know the very thing,' cried Annie; 'as bright as bright can be, and without any colour in it, except in the sun or candle-light. Dearest Lorna has the very thing, a necklace of some old glass-beads, or I think they called them jewels: she will be too glad to lend it to us. I will go for it, in a moment.'

So Annie found the necklace sparkling in the little secret hole, near the head of Lorna's bed, which she herself had recommended for its safer custody; and without a word to any one she brought it down, and danced it in the air before the Counsellor, for him to admire its lustre.

'Oh, that old thing!' said the gentleman, in a tone of some contempt; 'I remember that old thing well enough. However, for want of a better, no doubt it will answer our purpose. Three times three, I pass it over. Crinkleum, crankum, grass and clover! What are you feared of, you silly child?'

'Good sir, it is perfect witchcraft! I am sure of that, because it rhymes. Oh, what would mother say to me? Shall I ever go to heaven again? Oh, I see the cream already!'

'Now,' he said in a deep stern whisper; 'not a word of this to a living soul: go to your room, without so much as a single word to any one. Bolt yourself in, and for three hours now, read the Lord's Prayer backwards.'

Meanwhile the Counsellor was gone. He bade our mother adieu, with so much dignity of bearing, and such warmth and gratitude, and the high-bred courtesy of the old school (now fast disappearing), that when he was gone, dear mother fell back on the chair which he had used last night; as if it would teach her the graces.

'Oh the wickedness of the world! Oh the lies that are told

of people – or rather I mean the falsehoods – because a man is better born, and has better manners! Why, Lorna, how is it that you never speak about your charming uncle?'

'You had better marry him, madam,' said I, coming in very sternly; though I knew I ought not to say it: 'he can repay your adoration. He has stolen a hundred thousand pounds.'

'John,' cried my mother, 'you are mad!' And yet she turned as pale as death; for women are so quick at turning; and she inkled what it was.

Hereupon ensued a grim silence. It was not the value of the necklace – I am not so low a hound as that – nor was it even the damned folly shown by every one of us – it was the thought to Lorna's sorrow for her ancient plaything; and even more, my fury at the breach of hospitality.

But Lorna came up to me softly, and she laid one hand upon my shoulder; and she only looked at me.

'Darling John, did you want me to think that you cared for my money, more than for me?'

After this my heart was lighter (if they would only dry their eyes, and come round by dinner-time) than it had been since the day on which Tom Faggus discovered the value of that blessed and cursed necklace. Perhaps the Doones would let me have her; now that her property was gone.

But who shall tell of Annie's grief? The poor little thing fell against the wall, which had been whitened lately; and her face put all the white to scorn. My love, who was as fond of her, as if she had known her for fifty years, hereupon ran up and caught her, and abused all diamonds.

That same night Master Jeremy Stickles (of whose absence the Counsellor must have known) came back, with all equipment ready for the grand attack. Now the Doones knew, quite as well as we did, that this attack was threatening; and that, but for the weather, it would have been made long ago. Therefore we, or at least our people (for I was doubtful about going), were sure to meet with a good resistance, and due preparation.

Jeremy Stickles laughed heartily about Annie's new manner of charming cream; but he looked very grave at the loss of the jewels, so soon as he knew their value.

'My son,' he exclaimed, 'this is very heavy. It will go ill with all of you to make good this loss, as I fear that you will have to do.'

'What!' cried I, with my blood running cold. 'We make good the loss, Master Stickles! Every farthing we have in the world, and the labour of our lives to boot, will never make good the tenth of it.'

'My son,' replied Jeremy very gently, so that I could love him for it, 'not a word to your good mother of this unlucky matter. Keep it to yourself, my boy, and try to think but little of it. After all, I may be wrong: at any rate, least said best mended.'

'But Jeremy, dear Jeremy, how can I bear to leave it so? Do you suppose that I can sleep, and eat my food and go about, and look at other people, as if nothing at all had happened? And all the time have it on my mind, that not an acre of all the land, nor even our old sheep-dog, belongs to us of right at all. It is more than I can do, Jeremy. Let me talk, and know the worst of it.'

'Very well,' replied Master Stickles, seeing that both the doors were closed; 'I thought that nothing could move you, John; or I never would have told you. Likely enough I am quite wrong: and God send that I be so. But what I guessed at some time back seems more than a guess, now that you have told me about those wondrous jewels. Now will you keep as close as death every word I tell you? If I can ease you from this secret burden, will you bear, with strength and courage, the other which I plant on you?'

'I will do my best,' said I.

'No man can do more,' said he; and so began his story.

Jeremy Finds Out Something

'I WAS riding from Dulverton to Watchett, and it was late in the afternoon, and I was growing weary. The road (if road it could be called) turned suddenly down from the higher land to the very brink of the sea, and rounding a little jut of cliff I met the roar of the breakers.

'Watchett town was not to be seen, on account of a little foreland, a mile or more upon my course, and standing to the right of me. There was room enough below the cliffs for horse and man to get along, although the tide was running high with a northerly gale to back it. But close at hand and in a corner, drawn above the yellow sands and long eyebrows of wrack-weed, as snug a little house blinked on me as ever I saw, or wished to see.

'And so I made the old horse draw hand, which he was only too glad to do, and we clomb above the spring-tide mark, and over a little piece of turf, and struck the door of the hostelry. Some one came, and peeped at me through the lattice overhead, which was full of bulls' eyes; and then the bolt was drawn back, and a woman met me very courteously. A dark and foreign-looking woman, very hot of blood, I doubt, but not altogether a bad one. And she waited for me to be first to speak, which an Englishwoman would not have done.

' "Can I rest here for the night?" I asked, with a lift of my hat to her; for she was no provincial dame, who would stare at me for the courtesy: "my horse is weary from the sloughs, and myself but little better: besides that, we both are famished."

' "Yes, sir, you can rest and welcome. But of food, I fear, there is but little, unless of the common order. Our fishers would have drawn the nets, but the waves were violent.

However, we have – what you call it? I never can remember, it is so hard to say – the flesh of the hog salted."

' "Bacon!" said I; "what can be better? And half-a-dozen eggs with it, and a quart of fresh-drawn ale. You make me rage with hunger, madam. Is it cruelty, or hospitality?"

' "Ah, good!" she replied with a merry smile, full of southern sunshine: "you are not of the men round here: you can think, and you can laugh!"

' "And most of all, I can eat, good madam. In that way I shall astonish you; even more than by my intellect."

'She laughed aloud, and swung her shoulders, as your natives cannot do.

'However, not to dwell too much upon our little pleasantries (for I always get on with these foreign women, better than with your Molls and Pegs), I became not inquisitive, but reasonably desirous to know, by what strange hap or hazard a clever and a handsome woman could have settled here in this lonely inn, with only the waves for company, and a boorish husband who slaved all day in turning a potter's wheel at Watchett. And what was the meaning of the emblem set above her doorway, a very unattractive cat sitting in a ruined tree?

'However, I had not very long to strain my curiosity; for when she found out who I was, and how I held the King's commission, and might be called an officer, her desire to tell me all was more than equal to mine of hearing it. Many and many a day, she had longed for someone both skilful and trustworthy, most of all for someone bearing warrant from a court of justice. But the magistrates of the neighbourhood would have nothing to say to her, declaring that she was a crack-brained woman, and a wicked, and even a foreign one.

'By birth she was an Italian, from the mountains of Apulia, who had gone to Rome to seek her fortunes, after being badly treated in some love affair. Her name was Benita; being a quick and active girl, and resolved to work down her troubles, she found employment in a large hotel. And here she might have thriven well, and married well under sunny skies, and been a happy woman, but that some black day sent thither a rich and noble English family. It was not however their fervent longing for the Holy Father which had brought them to St Peter's roof; but rather their own bad luck in making their home too hot to hold them. For although in the main good Catholics, and pleasant receivers of anything, one of their number had given offence, by the folly of trying to think for himself. Some bitter feud had been among them, Benita knew not how it was; and the sister of the nobleman who had died quite lately was married to the rival claimant, whom they all detested. It was something about dividing land; Benita knew not what it was.

'But this Benita did know, that they were all great people, and rich, and very liberal; so that when they offered to take her, to attend to the children, and to speak the language for them, and to comfort the lady, she was only too glad to go, little foreseeing the end of it.

'And so they travelled through Northern Italy, and throughout the south of France, making their way anyhow; sometimes in coaches, sometimes in carts, sometimes upon mule-back, sometimes even a-foot and weary; but always as happy as could be.

'My Lord, who was quite a young man still, and laughed at English arrogance, rode on in front of his wife and friends, to catch the first of a famous view, on the French side of the Pyrenee hills. He kissed his hand to his wife, and said that he would save her the trouble of coming. For those two were so one in one, that they could make each other know, whatever he, or she, had felt. And so my Lord went round the corner, with a fine young horse leaping up at every step.

'They waited for him, long and long; but he never came

again; and within a week, his mangled body lay in a little chapel-yard.

'My Lady dwelled for six months more – it is a melancholy tale (what true tale is not so?) – scarcely able to believe that all her fright was not a dream. She would not wear a piece, or shape, of any mourning-clothes; she would not have a person cry, or any sorrow among us. She simply disbelieved the thing, and trusted God to right it.

'When the snow came down in autumn on the roots of the Pyrenees, and the chapel-yard was white with it, many people told the lady that it was time for her to go. And the strongest plea of all was this, that now she bore another hope of repeating her husband's virtues. So at the end of October, when wolves came down to the farm-lands, the little English family went home towards their England.

'They landed somewhere on the Devonshire coast, ten or eleven years agone, and stayed some days at Exeter; and set out thence in a hired coach, without any proper attendance, for Watchett, in the north of Somerset. For the lady owned a quiet mansion in the neighbourhood of that town, and her one desire was to find refuge there, and to meet her lord, who was sure to come (she said) when he heard of his new infant. But the roads were soft and very deep, and the sloughs were out in places; and the heavy coach broke down in the axle, and needed mending at Dulverton.

'Nevertheless, although it was afternoon, and the year now come to December, the horses were put to again, and the heavy coach went up the hill, with the lady and her two children, and Benita, sitting inside of it. Both the serving-men were scared, but the lady only said, "Drive on, I know a little of highwaymen; they never rob a lady."

'Through the fog, and through the muck, the coach went on till dark, as well as might be expected. But when they came, all thanking God, to the pitch and slope of the sea-bank, leading on towards Watchett town, there the little boy jumped up, and clapped his hands at the water; and there (as Benita said) they met their fate, and could not fly it.

'Although it was past the dusk of day, the silver light from the sea flowed in, and showed the cliffs, and the grey sand-line, and the drifts of wreck, and wrack-weed. It showed them also a troop of horsemen, waiting under a rock hard by, and ready to dash upon them. The postilions lashed towards the sea, and the horses strove in the depth of sand, and the serving-men cocked their blunderbusses, and cowered away behind them; but the lady stood up in the carriage bravely, and neither screamed nor spoke, but hid her son behind her. Meanwhile the drivers drove into the sea, till the leading horses were swimming.

'But before the waves came into the coach, a score of fierce men were round it. They cursed the postilions for mad cowards, and cut the traces, and seized the wheel-horses, all wild with dismay in the wet and the dark. Then, while the carriage was heeling over, and well-nigh upset in the water, the lady exclaimed, "I know that man! He is our ancient enemy:" and Benita snatched the most valuable of the jewels, a magnificent necklace of diamonds, and cast it over the little girl's head, and buried it under her travelling-cloak, hoping so to save it. Then a great wave, crested with foam, rolled in, and the coach was thrown on its side, and the sea rushed in at the top and the windows.

'What followed Benita knew not, as one might well suppose, herself being stunned by a blow on the head, beside being palsied with terror. "See, I have the mark now," she said, "where the jamb of the door came down on me!" But when she recovered her senses, she found herself upon the sand, the robbers were out of sight, and one of the serving-men was bathing her forehead with sea water. Then she ran to her mistress, who was sitting upright on a little rock, with her dead boy's face to her bosom, sometimes gazing upon him, and sometimes questing round for the other one.

'Although there were torches and links around, and she looked at her child by the light of them, no one dared to approach the lady, or speak, or try to help her. Each man whispered his fellow to go, but each hung back himself, and muttered that it was too awful to meddle with. And there she would have sat all night, with the fine little fellow stone dead in her arms, and her tearless eyes dwelling upon him, and her heart but not her mind thinking, only that the Italian woman stole up softly to her side, and whispered, "It is the will of God."

' "So it always seems to be," were all the words the mother answered; and then she fell on Benita's neck; and the men were ashamed to be near her weeping.

'Before the light of the morning came along the tide to Watchett my Lady had met her husband. She lies in Watchett little churchyard, with son and heir at her right hand, and a little babe, of sex unknown, sleeping on her bosom.'

'And what was the lady's name?' I asked; 'and what became of the little girl? And why did the woman stay there?'

'Well!' cried Jeremy Stickles, only too glad to be cheerful again: 'talk of a woman after that! Benita stayed in that blessed place, because she could not get away from it. The Doones – if Doones indeed they were, about which you of course know best – took every stiver out of the carriage; wet or dry they took it. And Benita could never get her wages; for the whole affair is in Chancery, and they have appointed a receiver.'

'Whew!' said I, knowing something of London, and sorry for Benita's chance.

'So the poor thing was compelled to drop all thought of Apulia, and settle down on the brink of Exmoor, where you get all its evils, without the good to balance them. She married a man who turned a wheel for making the blue Watchett ware, partly because he could give her a house, and partly because he proved himself a good soul towards my Lady. There they are, and have three children; and there you may go and visit them.'

'Now for my second question. What became of the little maid?'

'You great oaf!' cried Jeremy Stickles: 'you are rather more likely to know, I should think, than any one else in all the kingdoms. As certain sure as I stand here, that little maid is Lorna Doone.'

Mutual Discomfiture

JEREMY'S tale would have moved me greatly, both with sorrow and anger, even without my guess at first, and now my firm belief, that the child of those unlucky parents was indeed my Lorna.

For when he described the heavy coach, and the persons in and upon it, and the breaking down at Dulverton, and the place of their destination, as well as the time and the weather, and the season of the year, my heart began to burn within me, and my mind replaced the pictures, first of the foreign lady's-maid by the pump caressing me, and then of the coach struggling up the hill, and the beautiful dame, and the fine little boy, with the white cockade in his hat; but most of all the little girl, dark-haired and very lovely, and having even in those days the rich soft look of Lorna.

But when he spoke of the necklace thrown over the head of the little maiden, and of her disappearance, before my eyes arose at once the flashing of the beacon-fire, the lonely moors embrowned with light, the tramp of the outlaw cavalcade, and the helpless child head downward lying across the robber's saddle-bow. Then I remembered my own mad shout of boyish indignation, and marvelled at the strange long way by which the events of life come round. And while I thought of my own return, and childish attempt to hide myself from sorrow in the sawpit, and the agony of my mother's tears, it did not fail to strike me as a thing of omen, that the self-same day should be, both to my darling and myself, the blackest and most miserable of all youthful days.

Jeremy Stickles was quite decided – and of course the discovery being his, he had a right to be so – that not a word of all these things must be imparted to Lorna herself, or even to my mother, or any one whatever. 'Keep it tight as wax, my lad,' he cried, with a wink of great expression; 'this belongs to me, mind; and the credit, ay, and the premium, and the right of discount, are altogether mine. It would have taken you fifty years to put two and two together so, as I did, like a clap of thunder. Ah, God has given some men brains; and others have good farms and money, and a certain skill in the lower beasts. Each must use his special talent. You work your farm: I work my brains. You shall take the beauty, my son, and the elegance and the love, and all that – and my boy, I will take the money.'

This he said in a way so dry, and yet so richly unctuous, that being gifted somehow by God, with a kind of sense of queerness, I fell back in my chair, and laughed, though the underside of my laugh was tears.

'Now no more of that, my boy; a cigarro after schnapps, and go to meet my yellow boys.'

His 'yellow boys', as he called the Somerset trained bands, were even now coming down the valley. There was one good point about these men, that having no discipline at all, they made pretence to none whatever. Nay, rather they ridiculed the thing, as below men of any spirit. On the other hand, Master Stickles' troopers looked down on these native fellows from a height which I hope they may never tumble, for it would break the necks of all of them.

However, he had better hopes, when the sons of Devon

appeared, as they did in about an hour's time; fine fellows, and eager to prove themselves, quite prepared to fight the men of Somerset (if need be) in addition to the Doones. And there was scarcely a man among them but could have trounced three of the yellow men, and would have done it gladly too, in honour of the red facings.

The yellows and the reds together numbered a hundred and twenty men, most of whom slept in our barns and stacks; and besides these we had fifteen troopers of the regular army. You may suppose that all the country was turned upside down about it; and the folk who came to see them drill – by no means a needless exercise – were a greater plague than the soldiers.

Therefore all of us were right glad (except perhaps Farmer Snowe, from whom we had bought some victuals at rare price) when Jeremy Stickles gave orders to march, and we began to try to do it. A good deal of boasting went overhead, as our men defiled along the lane. The parish choir came part of the way, and the singing-loft from Countisbury; and they kept our soldiers' spirits up, with some of the most pugnacious Psalms. Parson Bowden marched ahead, leading all our van and file, as against the Papists; and promising to go with us, till we came to bullet distance. Therefore we marched bravely on, and children came to look at us. And I wondered where Uncle Reuben was, who ought to have led the culverins (whereof we had no less than three) if Stickles could only have found him.

When we reached the top of the hill, the sons of Devon marched on, and across the track leading into Doone-gate, so as to fetch round the western side, and attack with their culverin from the cliffs, whence the sentry had challenged me on the night of my passing the entrance. Meanwhile the yellow lads were to stay upon the eastern highland, whence Uncle Reuben and myself had reconnoitred so long ago; and whence I had leaped into the valley at the time of the great snowdrifts. And here they were not to show themselves; but keep their culverin in the woods, until their cousins of Devon appeared on the opposite parapet of the glen.

The third culverin was entrusted to the fifteen troopers; who with ten picked soldiers from either trained band, making in all five-and-thirty men, were to assault the Doone-gate itself, while the outlaws were placed between two fires from the eastern cliff and the western. And with this force went Jeremy Stickles, and with it went myself, as knowing more about the passage than any other stranger did. Therefore, you will see that the Doones must repulse at once three simultaneous attacks.

Now we five-and-thirty men lay back, a little way round the corner, in the hollow of the track which leads to the strong Doone-gate.

At last, we heard the loud bang-bang, which proved that Devon and Somerset were pouring their indignation hot into the den of malefactors, or at least so we supposed; therefore at double quick march we advanced round the bend of the cliff which had hidden us, hoping to find the gate undefended, and to blow down all barriers with the fire of our cannon. And indeed it seemed likely at first to be so, for the wild and mountainous gorge of rock appeared to be all in pure loneliness. Therefore we shouted a loud hurrah, as for an easy victory.

But while the sound of our cheer rang back among the crags above us, a shrill clear whistle cleft the air for a single moment, and then a dozen carbines bellowed, and all among us flew murderous lead. Several of our men rolled over, but the rest rushed on like Britons, Jeremy and myself in front, while we heard the horses plunging at the loaded gun behind us. 'Now, my lads,' cried Jeremy, 'one dash, and we are beyond them!' For he saw that the foe was overhead in the gallery of brushwood.

Our men with a brave shout answered him, for his courage was fine example; and we leaped in under the feet of the foe, before they could load their guns again. But here, when the foremost among us were past, an awful crash rang behind us, with the shrieks of men, and the din of metal, and the horrible screaming of horses. The trunk of the tree had been launched overhead, and crashed into the very midst of us. Our cannon was under it, so were two men and a horse with his poor back broken. Another horse vainly struggled to rise with his thighbone smashed and protruding.

Now I lost all presence of mind at this, and shouting for any to follow me, dashed headlong into the cavern. Some five or six men came after me, the foremost of whom was Jeremy, when a storm of shots whistled and pattered around me, with a blaze of light and a thunderous roar. On I leaped, like a madman, and pounced on one gunner, and hurled him across his culverin; but the others had fled, and a heavy oak door fell to with a bang, behind them. So utterly were my senses gone, and nought but strength remaining, that I caught up the Doone cannon with both hands, and dashed it, breech-first, at the doorway. The solid oak burst with the blow, and the gun stuck fast, like a builder's putlog.

But here I looked round in vain, for any to come and follow up my success. The scanty light showed me no figure moving through the length of the tunnel behind me; only a heavy groan or two went to my heart, and chilled it. So I hurried back to seek Jeremy, fearing that he must be smitten down.

And so indeed I found him, as well as three other poor fellows, struck by the charge of the culverin, which had passed so close beside me. Two of the four were as dead as stones, and growing cold already, but Jeremy and the other could manage to groan, just now and then.

The shot had taken him in the mouth; about that no doubt could be, for two of his teeth were in his beard, and one of his lips was wanting. I laid his shattered face on my breast, and nursed him, as a woman might. But he looked at me with a jerk at this; and I saw that he wanted coolness.

While here we stayed, quite out of danger, a boy who had no business there (being in fact our clerk's apprentice to the art of shoe-making) came round the corner upon us.

'Got the worst of it!' cried the boy: 'better be off all of you. Zomerzett and Devon a vighting; and the Doones have drashed 'em both. Maister Ridd even thee be drashed.'

We few, who yet remained of the force which was to have won the Doone-gate, gazed at one another, like so many fools, and nothing more. For we still had some faint hopes of winning the day, and recovering our reputation, by means of what the other men might have done without us. And we could not understand at all how Devonshire and Somerset, being embarked in the same cause, should be fighting with one another.

Finding nothing more to be done in the way of carrying on the war, we laid poor Master Stickles and two more of the wounded upon the carriage of bark and hurdles, whereon our gun had laid; and we rolled the gun into the river, and harnessed the horses yet alive, and put the others out of their pain, and sadly wended homewards, feeling ourselves to be thoroughly beaten, yet ready to maintain that it was no fault of ours whatever.

Now this enterprise having failed so, I prefer not to dwell too long upon it; only just to show the mischief which lay at the root of the failure. And this mischief was the vile jealousy betwixt red and yellow uniform.

The men of Devon, who bore red facings, had a long way to go round the hills, before they could get into due position on the western side of the Doone Glen. And knowing that their cousins in yellow would claim the whole of the glory, if allowed to be first with the firing, these worthy fellows waited not to take good aim with their cannon, seeing the others about to shoot; but fettled it anyhow on the slope pointing in a general direction; and trusting in God for aim-worthiness, laid the rope to the breech, and fired. Now as Providence ordained it, the shot, which was a casual mixture of anything considered hard – for instance jug-bottoms and knobs of doors – the whole of this pernicious dose came scattering and shattering among the unfortunate yellow men upon the opposite cliff; killing one and wounding two.

Now what did the men of Somerset do, but instead of waiting for their friends to send around and beg pardon, train their gun full mouth upon them, and with a vicious meaning shoot? Nor only this, but they loudly cheered, when they saw four or five red coats lie low; for which savage feeling not even the remarks of the Devonshire men concerning their coats could entirely excuse them.

This was a melancholy end of our brave setting out: and everybody blamed every one else: and several of us wanted to have the whole thing over again, as then we must have righted it. But upon one point all agreed, by some reasoning not clear to me, that the root of the evil was to be found in the way Parson Bowden went up the hill, with his hat on, and no cassock.

Getting into Chancery

To me the whole thing was purely grievous; not from any sense of defeat (though that was bad enough), but from the pain and anguish caused by death, and wounds, and mourning.

Jeremy Stickles lay and tossed, and thrust up his feet in agony, and bit with his lipless mouth the clothes, and was proud to see blood upon them. He looked at us ever so many times, as much as to say, 'Fools, let me die; then I shall have some comfort'; but we nodded at him sagely, especially the women, trying to convey to him, on no account to die yet. And then we talked to one another (on purpose for him to hear us), how brave he was, and not the man to knock under in a hurry, and how he should have the victory yet; and how well he looked, considering.

These things cheered him, a little now, and a little more next time; and every time we went on so, he took it with less impatience. And after that he came round gently; though never to the man he had been, and never to speak loud again.

To myself (though by rights the last to be thought of, among so much pain and trouble) Jeremy's wound was a great misfortune, in more ways than one. In the first place, it deferred my chance of imparting either to my mother or to Mistress Lorna my firm belief that the maid I loved was not sprung from the race which had slain my father; neither could he in any way have offended against her family. And this discovery I was yearning more and more to declare to them; being forced to see (even in the midst of all our warlike troubles) that a certain difference was growing betwixt them both. And the saddest, and most hurtful thing, was that neither could ask the other of the shadow falling between them. And so it went on, and deepened.

In the next place Colonel Stickles' illness was a grievous thing to us, in that we had no one now to command the troopers. Ten of these were still alive, and so well approved to us, that they could never fancy aught, whether for dinner or supper, without its being forthcoming. For we knew that if they once resolved to go (as they might do at any time, with only a corporal over them), all our house, and all our goods, ay, and our own precious lives, would and must be at the mercy of embittered enemies.

But yet another cause arose, and this the strongest one of all, to prove the need of Stickles' aid, and calamity of his illness. And this came to our knowledge first, without much time to think of it.

It fell on a very black day (for all except the lawyers), that His Majesty's Court of Chancery, if that be what it called itself, gained scent of poor Lorna's life, and of all that might be made of it. Whether through that brave young lord who ran into such peril; or whether through that deep old Counsellor, whose game none might penetrate; or through any disclosures of the Italian woman, or even of Jeremy himself; none just now could tell us: only this truth was too clear – Chancery had heard of Lorna, and then had seen how rich she was: and never delaying in one thing, had opened mouth, and swallowed her.

But now having Jeremy Stickles' leave, which he gave with a nod when I told him all, and at last made him understand it, I laid bare to my mother as well what I knew, as what I merely surmised, or guessed, concerning Lorna's parentage. All this she received with great tears, and wonder, and fervent thanks to God. However, now the question was, how to act about these writs.

Feeling many things, but thinking without much to guide me, I went up to Lorna.

'Now, Lorna,' said I, as she hung on my arm, willing to trust me anywhere, 'come to your little plant-house, and hear a moving story.'

'No story can move me much, dear,' she answered, 'since I know your strength of kindness, scarcely any tale can move me, unless it be of yourself, love; or of my poor mother.'

'It is of your poor mother, darling. Can you bear to hear it?' And yet I wondered why she did not say as much of her father.

'Yes, I can hear anything. But although I cannot see her, and have long forgotten, I could not bear to hear ill of her.'

'There is no ill to hear, sweet child, except of evil done to her. Lorna, you are of an ill-starred race.'

'Better that than a wicked race,' she answered with her

usual quickness, leaping at conclusion: 'tell me I am not a Doone, and I will – but I cannot love you more.'

'You are not a Doone, my Lorna, for that, at least, I can answer; though I know not what your name is.'

'And my father – your father – what I mean is' –

'Your father and mine never met one another. Your father was killed by an accident in the Pyrenean mountains, and your mother by the Doones; or at least they caused her death, and carried you away from her.'

When at last my tale was done, she turned away, and wept bitterly for the sad fate of her parents. But to my surprise, she spoke not even a word of wrath or rancour. She seemed to take it all as fate.

'Lorna, darling,' I said at length, for men are more impatient in times of trial than women are, 'do you not even wish to know what your proper name is?'

'How can it matter to me, John?' she answered, with a depth of grief which made me seem a trifler. 'It can never matter now, when there are none to share it.'

'Poor little soul!' was all I said, in a tone of purest pity; and to my surprise she turned upon me, caught me in her arms, and loved me, as she never had done before.

'Dearest, I have you,' she cried; 'you, and only you, love. Having you, I want no other. All my life is one with yours. Oh, John, how can I treat you so?'

'I cannot believe, in the pride of my joy,' I whispered into one little ear, 'that you could ever so love me, beauty, as to give up the world for me.'

'Would you give up your farm for me, John?' cried Lorna, leaping back and looking, with her wondrous power of light, at me; 'would you give up your mother, your sisters, your home, and all that you have in the world, and every hope of your life, John?'

'Of course I would. Without two thoughts. You know it; you know it, Lorna.'

'It is true that I do,' she answered in a tone of deepest sadness; 'and it is this power of your love which has made me love you so. No good can come of it; no good. God's face is set against selfishness.'

As she spoke in that low tone, I gazed at the clear lines of her face (where every curve was perfect), not with love and wonder only, but with a strange new sense of awe.

Lorna Knows Her Nurse

ONE day, not knowing what might happen, or even how soon poor Lorna might be taken from our power, and, falling into lawyer's hands, have cause to wish herself most heartily back among robbers, I set forth for Watchett, taking advantage of the visit of some troopers from an outpost, who would make our house quite safe.

Riding along, I meditated upon Lorna's history; how many things were now beginning to unfold themselves, which had been obscure and dark! For instance, Sir Ensor Doone's consent, or to say the least his indifference, to her marriage with a yeoman; which in a man so proud (though dying) had greatly puzzled both of us. But now, if she not only proved to be no grandchild of the Doone, but even descended from his enemy, it was natural enough that he should feel no great repugnance to her humiliation. And that Lorna's father had been a foe to the house of Doone I gathered from her mother's cry when she beheld their leader. Moreover that fact would supply their motive in carrying off the unfortunate little creature, and rearing her among them, and as one of their own family; yet hiding her true birth from her. If one of them could marry her, before she learned of right and wrong, vast property, enough to buy pardons for a thousand Doones, would be at their mercy.

Then as her beauty grew richer and brighter, Carver Doone was smitten strongly, and would hear of no one else as a suitor for her; and by the terror of his claim drove off all the others. Here too lay the explanation of a thing which seemed to be against the laws of human nature, and upon which I had longed, but dared not, to cross-question Lorna. How could such a lovely maid, although so young, and brave, and distant, have escaped the vile affections of a lawless company?

But now it was as clear as need be. For any proven violence would have utterly vitiated all claim upon her grand estates; at least as those claims must be urged before a court of equity. And therefore all the elders (with views upon her real estate) kept strict watch on the youngers, who confined their views to her personality.

When I knocked at the little door, whose sill was gritty and grimed with sand, no one came for a very long time to answer me, or to let me in. After a while I knocked again, for my horse was becoming hungry; and a good while after that again, a voice came through the key-hole –

'Who is it that wishes to enter?'

'The boy who was at the pump,' said I, 'when the carriage broke down at Dulverton. The boy that lives at oh – ah; and some day you would come seek for him.'

'Oh yes, I remember certainly. My leetle boy, with the fair white skin. I have desired to see him, oh many, yes, many times.'

She was opening the door, while saying this; and then she started back in affright, that the little boy should have grown so.

'You cannot be that leetle boy. It is quite impossible. Why do you impose on me?'

'Not only am I that little boy, who made the water to flow for you, till the nebule came upon the glass; but also I am come to tell you all about your little girl.'

'Come in, you very great leetle boy,' she answered, with her dark eyes brightened. And I went in, and looked at her. She was altered by time, as much as I was. Yet her face was comely still, and full of strong intelligence. I gazed at her, and she at me: and we were sure of one another.

Madame Benita Odam – for the name of the man who turned the wheel proved to be John Odam – showed me into a little room containing two chairs and a fir-wood table, and sat down on a three-legged seat and studied me very steadfastly. This she had a right to do; and I, having all my clothes on now, was not disconcerted. It would not become me to repeat her judgment upon my appearance, which she delivered as calmly as if I were a pig at market, and as proudly as if her own pig.

Not wanting to talk about myself (though very fond of doing so, when time and season favour), I led her back to that fearful night of the day when first I had seen her. She was not desirous to speak of it, because of her own little children: however, I drew her gradually to recollection of Lorna, and then of the little boy who died, and the poor mother buried with him. And her strong hot nature kindled, as she dwelled upon these things: and my wrath waxed within me; and we forgot reserve and prudence under the sense of so vile a wrong. She told me (as nearly as might be) the very same story which she had told to Master Jeremy Stickles; only she dwelled upon it more, because of my knowing the outset. And being a woman, with an inkling of my situation, she enlarged upon the little maid, more than to dry Jeremy.

'Would you know her again?' I asked, being stirred by these accounts of Lorna, when she was five years old: 'would you know her as a full-grown maiden?'

'I think I should,' she answered; 'it is not possible to say, until one sees the person: but from the eyes of the little girl, I think that I must know her. Oh, the poor young creature!'

'Now she is a tall young lady, and as beautiful as can be. If I sleep in your good hostel tonight, will you come with me to Oare tomorrow, and see your little maiden?'

At last I made her promise to come with me, presuming that Master Odam could by any means be persuaded to keep her company in the cart, as propriety demanded. But having little doubt that Master Odam was entirely at his wife's command, I looked upon that matter as settled.

Therefore we set out pretty early, three of us, and a baby, who could not well be left behind. The wife of the man who owned the cart had undertaken to mind the business and the other babies, upon condition of having the keys of all the taps left with her.

As luck would have it, the first who came to meet us at the gate was Lorna, with nothing whatever upon her head (the weather being summerly), but her beautiful hair shed round her; and wearing a sweet white frock tucked in, and showing her figure perfectly. In her joy she ran straight up to the cart; and then stopped and gazed at Benita. At one glance her old nurse knew her: 'Oh, the eyes, the eyes!' she cried, and was over the rail of the cart in a moment, in spite of all her substance. Lorna, on the other hand, looked at her with some doubt and wonder; as though having right to know much about her, and yet unable to do so. But when the foreign woman said something in Roman language, and flung new hay from the cart upon her, as if in a romp of childhood, the young maid cried 'Oh, Nita, Nita!' and fell upon her breast, and wept; and after that looked round at us.

This being so, there could be no doubt as to the power of proving Lady Lorna's birth, and rights, both by evidence and token. For though we had not the necklace now – thanks to Annie's wisdom – we had the ring of heavy gold. And Benita knew this ring as well as she knew her own fingers, having heard a long history about it; and the effigy on it of the wild cat was the bearing of the house of Lorne.

For though Lorna's father was a nobleman of high and goodly lineage, her mother was of yet more ancient and renowned descent, being the last in line direct from the great and kingly chiefs of Lorne. A wild and headstrong race they were, and must have everything their own way. Hot blood was ever among them, even of one household; and their sovereignty (which more than once had defied the King of Scotland) waned and fell among themselves, by continual quarrelling. And it was of a piece with this, that the Doones (who were an offset, by the mother's side, holding in co-partnership some large property, which had come by the spindle, as we say) should fall out with the Earl of Lorne, the last but one of that title.

The daughter of this nobleman had married Sir Ensor Doone; but this, instead of healing matters, led to fierce conflict.

Therefore knowing Lorna to be direct in heirship to vast property, and bearing especial spite against the house of which she was the last, the Doones had brought her up with full intention of lawful marriage; and had carefully secluded her from the wildest of their young gallants. Of course, if they had been next in succession, the child would have gone down the waterfall to save any further trouble; but there was an intercepting branch of some honest family; and they being outlaws, would have a poor chance (though the law loves outlaws) against them. Only Lorna was of the stock; and Lorna they must marry. And what a triumph against the old Earl, for a cursed Doone to succeed him!

As for their outlawry, great robberies, and grand murders, the veriest child, now-a-days, must know that money heals the whole of that. Even if they had murdered people of a good position, it would only cost twice as much to prove their motives loyal. But they had never slain any man above the rank of yeoman; and folk even said that my father was the highest of their victims; for the death of Lorna's mother, and brother, was never set to their account.

How truly we discern clear justice, and how well we deal it! If any poor man steals a sheep, having ten children starving, and regarding it as mountain game (as a rich man does a hare), to the gallows with him. If a man of rank beats down a door, smites the owner upon the head, and honours the wife with attention, it is a thing to be grateful for, and to slouch smitten head the lower.

Jeremy Proved Right

WHILE we were full of all these things, and wondering what would happen next, or what we ought ourselves to do, another very important matter called for our attention. This was no less than Annie's marriage to the Squire, Faggus.

When the time for the wedding came, there was such a stir and commotion as had never been known in the parish of Oare since my father's marriage. For Annie's beauty and kindliness had made her the pride of the neighbourhood; and the presents sent her, from all around, were enough to stock a shop with.

I myself set off to Dulverton, bearing more commissions, more messages, and more question, than a man of thrice my memory might carry so far as the corner where the saw-pit is. And to make things worse, one girl, or other, would keep on running up to me, or even after me (when started), with something or other she had just thought of, which she could not possibly do without, and which I must be sure to remember, as the most important of the whole.

To my dear mother, who had partly outlived the exceeding value of trifles, the most important matter seemed to ensure Uncle Reuben's countenance and presence at the marriage. And if I succeeded in this, I might well forget all the maidens' trumpery.

Uncle Reuben was not at home; but Ruth, who received me very kindly, was sure of his return in the afternoon, and persuaded me to wait for him. And by the time that I had finished all I could recollect of my orders, even with paper to help me, the old gentleman rode into the yard, and was more surprised than pleased to see me. But if he was surprised, I was more than that – I was utterly astonished at the change in his appearance since the last time I had seen him. From a hale, and rather heavy man, grey-haired, but plump, and ruddy, he was altered to a shrunken, wizened, trembling, and almost decrepit figure. Instead of curly and comely locks, grizzled indeed, but plentiful, he had only a few lank white hairs scattered and flattened upon his forehead. But the greatest change of all was in the expression of his eyes, which had been so keen, and restless, and bright, and a little sarcastic. Bright indeed they still were, but with a slow unhealthy lustre; their keenness was turned to perpetual outlook, their restlessness to a haggard want. As for the humour which once gleamed there (which people who fear it call sarcasm), it had been succeeded by stares of terror, and then mistrust, and shrinking. There was none of the interest in mankind, which is needful even for satire.

'Now what can this be?' thought I to myself: 'has the old man lost all his property, or taken too much to strong waters?'

'Come inside, John Ridd,' he said: 'I will have a talk with you. It is cold out here: and it is too light. Come inside, John Ridd, boy.'

I followed him into a little dark room. It was closed from the shop by an old division of boarding, hung with tanned canvas; and the smell was very close and faint. Here there was a ledger-desk, and a couple of chairs, and a long-legged stool.

'Take the stool,' said Uncle Reuben, showing me in very quietly, 'it is fitter for your height, John. Wait a moment; there is no hurry.'

Then he slipped out by another door, and closing it quickly after him, told the foreman, and waiting-men, that the business of the day was done. They had better all go home at once; and he would see to the fastenings. Of course they were only too glad to go; but I wondered at his sending them, with at least two hours of daylight left.

Uncle Ben came reeling in, not from any power of liquor, but because he was stiff from horse-back, and weak from work and worry.

'Let me be, John, let me be,' he said, as I went to help him: 'this is an unkid dreary place; but many a hundred of good gold Carolus has been turned in this place, John.'

'Not a doubt about it, sir,' I answered, in my loud and cheerful manner; 'and many another hundred, sir; and may you long enjoy them!'

'My boy, do you wish me to die?' he asked, coming up close to my stool, and regarding me with a shrewd, though blear-eyed gaze: 'many do. Do you, John?'

'Come,' said I, 'don't ask such nonsense. You know better than that, Uncle Ben. Or else, I am sorry for you. I want you to live as long as possible. Here's to your health and dear little Ruth's; and may you live to knock off the cobwebs from every bottle in under the arch! Uncle Reuben, your life and health, sir!'

With that, I took my glass thoughtfully, for it was wondrous good; and Uncle Ben was pleased to see me dwelling pleasantly on the subject, with parenthesis, and self-commune, and oral judgment unpronounced, though smacking of fine decision. '*Curia vult advisari*,' as the lawyers say; which means, 'Let us have another glass, and then we can think about it.'

'Come now, John,' said Uncle Ben, laying his wrinkled hand on my knee, 'I have at last resolved to let you know my secret; and for two good reasons. The first is, that it wears me out to dwell upon it, all alone: and the second is, that I can trust you to fulfil a promise. Moreover you are my next of kin, except among the womenkind; and you are just the man I want to help me in my enterprise.'

'And I will help you, sir,' I answered, fearing some conspiracy, 'in anything that is true, and loyal, and according to the laws of the realm.'

'Ha, ha!' cried the old man, laughing until his eyes ran over, and spreading out his skinny hands upon his shining breeches, 'thou hast gone the same fool's track as the rest; even as spy Stickles went, and all his precious troopers. Landing of arms at Glenthorne and Lynmouth, waggons escorted across the moor, sounds of metal, and booming noises! Ah, but we managed it cleverly, to cheat even those so near to us. Disaffection at Taunton, signs of insurrection at Dulverton! We set it all abroad, right well. And not even you to suspect our work; though we thought at one time that you watched us. Now who, do you suppose, is at the bottom of all this Exmoor insurgency, all this western rebellion – not that I say there is none, mind – but who is at the bottom of it?'

'Either Mother Melldrum,' said I, being now a little angry, 'or else old Nick himself.'

'Nay, old Uncle Reuben!' Saying this, Master Huckaback cast back his coat, and stood up, and made the most of himself.

'Well!' cried I, being now quite come to the limits of my intellect, 'then after all Captain Stickles was right in calling you a rebel, sir!'

'Of course he was: could so keen a man be wrong, about an old fool like me? But come, and see our rebellion, John. I will trust you now with everything. I will take no oath from you; only your word to keep silence; and most of all from your mother.'

'I will give you my word,' I said, although liking not such pledges; which make a man think before he speaks in ordinary company, against his usual practice. However, I was now so curious, that I thought of nothing else; and scarcely could believe at all that Uncle Ben was quite right in his head.

'Take another glass of wine, my son,' he cried with a cheerful countenance, which made him look more than ten years younger; 'you shall come into partnership with me: your strength will save us two horses, and we always fear the horse work. Come and see our rebellion, my boy; you are a made man from tonight.'

'But where am I to come and see it? Where am I to find it, sir?'

'Meet me,' he answered, yet closing his hands, and wrinkling with doubt his forehead; 'come alone, of course; and meet me at the Wizard's Slough, at ten tomorrow morning.'

Master Huckaback's Secret

KNOWING Master Huckaback to be a man of his word, as well as one who would have others so, I was careful to be in good time the next morning, by the side of the Wizard's Slough. Starting about eight o'clock, without mentioning my business, I arrived at the mouth of the deep descent, such as John Fry described it.

When I came to the foot of this ravine, and over against the great black slough, there was no sign of Master

Huckaback, nor of any other living man, except myself, in the silence.

Then a man on horseback appeared as suddenly as if he had risen out of the earth, on the other side of the great black slough. At first I was a little scared, my mind being in the tune for wonders; but presently the white hair, whiter from the blackness of the bog between us, showed me that it was Uncle Reuben come to look for me, that way. Then I left my chair of rock, and waved my hat, and shouted to him, and the sound of my voice among the crags and lonely corners frightened me.

Old Master Huckaback made no answer, but (so far as I could guess) beckoned me to come to him. There was just room between the fringe of reed and the belt of rock around it, for a man going very carefully to escape that horrible pit-hole. And so I went round to the other side, and there found open space enough, with stunted bushes, and starveling trees, and straggling tufts of rushes.

'You fool, you are frightened,' said Uncle Ben, as he looked at my face after shaking hands: 'I want a young man of steadfast courage, as well as of strength and silence. And after what I heard of the battle at Glen Doone, I thought I might trust you for courage.'

'So you may,' said I, 'wherever I see mine enemy; but not where witch and wizard be.'

'Tush, great fool!' cried Master Huckaback; 'the only witch, or wizard, here is the one that bewitcheth all men. Now fasten up my horse, John Ridd, and not too near the slough, lad. Ah, we have chosen our entrance wisely. Two good horsemen, and their horses, coming hither to spy us out, are gone mining on their own account (and their last account it is) down this good wizard's boghole. Now follow me, step for step,' he said, when I had tethered his horse to a tree; 'the ground is not death (like the wizard's hole), but parts are treacherous. I know it well by this time.'

Without any more ado, he led me, in and out of the marshy places, to a great round hole or shaft, bratticed up with timber. I never had seen the like before, and wondered how they could want a well, with so much water on every side.

He signed to me to lift a heavy wooden corb, with an iron loop across it, and sunk in a little pit of earth, a yard or so from the mouth of the shaft. I raised it, and by his direction dropped it into the throat of the shaft, where it hung and shook from a great cross-beam laid at the level of the earth. A very stout thick rope was fastened to the handle of the corb, and ran across a pulley hanging from the centre of the beam, and thence out of sight in the nether places.

'I will first descend,' he said; 'your weight is too great for safety. When the bucket comes up again, follow me, if your heart is good.'

Then he whistled down, with a quick sharp noise, and a whistle from below replied: and he clomb into the vehicle, and the rope ran through the pulley, and Uncle Ben went merrily down, and was out of sight before I had time to think of him. At last up came the bucket; and, with a short sad prayer, I went into whatever might happen.

The scoopings of the side grew black, and the patch of sky above more blue, as, with many thoughts of Lorna, a long way underground I sank. Then I was fetched up at the bottom, with a jerk and rattle; and but for holding by the rope so, must have tumbled over. Two great torches of bale-resin showed me all the darkness, one being held by Uncle Ben and the other by a short square man with a face which seemed well known to me.

'Hail to the world of gold, John Ridd,' said Master Huckaback, smiling in the old dry manner: 'bigger coward never came down the shaft, now did he, Carfax?'

'They be all alike,' said the short square man, 'fust time as they doos it.'

'Come on then, my lad; and we will show you something better. We want your great arm on here, for a job that has beaten the whole of us.'

With these words, Uncle Ben led the way along a narrow passage, roofed with rock, and floored with slate-coloured shale and shingle, and winding in and out, until we stopped at a great stone block or boulder, lying across the floor, and as large as my mother's best oaken wardrobe. Beside it were several sledgehammers, some battered, and some with broken helves.

'Thou great villain!' cried Uncle Ben, giving the boulder a little kick; 'I believe thy time has come at last. Now, John, give us a sample of the things they tell of thee. Take the biggest of them sledge-hammers and crack this rogue in two for us. We have tried at him for a fortnight, and he is a nut worth cracking. But we have no man who can swing that hammer, though all in the mine have handled it.'

'I will do my very best,' said I, pulling off my coat and waistcoat, as if I were going to wrestle; 'but I fear he will prove too tough for me.'

'Ay, that her wull,' grunted Master Carfax; 'lack'th a Carnishman, and a beg one too, not a little charp such as I be. There be no man outside Carnwall, as can crack that boolder.'

'Bless my heart,' I answered; 'but I know something of you, my friend, or at any rate of your family. Well I have beaten most of your Cornish men, though not my place to talk of it.'

I took up the hammer, and swinging it far behind my head fetched it down, with all my power, upon the middle of the rock. The roof above rang mightily, and the echo went down delven galleries, so that all the miners flocked to know what might be doing. But Master Carfax only smiled, although the blow shook him where he stood, for behold the stone was still unbroken, and as firm as ever. Then I smote it again, with no better fortune, and Uncle Ben looked vexed and angry, but all the miners grinned with triumph.

'This little tool is too light,' I cried; 'one of you give me a piece of strong cord.'

Then I took two more of the weightiest hammers, and lashed them fast to the back of mine, not so as to strike, but to burden the fall. Having made this firm, and with room to grasp the handle of the largest one only – for the helves of the others were shorter – I smiled at Uncle Ben, and whirled the mighty implement round my head, just to try whether I could manage it. Upon that, the miners gave a cheer, being honest men, and desirous of seeing fair play between this stone and me with my hammer hammering.

Then I swung me on high, to the swing of the sledge, as a thresher bends back to the rise of his flail, and with all my power descending delivered the ponderous onset. Crashing and crushed the great stone fell over, and threads of sparkling gold appeared in the jagged sides of the breakage.

'How now, Simon Carfax?' cried Uncle Ben triumphantly; 'wilt thou find a man in Cornwall can do the like of that?'

'Ay, and more,' he answered: 'however, it be pretty fair for a lad of these outlandish parts. Get your rollers, my lads, and lead it to the crushing engine.'

'Thou hast done us a good turn, my lad,' said Uncle Reuben, as the others passed out of sight at the corner; 'and now I will show thee the bottom of a very wondrous mystery. But we must not do it more than once, for the time of day is the wrong one.'

The whole affair being a mystery to me, and far beyond my understanding, I followed him softly, without a word, yet thinking very heavily, and longing to be above ground again. He led me through small passages, to a hollow place near the descending-shaft, where I saw a most extraordinary monster fitted up. In form it was like a great coffee-mill, such as I had seen in London, only a thousand times larger, and with a heavy windlass to work it.

'Put in a barrow-load of the smoulder,' said Uncle Ben to Carfax; 'and let them work the crank, for John to understand a thing or two.'

'At this time of day!' cried Simon Carfax; 'and the watching as has been o' late!'

However, he did it without more remonstrance; pouring into the scuttle at the top of the machine about a basketful of broken rock; and then a dozen men went to the wheel, and forced it round, as sailors do. Upon that such a hideous noise arose, as I never should have believed any creature capable of making: and I ran to the well of the mine for air, and to ease my ears, if possible.

'Enough, enough!' shouted Uncle Ben, by the time I was nearly deafened; 'we will digest our goodly boulder, after the devil is come abroad for his evening work. Now, John, not a word about what you have learned: but henceforth you will not be frightened by the noise we make at dusk.'

I could not deny but what this was very clever management. If they could not keep the echoes of the upper air from moving, the wisest plan was to open their valves during the discouragement of the falling evening; when folk would rather be driven away, than drawn into the wilds and quagmires, by a sound so deep and awful coming through the darkness.

Truth Down a Mine

Now I had enough of that underground work to last me for a year to come; neither would I, for sake of gold, have ever stepped into that bucket, of my own good will again. But when I told Lorna – whom I could trust in any matter of secrecy, as if she had never been a woman – all about my great descent, and the honeycombing of the earth, and the mournful noise at eventide, when the gold was under the crusher, and bewailing the mischief it must do, then Lorna's chief desire was to know more about Simon Carfax.

'It must be our Gwenny's father,' she cried; 'the man who disappeared underground, and whom she has ever been seeking. How grieved the poor little thing will be, if it should turn out, after all, that he left his child on purpose! I can hardly believe it, can you, John?'

Being resolved to seek this out, and do a good turn, if I could, to Gwenny, who had done me many a good one, I begged my Lorna to say not a word of this matter to the handmaiden, until I had further searched it out.

Having now true right of entrance, and being known to the watchman, and regarded (since I cracked the boulder) as one who could pay his footing, and perhaps would be the master, when Uncle Ben should be choked with money, I found the corb sent up for me rather sooner than I wished it. At the bottom Master Carfax met me, being captain of the mine, and desirous to know my business. He wore a loose sack round his shoulders, and his beard was two feet long.

'My business is to speak with you,' I answered rather sternly; for this man, who was nothing more than Uncle Reuben's servant, had carried things too far with me, showing no respect whatever; and though I do not care for much, I liked to receive a little, even in my early days.

'Coom into the muck-hole, then,' was his gracious answer; and he led me into a filthy cell, where the miners changed their jackets.

'Simon Carfax,' I began, with a manner to discourage him; 'I fear you are a shallow fellow, and not worth my trouble.'

'Then don't take it,' he replied; 'I want no man's trouble.'

'For your sake I would not,' I answered; 'but for your

daughter's sake I will: the daughter whom you left to starve so pitifully in the wilderness.'

The man stared at me with his pale grey eyes, whose colour was lost from candle-light; and his voice as well as his body shook, while he cried, –

'It is a lie, man. No daughter and no son have I. Nor was ever child of mine left to starve in the wilderness. You are too big for me to tackle, and that makes you a coward for saying it.' His hands were playing with a pickaxe-helve, as if he longed to have me under it.

'Perhaps I have wronged you, Simon,' I answered very softly; for the sweat upon his forehead shone in the smoky torchlight: 'if I have, I crave your pardon. But did you not bring up from Cornwall a little maid named "Gwenny", and supposed to be your daughter?'

'Ay, and she was my daughter, my last and only child of five; and for her I would give this mine, and all the gold will ever come from it.'

'You shall have her, without either mine or gold; if you only prove to me that you did not abandon her.'

'Abandon her! I abandon Gwenny!' he cried, with such a rage of scorn that I at once believed him. 'They told me she was dead, and crushed, and buried in the drift here; and half my heart died with her. The Almighty blast their mining-work, if the scoundrels lied to me!'

'The scoundrels must have lied to you,' I answered, with a spirit fired by his heat of fury: 'the maid is living, and with us. Come up; and you shall see her.'

'Rig the bucket,' he shouted out along the echoing gallery; and then he fell against the wall, and through the grimy sack I saw the heaving of his breast, as I have seen my opponent's chest, in a long hard bout of wrestling. For my part, I could do no more than hold my tongue, and look at him.

Without another word, we rose to the level of the moors and mires; neither would Master Carfax speak, as I led him across the barrows. In this he was welcome to his own way, for I do love silence; so little harm can come of it. And though Gwenny was no beauty, her father might be fond of her.

So I put him in the cow-house (not to frighten the little maid), and the folding shutters over him, such as we used at the beestings; and he listened to my voice outside, and held on, and preserved himself.

I went and fetched his Gwenny forth from the back kitchen.

'Come, and see who is in the cow-house.'

Gwenny knew; she knew in a moment. Looking into my eyes, she knew; and hanging back from me to sigh, she knew it even better.

She had not much elegance of emotion, being flat and square all over; but none the less for that her heart came quick, and her words came slowly.

'Oh, Jan, you are too good to cheat me. Is it joke you are putting upon me?'

I answered her with a gaze alone; and she tucked up her clothes and followed me, because the road was dirty. Then I opened the door just wide enough for the child to go to her father; and left those two to have it out, as might be most natural. And they took a long time about it.

Without intending any harm, and meaning only good indeed, I had now done serious wrong to Uncle Reuben's prospects. For Captain Carfax was full as angry at the trick played on him, as he was happy in discovering the falsehood and the fraud of it. Nor could I help agreeing with him, when he told me all of it.

For when this poor man left his daughter, (asleep as he supposed, and having his food, and change of clothes, and Sunday hat to see to,) he meant to return in an hour or so, and settle about her sustenance in some house of the neighbourhood. But this was the very thing of all things which the leaders of the enterprise, who had brought him up from Cornwall, for his noted skill in metals, were determined, whether by fair means or foul, to stop at the very outset. Secrecy being their main object, what chance could be there of it, if the miners were allowed to keep their children in the neighbourhood? Hence, on the plea of feasting Simon, they kept him drunk for three days and three nights, assuring him (whenever he had gleams enough to ask for her) that his daughter was as well as could be, and enjoying herself with the children. Not wishing the maid to see him tipsy, he pressed the matter no further; but applied himself to the bottle again, and drank her health with pleasure.

However, after three days of this, his constitution rose against it, and he became quite sober. He sought for Gwenny high and low; first with threats, and then with fears, and then with tears and wailing. And so he became to the other men a warning and great annoyance. Therefore they combined to swear what seemed a very likely thing, and might be true for all they knew; to wit, that Gwenny had come to seek her father down the shaft-hole, and peering too eagerly into the dark, had toppled forward, and gone down, and lain at the bottom as dead as a stone.

'And thou being so happy with drink,' the villains finished up to him, 'and getting drunker every day, we thought it shame to trouble thee, and we buried the wench in the lower drift; and no use to think more of her; but come and have a glass, Sim.'

But Simon Carfax swore that drink had lost him his wife, and now had lost him the last of his five children, and would lose him his own soul, if further he went on with it; and from that day to his death he never touched strong drink again.

Lorna Gone Away

Now a mighty giant had arisen in a part of Cornwall; and his calf was twenty-five inches round, and the breadth of his shoulders two feet and a quarter; and his stature seven feet and three quarters. Round the chest he was seventy inches, and his hand a foot across, and there were no scales strong enough to judge of his weight in the market-place. Now this man – or I should say, his backers and boasters, for the giant himself was modest – sent me a brave and haughty challenge, to meet him in the ring at Bodmin-town, on the first day of August, or else to return my champion's belt to them by the messenger.

It is no use to deny that I was greatly dashed and scared at first. For my part, I was only, when measured without clothes on, sixty inches round the breast, and round the calf scarce twenty-one, only two feet across the shoulders, and in height not six and three quarters. However, I resolved to go and try him, as they would pay all expenses, and a hundred pounds, if I conquered him.

Now this story is too well-known for me to go through it again. Enough that, trusting in my practice and study of the art, I resolved to try a back with him; and when my arms were round him once, the giant was but a farthingale put into the vice of a blacksmith. The man had no bones; his frame sank in, and I was afraid of crushing him. He lay on his back, and smiled at me; and I begged his pardon. I got my hundred pounds, and made up my mind to spend every farthing in presents for mother and Lorna.

Now coming into the kitchen, with all my cash in my breeches pocket (golden guineas, with an elephant on them, for the stamp of the guinea company), I found dear mother most heartily glad to see me safe and sound again, but by the way they hung about, I knew that something was gone wrong.

'Where is Lorna?' I asked at length, after trying not to ask it: 'I want her to come, and see my money. She never saw so much before.'

'Alas!' said mother, with a heavy sigh; 'she will see a great deal more, I fear; and a deal more than is good for her. Whether you ever see her again will depend upon her nature, John.'

'What do you mean, mother?' cried I, being wild by this time; 'Lizzie, you have a little sense; will you tell me where is Lorna?'

'The Lady Lorna Dugal,' said Lizzie, screwing up her lips, as if the title were too grand, 'is gone to London, brother John; and not likely to come back again. We must try to get on without her. The lady spoke very little to any one except indeed to mother, and to Gwenny Carfax: and Gwenny is gone with her, so that the benefit of that is lost. But she left a letter for "poor John", as in charity she called him. How grand she looked, to be sure, with the fine clothes on that were come for her! It's in the little cupboard, near the head of Lady Lorna's bed, where she used to keep the diamond necklace, which we contrived to get stolen.'

Without another word, I rushed (so that every board in the house shook) up to my lost Lorna's room, and tore the little wall-niche open, and espied my treasure. It was as simple, and as homely, and loving, as even I could wish. 'My own love, and sometime lord, – Take it not amiss of me, that even without farewell, I go; for I cannot persuade the men to wait, your return being doubtful. My great uncle, some grand lord, is awaiting me at Dunster, having fear of venturing too near this Exmoor country. I, who have been so lawless always, and the child of outlaws, am now to atone for this, it seems, by living in a court of law, and under special surveillance (as they call it, I believe) of His Majesty's Court of Chancery. My uncle is appointed my guardian and master; and I must live beneath his care, until I am twenty-one years old. The men had their orders and must obey them; and Master Stickles was ordered too to help, as the King's Commissioner. Of one thing rest you well assured: no difference of rank, or fortune, or of life itself, shall ever make me swerve from truth to you. Though they tell you I am false, though your own mind harbours it, from the sense of things around, and your own under-valuing, yet take counsel of your heart, and cast such thoughts away from you; being unworthy of itself, they must be unworthy also of the one who dwells there: and that one is, and ever shall be, your own Lorna Dugal.'

'No doubt it is all over!' my mind said to me bitterly: 'Trust me, all shall yet be right!' my heart replied very sweetly.

Tom Faggus Goes to War

ALL our neighbourhood was surprised, that the Doones had not ere now attacked, and probably made an end of us. For we lay almost at their mercy now, having only a Serjeant and three men, to protect us, Captain Stickles having been ordered southwards with all his force, except such as might be needful for collecting toll, and watching the imports at Lynmouth, and thence to Porlock.

Now the reason, why the Doones did not attack us, was that they were preparing to meet another, and more powerful assault, upon their fortress; being assured that their repulse of King's troops could not be looked over when brought before the authorities. And no doubt they were right; for although the conflicts in the Government during that summer, and autumn, had delayed the matter, yet positive orders had been issued, that these outlaws and malefactors should at any price be brought to justice; when the sudden death of King Charles the Second threw all things into confusion, and all minds into a panic.

The next fortnight, we were daily troubled with conflicting rumours, each man relating what he desired, rather than what he had right, to believe. We were told that the Duke had been proclaimed King of England, in every town of Dorset and of Somerset; that he had won a great battle at Axminster, and another at Bridport, and another somewhere else; that all the western counties had risen as one man for him, and all the militia joined his ranks; that Taunton, and Bridgewater, and Bristowe, were all mad with delight, the two former being in his hands, and the latter craving to be so. And then, on the other hand, we heard that the Duke had been vanquished, and put to flight, and upon being apprehended had confessed himself an impostor, and a papist, as bad as the King was.

We longed for Colonel Stickles (as he always became in time of war, though he fell back to Captain, and even Lieutenant, directly the fight was over), for then we should have won trusty news, as well as good consideration. But all the soldiers had been ordered away at full speed for Exeter, to join the Duke of Albemarle, or if he were gone, to follow him. As for us, who had fed them so long (although not quite for nothing), we must take our chance of Doones, or any other enemies.

I myself became involved (God knows how much against my will and my proper judgment) in the troubles, and the conflict, and the cruel work coming afterwards. If ever I had made up my mind to anything in all my life, it was at this particular time, and as stern and strong as could be. I had resolved to let things pass. But all my policy went for nothing, through a few touches of feeling.

One day at the beginning of July, I came home from mowing about noon, to fetch some cider for all of us, and to eat a morsel of bacon.

In the courtyard I saw a little cart, with iron breaks underneath it, such as fastidious people use to deaden the jolting of the road; but few men under a lord or baronet would be so particular. Therefore I wondered who our noble visitor could be. But when I entered the kitchen-place, brushing up my hair for somebody, behold it was no one greater than our Annie, with my godson in her arms, and looking pale and tear-begone. And at first she could not speak to me.

'Tell me what it is, my dear. Any grief of yours will vex me greatly; but I will try to bear it.'

'Then, John, it is just this. Tom has gone off with the rebels: and you must, oh, you must go after him.'

'Now,' I said, 'be in no such hurry;' for while I was gradually yielding, I liked to pass it through my fingers, as if my fingers shaped it: 'there are many things to be thought about, and many ways of viewing it.'

'Oh, you never can have loved Lorna! No wonder you gave her up so! John, you can love nobody, but your oat-ricks, and your hay-ricks.'

'Sister mine, because I rant not, neither rave of what I feel, can you be so shallow as to dream that I feel nothing? What is your love for Tom Faggus? What is your love for your baby (pretty darling as he is) to compare with such a love as for ever dwells with me? Because I do not prate of it; because it is beyond me, not only to express, but even form to my own heart in thoughts; because I do not shape my face, and would scorn to play to it, as a thing of acting, and lay it out before you, are you fools enough to think – ' but here I stopped, having said more than was usual with me.

'I am very sorry, John. Dear John, I am so sorry. What a shallow fool I am!'

'I will go seek your husband,' I said, to change the subject, for even to Annie I would not lay open all my heart about Lorna.

But when my poor mother heard that I was committed, by word of honour, to a wild-goose chase, among the rebels, after that runagate Tom Faggus, she simply stared, and would not believe it.

Slaughter in the Marshes

RIGHT early in the morning I was off, without a word to any one.

We went away in merry style; my horse being ready for anything, and I only glad of a bit of change, after months of working and brooding; with no content to crown the work; no hope to hatch the brooding, or without hatching to reckon it. Who could tell but what Lorna might be discovered, or at any rate heard of, before the end of this campaign; if campaign it could be called of a man who went to fight nobody, only to redeem a runagate?

Yet there was one thing rather unfavourable to my present enterprise, namely, that I knew nothing of the country I was bound to, not even in what part of it my business might be supposed to lie. For beside the uncertainty caused by the conflict of reports, it was likely that King Monmouth's army would be moving from place to place, according to the prospect of supplies and of reinforcements. However there would arise more chance of getting news as I went on: but the manner in which I was bandied about, by false information, from pillar to post, or at other times driven quite out of my way by the presence of the King's soldiers, may be known by the names of the following towns, to which I was sent in succession, Bath, Frome, Wells, Wincanton, Glastonbury, Shepton, Bradford, Axbridge, Somerton, and finally Bridgewater.

There I was guided mainly by the sound of guns and trumpets, in riding out of the narrow ways, and into the open marshes. And thus I might have found my road, in spite of all the spread of water, and the glaze of moonshine; but that, as I followed sound (far from hedge or causeway), fog (like a chestnut tree in blossom, touched with moonlight) met me. Now fog is a thing that I understand, and can do with well enough, where I know the country: but here I had never been before. It was nothing to our Exmoor fogs; not to be compared with them; and all the time one could see the moon; which we cannot do in our fogs. Yet the gleam of water always makes a fog more difficult; like a curtain on a mirror; none can tell the boundaries.

At last, when I almost despaired of escaping from this tangle of spongy banks, and of hazy creeks, and reed-fringe, my horse heard the neigh of a fellow-horse, and was only too glad to answer it; upon which the other, having lost his rider, came up, and pricked his ears at us, and gazed through the fog very steadfastly. Therefore I encouraged him with a soft and genial whistle, and my horse did his best to tempt him with a snort of inquiry. However, nothing would suit that nag, except to enjoy his new freedom; and he capered away with his tail set on high, and the stirrup-irons clashing under him. Therefore, as he might know the way, and appeared to have been in the battle, we followed him very carefully; and he led us to a little hamlet, called (as I found afterwards) West Zuyland, or Zealand, so named perhaps from its situation amid this inland sea.

Here the King's troops had been quite lately, and their fires were still burning; but the men themselves had been summoned away by the night attack of the rebels. Hence I procured for my guide a young man who knew the district thoroughly, and who led me by many intricate ways to the rear of the rebel army. We came upon a broad open moor, striped with sullen water-courses, shagged with sedge, and yellow iris, and in the drier part with bilberries. For by this time it was four o'clock, and the summer sun, arising wanly, showed us all the ghastly scene.

Would that I had never been there! Often in the lonely hours, even now it haunts me. Flying men, flung back from dreams of victory and honour, only glad to have the luck of life and limbs to fly with, mud-bedraggled, foul with slime, reeking both with sweat and blood, which they could not stop to wipe, cursing, with their pumped out lungs, every stick that hindered them, or gory puddle that slipped the step, scarcely able to leap over the corpses that had dragged to die. And to see how the corpses lay; some had bloodless hands put upwards, white as wax, and firm as death, clasped (as on a monument) in prayer for dear ones left behind, or in high thanksgiving. And of these men there was nothing in their broad blue eyes to fear. But others were of different sort; simple fellows unused to pain, accustomed to the bill-hook, perhaps, or rasp of the knuckles in a quick-set hedge, or making some to-do, at breakfast, over a thumb cut in sharpening a scythe, and expecting their wives to make more to-do. Yet here lay these poor chaps, dead; dead, after a deal of pain, with little mind to bear it, and a soul they had never thought of.

I stopped my horse, desiring not to be shot for nothing; and eager to aid some poor sick people, who tried to lift their arms to me. And this I did to the best of my power, though void of skill in the business ; and more inclined to weep with them than to check their weeping.

In the midst of this, I felt warm lips laid against my cheek quite softly, and then a little push; and behold it was a horse leaning over me! I arose in haste, and there stood Winnie, looking at me with beseeching eyes, enough to melt a heart of stone. Then seeing my attention fixed, she turned her head, and glanced back sadly towards the place of battle, and gave a little wistful neigh: and then looked me full in the face again, as much as to say, 'Do you understand?' while she scraped with one hoof impatiently. I went to her side and patted her; but that was not what she wanted. Then I offered to leap into the empty saddle; but neither did that seem good to her; for she ran away towards the part of the field, at which she had been glancing back, and then turned round, and shook her mane, entreating me to follow her. I mounted my own horse again, and to Winnie's great delight, professed myself at her service. With her ringing silvery neigh, such as no other horse of all I ever knew could equal, she at once proclaimed her triumph, and told her master (or meant to tell, if death should not have closed his ears), that she was coming to his aid, and bringing one who might be trusted, of the higher race that kill.

A Cold Sweat

THAT faithful creature, whom I began to admire as if she were my own (which is no little thing for a man to say of another man's horse) stopped in front of a low black shed, such as we call a 'linhay'. And here she uttered a little greeting, in a subdued and softened voice, hoping to obtain answer, such as her master was wont to give in a cheery manner. Receiving no reply, she entered; and I followed. There I found her sniffing gently, but with great emotion, at the body of Tom Faggus. A corpse poor Tom appeared to be, if ever there was one in this world; and I turned away, and felt unable to keep altogether from weeping. But the mare either could not understand, or else would not believe it. She reached her long neck forth, and felt him with her under lip, passing it over his skin as softly as a mother would do an infant; and then she looked up at me again; as much as to say, 'He is all right.'

Upon this I took courage, and handled poor Tom, which being young I had feared at first to do. He groaned very feebly, as I raised him up; and there was the wound, a great savage one (whether from pike-thrust or musket-ball), gaping and welling in his right side, from which a piece seemed to be torn away. I bound it up with some of my linen, so far as I knew how; just to stanch the flow of blood, until we could get a doctor. Then I gave him a little weak brandy and water, which he drank with the greatest eagerness, and made sign to me for more of it.

After that he seemed better, and a little colour came into his cheeks; and he looked at Winnie and knew her; and would have her nose in his clammy hand, though I thought it not good for either of them. With the stay of my arm he sat upright, and faintly looked about him; as if at the end of a violent dream, too much for his power of mind. Then he managed to whisper, 'Is Winnie hurt?'

'As sound as a roach,' I answered. 'Then so am I,' said he: 'put me upon her back, John; she and I die together.'

While I was yet hesitating, a storm of horse at full gallop went by, tearing, swearing, bearing away all the country before them. Only a little pollard hedge kept us from their blood-shot eyes. 'Now is the time,' said my cousin Tom, so far as I could make out his words; 'on their heels, I am safe, John, if I only have Winnie under me. Winnie and I die together.'

Seeing this strong bent of his mind, stronger than any pains of death, I even did what his feeble eyes sometimes implored, and sometimes commanded. With a strong sash, from his own hot neck, bound and twisted, tight as wax, around his damaged waist, I set him upon Winnie's back, and placed his trembling feet in stirrups, with a band from one to other, under the good mare's body; so that no swerve could throw him out: and then I said, 'Lean forward, Tom; it will stop your hurt from bleeding.' He leaned almost on the neck of the mare, which, as I knew, must close the wound; and the light of his eyes was quite different, and the pain of his forehead unstrung itself, as he felt the undulous readiness of her volatile paces under him.

'God bless you, John; I am safe,' he whispered, fearing to open his lungs much: 'who can come near my Winnie mare? A mile of her gallop is ten years of life. Look out for yourself, John Ridd.' He sucked his lips, and the mare went off, as easy and swift as a swallow.

'Well,' thought I, 'I have done a very good thing, no doubt, and ought to be thankful to God for the chance. But as for getting away unharmed, with all these scoundrels about me, and only a foundered horse to trust in upon the whole, I begin to think that I have made a fool of myself, according to my habit. No wonder Tom said, "Look out for yourself!" I shall look out from a prison window, or perhaps even out of a halter. And then, what will Lorna think of me?'

But while thinking these things, and desiring my breakfast, beyond any power of describing, and even beyond my remembrance, I fell into a troop of men, from which there was no exit. These, like true crusaders, met me, swaggering very heartily, and with their barrels of cider set, like so many cannon, across the road, over against a small hostel.

'We have won the victory, my lord King, and we mean to enjoy it. Down from thy horse, and have a stoup of cider, thou big rebel.'

'No rebel am I. My name is John Ridd. I belong to the side of the King: and I want some breakfast.'

Even while I was hesitating, a superior officer rode up, with his sword drawn, and his face on fire.

'Who is this young fellow we have here? Speak up, sirrah; what are thou, and how much will thy good mother pay for thee?'

'My mother will pay naught for me,' I answered; 'so please your worship, I am no rebel; but an honest farmer, and well-proved of loyalty.'

'Ha, ha! a farmer art thou? Those fellows always pay the best. Good farmer, come to yon barren tree; thou shalt make it fruitful.'

Colonel Kirke made a sign to his men, and before I could think of resistance, stout new ropes were flung around me; and with three men on either side, I was led along very painfully. The face of the Colonel was hard and stern as a block of bogwood oak; and though the men might pity me, and think me unjustly executed, yet they must obey their orders, or themselves be put to death. Therefore I addressed myself to the Colonel, in a most ingratiating manner; begging him not to sully the glory of his victory, and dwelling upon my pure innocence, and even good service to our lord the King.

It is not in my power to tell half the thoughts that moved me, when we came to the fatal tree, and saw two men hanging there already, as innocent perhaps as I was, and henceforth entirely harmless. Though ordered by the Colonel to look steadfastly upon them, I could not bear to do so; upon which he called me a paltry coward, and promised my breeches to any man who would spit upon my countenance. One bravely stepped forward to do for me, trusting no doubt to the rope I was led with. But, unluckily as it proved for him, my right arm was free for a moment; and therewith I dealt him such a blow, that he never spake again. At the sound and sight of that bitter stroke, the other men drew back; and Colonel Kirke, now black in the face with fury and vexation, gave orders for to shoot me, and cast me into the ditch hard by. The men raised their pieces, and pointed at me, waiting for the word to fire; and I, being quite overcome by the hurry of these events, and quite unprepared to die yet, could only think all upside down about

Lorna, and my mother, and wonder what each would say to it. I spread my hands before my eyes, not being so brave as some men; and hoping, in some foolish way, to cover my heart with my elbows. I heard the breath of all around, as if my skull were a sounding-board; and knew even how the different men were fingering their triggers. And a cold sweat broke all over me, as the Colonel, prolonging his enjoyment, began slowly to say, 'Fire'.

But while he was yet dwelling on the 'F', the hoofs of a horse dashed out on the road, and horse and horseman flung themselves betwixt me and the gun-muzzles. So narrowly was I saved, that one man could not check his trigger: his musket went off, and the ball struck the horse on the withers, and scared him exceedingly. He began to lash out with his heels all around, and the Colonel was glad to keep clear of him; and the men made excuse to lower their guns, not really wishing to shoot me.

'How now, Captain Stickles?' cried Kirke, the more angry because he had shown his cowardice; 'dare you, sir, to come betwixt me and my lawful prisoner?'

'Nay, hearken one moment, Colonel,' replied my old friend Jeremy; and his damaged voice was the sweetest sound I had heard for many a day; 'for your own sake hearken.' He looked so full of momentous tidings, that Colonel Kirke made a sign to his men, not to shoot me till further orders; and then he went aside with Stickles, so that in spite of all my anxiety I could not catch what passed between them. But I fancied that the name of Lord Chief Justice Jeffreys was spoken more than once, and with emphasis, and deference.

'Then I leave him in your hands, Captain Stickles,' said Kirke at last so that all might hear him; and though the news was so good for me, the smile of baffled malice made his dark face look most hideous; 'and I shall hold you answerable for the custody of this prisoner.'

'Colonel Kirke, I will answer for him,' Master Stickles replied, with a grave bow, and one hand on his breast: 'John Ridd, you are my prisoner. Follow me, John Ridd.'

Being free of my arms again, I touched my hat to Colonel Kirke, as became his rank and experience; but he did not condescend to return my short salutation, having espied in the distance a prisoner, out of whom he might make money.

I wrung the hand of Jeremy Stickles, for his truth and goodness; and he almost wept (for since his wound, he had been a weakened man) as he answered, 'Turn for turn, John. You saved my life from the Doones; and by the mercy of God, I have saved you from a far worse company.'

Suitable Devotion

JEREMY STICKLES assured me, as we took the road to Bridgewater, that the only chance for my life was to obtain an order forthwith for my dispatch to London, as a suspected person indeed, but not found in open rebellion, and believed to be under the patronage of the great Lord Jeffreys.

'An hour agone I would have fled, for the sake of my mother, and the farm. But now that I have been taken prisoner, and my name is known, if I fly, the farm is forfeited; and my mother and sister must starve. Moreover, I have done no harm; I have borne no weapons against the King, nor desired the success of his enemies. I like not that the son of a bona-roba should be King of England; neither do I count the papists any more than we are. If they have aught to try me for, I will stand my trial.'

'Then to London thou must go, my son. There is no such thing as trial here: we hang the good folk without it, which saves them much anxiety. But quicken thy step, good John; I have influence with Lord Churchill, and we must contrive to see him, ere the foreigner falls to work again. Lord Churchill is a man of sense, and imprisons nothing but his money.'

We were lucky enough to find this nobleman, who has since become so famous by his foreign victories. Now this good Lord Churchill – one might call him good, by comparison with the very bad people around him – granted, without any long hesitation, the order for my safe deliverance to the Court of King's Bench at Westminster; and Stickles, who had to report in London, was empowered to convey me, and made answerable for producing me.

For fear of any unpleasant change, we set forth at once for London; and truly thankful may I be that God in His mercy spared me the sight of the cruel and bloody work, with which the whole country reeked and howled, during the next fortnight. I have heard things that set my hair on end, and made me loathe good meat for days; but I make a point of setting down only the things which I saw done: and in this particular case, not many will quarrel with my decision. Enough, therefore, that we rode on as far as Wells, where we slept that night; and being joined in the morning by several troopers and orderlies, we made a slow but safe journey to London, by way of Bath, and Reading.

What moved me most, when I saw again the noble oil and tallow of the London lights, and the dripping torches at almost every corner, and the handsome sign-boards, was the thought that here my Lorna lived, and walked, and took the air, and perhaps thought, now and then, of the old days in the good farmhouse. Although I would make no approach to her, any more than she had done to me (upon which grief I have not dwelt, for fear of seeming selfish), yet there must be some large chance, or the little chance might be enlarged, of falling in with the maiden somehow, and learning how her mind was set. If against me, all should be over. I was not the man to sigh and cry for love, like a hot-brained Romeo: none should even guess my grief, except my sister Annie.

But if Lorna loved me still – as in my heart of hearts I hoped – then would I for no one care, except her own delicious self. Rank and title, wealth and grandeur, all should go to the winds, before they scared me from my own true love.

But I abode in London betwixt a month and five weeks' time, ere ever I saw Lorna. Nevertheless I heard of Lorna, from the worthy furrier, with whom I had lodged before also, almost every day, and with a fine exaggeration. This honest man was one of those who, in virtue of their trade, and nicety of behaviour, are admitted into noble life, to take measurements, and show patterns. And while so doing, they contrive to acquire what is to the English mind at once the most important, and most interesting of all knowledge, – the science of being able to talk about the titled people. So my furrier (whose name was Ramsack), having to make robes for peers, and cloaks for their wives and otherwise, knew the great folk, sham or real, as well as he knew a fox, or skunk, from a wolverine skin.

From Master Ramsack I discovered that the nobleman, to whose charge Lady Lorna had been committed, by the Court of Chancery, was Earl Brandir of Lochawe, her poor mother's uncle. For the Countess of Dugal was daughter, and only child, of the last Lord Lorne, whose sister had married Sir Ensor Doone; while he himself had married the sister of Earl Brandir. This nobleman had a country house near the village of Kensington; and here his niece dwelled with him, when she was not in attendance on Her Majesty the Queen, who had taken a liking to her. Now since the King had begun to attend the celebration of mass in the chapel at Whitehall, – and not at Westminster Abbey, as our gossips had averred – he had given order that the doors should be thrown open, so that all who could make interest to get into the antechamber, might see this form of worship. Master Ramsack told me that Lorna was there almost every Sunday;

their Majesties being most anxious to have the presence of all the nobility of the Catholic persuasion, so as to make a goodly show. And the worthy furrier, having influence with the door keepers, obtained admittance for me, one Sunday, into the antechamber.

Here I took care to be in waiting, before the Royal procession entered; but being unknown, and of no high rank, I was not allowed to stand forward among the better people, but ordered back into a corner very dark and dismal.

You may suppose that my heart beat high, when the King, and the Queen, appeared, and entered, followed by the Duke of Norfolk bearing the sword of state, and by several other noblemen, and people of repute. After all the men were gone, some to this side, some to that, according to their feelings, a number of ladies, beautifully dressed, being of the Queen's retinue, began to enter, and were stared at three times as much as the men had been. And indeed they were worth looking at (which men never are to my ideas, when they trick themselves with gewgaws), but none was so well worth eye-service as my own beloved Lorna. She entered modestly and shyly, with her eyes upon the ground, knowing the rudeness of the gallants, and the large sum she was priced at. Her dress was of the purest white, very sweet and simple, without a line of ornament, for she herself adorned it. The way she walked, and touched her skirt (rather than seemed to hold it up), with a white hand bearing one red rose, this, and her stately supple neck, and the flowing of her hair would show, at a distance of a hundred yards, that she could be none but Lorna Doone – Lorna Doone of my early love; in the days when she blushed for her name before me, by reason of dishonesty; but now the Lady Lorna Dugal; as far beyond reproach as above my poor affection. All my heart, and all my mind, gathered themselves upon her. Would she see me, or would she pass? Was there instinct in our love?

By some strange chance she saw me. Or was it through our destiny? While with eyes kept sedulously on the marble floor, while with shy quick steps she passed, some one (perhaps with purpose) trod on the skirt of her clear white dress, – with the quickness taught her by many a scene of danger, she looked up, and her eyes met mine.

As I gazed upon her, steadfastly, yearningly, yet with some reproach, and more of pride than humility, she made me one of the courtly bows which I do so much detest; yet even that was sweet and graceful, when my Lorna did it. But the colour of her pure clear cheeks was nearly as deep as that of my own, when she went on for the religious work. And the shining of her eyes was owing to an unpaid debt of tears.

All these proud thoughts arose within me, as the lovely form of Lorna went inside, and was no more seen.

Nevertheless, I waited on; as my usual manner is. For to be beaten, while running away, is ten times worse than to face it out, and take it, and have done with it.

While I stored up, in my memory, enough to keep our parson going through six pipes on a Saturday night – to have it as right as could be next day – a lean man with a yellow beard, too thin for a good Catholic (which religion always fattens,) came up to me, working sideways, in the manner of a female crab.

'This is not to my liking,' I said: 'if aught thou hast, speak plainly; while they make that musical roar inside.'

Nothing had this man to say; but with many sighs, because I was not of the proper faith, he took my reprobate hand to save me: and with several religious tears, looked up at me, and winked with one eye. Although the skin of my palms was thick, I felt a little suggestion there, as of a gentle leaf in spring, fearing to seem too forward.

Then I lifted up my little billet; and in that dark corner read it, with a strong rainbow of colours coming from the angled light. And in mine eyes there was enough to make rainbow of strongest sun, as my anger clouded off.

All of it was done in pencil; but as plain as plain could be. In my coffin it shall lie, with my ring, and something else. Therefore will I not expose it to every man who buys this book, and haply thinks that he has bought me to the bottom of my heart. Enough for men of gentle birth (who never are inquisitive) that my love told me, in her letter, just to come and see her.

Lorna Still is Lorna

I FELT myself to be getting on better than at any time since the last wheat-harvest, as I took the lane to Kensington upon the Monday evening. For although no time was given in my Lorna's letter, I was not inclined to wait any more than decency required. And though I went and watched the house, decency would not allow me to knock on the Sunday evening, especially when I found at the corner that his lordship was at home.

The lanes, and fields, between Charing Cross and the village of Kensington, are, or were at that time, more than reasonably infested with footpads, and with highwaymen. However, my stature and holly club kept these fellows from doing more than casting sheep's eyes at me. For it was still broad daylight, and the view of the distant villages, Chelsea, Battersea, Tyburn, and others, as well as a few large houses, among the hams, and towards the river, made it seem less lonely.

When I came to Earl Brandir's house, my natural modesty forbade me to appear at the door for guests; therefore I went to the entrance for servants and retainers. Here, to my great surprise, who should come and let me in but little Gwenny

Carfax, whose very existence had almost escaped my recollection. Her mistress, no doubt, had seen me coming, and sent her to save trouble. But when I offered to kiss Gwenny, in my joy and comfort to see a farmhouse face again, she looked ashamed, and turned away, and would hardly speak to me.

I followed her to a little room, furnished very daintily; and there she ordered me to wait, in a most ungracious manner. 'Well,' thought I, 'if the mistress and the maid are alike in temper, better it had been for me to abide at Master Ramsack's.'

Almost ere I hoped – for fear and hope were so entangled, that they hindered one another – the velvet hangings of the doorway parted, with a little doubt, and then a good face put on it. Lorna, in her perfect beauty, stood before the crimson folds, and her dress was all pure white, and her cheeks were rosy pink, and her lips were scarlet.

Like a maiden, with skill and sense, checking violent impulse, she stayed there for one moment only, just to be admired: and then like a woman, she came to me, seeing how alarmed I was. The hand she offered me I took, and raised it to my lips with fear, as a thing too good for me. 'Is that all?' she whispered; and then her eyes gleamed up at me: and in another instant she was weeping on my breast.

'Darling Lorna, Lady Lorna,' I cried, in astonishment, yet unable but to keep her closer to me, and closer; 'surely, though I love you so, this is not as it should be.'

'Yes, it is, John. Yes, it is. Nothing else should ever be. Oh, why have you behaved so?'

'I am behaving,' I replied, 'to the very best of my ability. There is no other man in the world could hold you so, without kissing you.'

'Then why don't you do it, John?' asked Lorna, looking up at me, with a flash of her old fun.

Now this matter, proverbially, is not so meet for discussion, as it is for repetition. Enough that we said nothing more than, 'Oh, John, how glad I am!' and, 'Lorna, Lorna, Lorna!' for about five minutes. Then my darling drew back proudly; with blushing cheeks, and tear-bright eyes, she began to cross-examine me.

'Master John Ridd, you shall tell the truth, the whole truth, and nothing but the truth. I have been in Chancery, sir; and can detect a story. Now why have you never for more than a twelvemonth, taken the smallest notice of your old friend, Mistress Lorna Doone?' Although she spoke in this light-some manner, as if it made no difference, I saw that her quick heart was moving, and the flash of her eyes controlled.

'Simply for this cause,' I answered, 'that my old friend, and true love, took not the smallest heed of me. Nor knew I where to find her.'

'What!' cried Lorna; and nothing more; being overcome with wondering. I told her, over and over again, that not a single syllable of any message from her, or tidings of her welfare, had reached me, or any one of us, since the letter she left behind.

Then she moved an implement such as I had not seen before, and which made a ringing noise at a serious distance. And before I had ceased wondering – for if such things go on, we might ring the church bells, while sitting in our back-kitchen – little Gwenny Carfax came, with a grave and sullen face.

'Gwenny,' began my Lorna, in a tone of high rank and dignity, 'go and fetch the letters, which I gave you at various times for dispatch to Mistress Ridd.'

'How can I fetch them, when they are gone? It be no use for him to tell no lies' –

'Now, Gwenny, can you look at me?' I asked very sternly; for the matter was no joke to me, after a year's unhappiness.

'I don't want to look at 'ee. What should I look at a young man for, although he did offer to kiss me?'

I saw the spite and impudence of this last remark; and so did Lorna, although she could not quite refrain from smiling.

'Now, Gwenny, not to speak of that,' said Lorna very demurely, 'if you thought it honest to keep the letters, was it honest to keep the money?'

At this the Cornish maiden broke into a rage of honesty: 'A' putt the money by for 'ee. 'Ee shall have every farden of it.' And so she flung out of the room.

'And Gwenny,' said Lorna very softly, following under the door-hangings; 'if it is not honest to keep the money, it is not honest to keep the letters, which would have been worth more than any gold, to those who were so kind to you. Your father shall know the whole, Gwenny, unless you tell the truth.'

'Now, a' will tell all the truth,' this strange maiden answered, talking to herself at least as much as to her mistress, while she went out of sight and hearing. And then I was so glad at having my own Lorna once again, cleared of all contempt for us, and true to me through all of it, that I would have forgiven Gwenny for treason, or even forgery. She came back with a leathern bag, and tossed it upon the table. Not a word did she vouchsafe to us; but stood there, looking injured.

'What made you treat me so, little Gwenny?' I asked, for Lorna would not ask, lest the reply should vex me.

'Because 'ee be'est below her so. Her shanna' have a poor farmering chap, not even if her were a Carnishman. All her land, and all her birth – and who be you, I'd like to know?'

'Gwenny, you may go,' said Lorna, reddening with quiet anger; 'and remember that you come not near me for the next three days. It is the only way to punish her,' she continued to me, when the maid was gone, in a storm of sobbing and weeping. 'Now, for the next three days, she will scarcely touch a morsel of food, and scarcely do a thing but cry. Make up your mind to one thing, John; if you mean to take me, for better for worse, you will have to take Gwenny with me.'

'I would take you with fifty Gwennies,' said I, 'although every one of them hated me; which I do not believe this little maid does, in the bottom of her heart.'

After this, we spoke of ourselves, and the way people would regard us, supposing that when Lorna came to be her own free mistress (as she must do in the course of time) she were to throw her rank aside, and refuse her title, and caring not a fig for folk who cared less than a fig-stalk for her, should shape her mind to its native bent, and to my perfect happiness.

'Will you allow me just to explain my own view of this matter, John?' said she. 'It may be a very foolish view, but I shall never change it. In the first place, it is quite certain, that neither you nor I can be happy without the other. Then what stands between us? Worldly position, and nothing else. I have no more education than you have, John Ridd; nay, and not so much. My birth and ancestry are not one whit more pure than yours, although they may be better known. Your descent from ancient freeholders, for five-and-twenty generations of good, honest men, although you bear no coat of arms, is better than the lineage of nine proud English noblemen out of every ten I meet with. And worldly position means only wealth, and title, and the right to be in great houses, and the pleasure of being envied. I have not been here for a year, John, without learning something. Oh, I hate it; how I hate it!

'But there is no time now,' she added, glancing at a jewelled timepiece, scarcely larger than an oyster, which she drew from near her waist-band; and then she pushed it away, in confusion, lest its wealth should startle me. 'My uncle will come home in less than half an hour, dear: and you are not the one to take a side passage, and avoid him. I shall tell him that you have been here: and that I mean you to come again.'

As Lorna said this, with a manner as confident as need be, I saw that she had learned in town the power of her beauty, and knew that she could do with most men aught she set her mind upon. And as she stood there, flushed with pride and faith in her own loveliness, and radiant with the love itself, I felt that she must do exactly as she pleased with every one. For now, in turn, and elegance, and richness, and variety, there was nothing to compare with her face, unless it were her figure. Therefore I gave in and said, –

'Darling, do just what you please. Only make no rogue of me.'

For that she gave me the simplest, kindest, and sweetest of all kisses; and I went down the great stairs grandly, thinking of nothing else but that.

John is John no Longer

HOWEVER, I soon was able to help Lord Brandir, as I think, in two different ways; first of all, as regarded his mind, and then as concerned his body: and the latter perhaps was the greatest service, at his time of life.

Lorna said to me one day, 'You know, John, well enough that my poor uncle still believes that his one beloved son will come to light and life again. He has made all arrangements accordingly: all his property is settled on that supposition. He cannot believe that he will die, without his son coming back to him; and he always has a bedroom ready, and a bottle of Alan's favourite wine cool from out the cellar; he has made me work him a pair of slippers, from the size of a mouldy boot; and if he hears of a new tobacco –

much as he hates the smell of it – he will go to the other end of London, to get some for Alan. Now you know how deaf he is; but if any one say "Alan", even in the place outside the door, he will make his courteous bow to the very highest visitor, and be out here in a moment, and search the entire passage, and yet let no one know it.'

'It is a piteous thing,' I said; for Lorna's eyes were full of tears.

'And he means me to marry him. It is the pet scheme of his life. I am to grow more beautiful, and more highly taught, and graceful; until it pleases Alan to come back, and demand me. Can you understand this matter, John? Or do you think my uncle mad?'

'Lorna, I should be mad myself, to call any man mad, for hoping.'

'Then will you tell me what to do? It makes me very sorrowful. For I know that Alan Brandir lies below the sod in Doone-valley.'

'And if you tell his father,' I answered softly, but clearly, 'in a few weeks he will lie below the sod in London; at least if there is any.'

'Perhaps you are right, John,' she replied: 'to lose hope must be a dreadful thing, when one is turned of seventy. Therefore I will never tell him.'

The other way in which I managed to help the good Earl Brandir was of less true moment to him; but as he could not know of the first, this was the one which moved him.

The good Earl of Brandir was a man of the noblest charity. True charity begins at home, and so did his; and was afraid of losing the way, if it went abroad. So this good nobleman kept his money in a handsome pewter box, with his coat of arms upon it, and a double lid, and locks. Moreover, there was a heavy chain, fixed to a staple in the wall, so that none might carry off the pewter with the gold inside of it.

Now one evening towards September, when the days were drawing in, looking back at the house, to see whether Lorna were looking after me, I espied a pair of villainous fellows watching from the thicket-corner, some hundred yards or so behind the good Earl's dwelling. 'There is mischief a-foot,' thought I to myself, being thoroughly conversant with theft, from my knowledge of the Doones; 'how will be the moon tonight, and when may we expect the watch?'

I found that neither moon, nor watch, could be looked for until the morning; the moon, of course, before the watch, and more likely to be punctual. Therefore I resolved to wait, and see what those two villains did, and save (if it were possible) the Earl of Brandir's pewter box. But, inasmuch as those bad men were almost sure to have seen me leaving the house, and looking back, and striking out on the London road, I marched along at a merry pace, until they could not discern me; and then I fetched a compass round, and refreshed myself at a certain inn, entitled 'The Cross-bones, and Buttons'. Then I took up my position, two hours before midnight, among the shrubs at the eastern end of Lord Brandir's mansion.

When all the lights were quenched, and all the house was quiet, I heard a low and wily whistle from a clump of trees close-by; and then three figures passed between me and a whitewashed wall, and came to a window which opened into a part of the servants' basement. This window was carefully raised by some one inside the house: and after a little whispering, and something which sounded like a kiss, all the three men entered. I crept along the wall, and entered very quietly after them; being rather uneasy about my life, because I bore no fire-arms, and had nothing more than my holly staff, for even a violent combat.

Now, keeping well away in the dark, yet nearer than was necessary to my own dear Lorna's room, I saw these fellows try the door of the good Earl Brandir, knowing from the maid, of course, his lordship could hear nothing, except the name of Alan. They tried the lock, and pushed at it, and even set their knees upright; but a Scottish nobleman may be trusted to secure his door at night. So they were forced to break it open; and at this the guilty maid, or woman, ran away. These three rogues burst into Earl Brandir's room, with a light, and a crowbar, and fire-arms.

When I came to the door of the room, being myself in shadow, I beheld two bad men trying vainly to break open the pewter box, and the third with a pistol muzzle laid to the nightcap of his lordship. With foul face, and yet fouler words, this man was demanding the key of the box, which the other men could by no means open, neither drag it from the chain. 'I tell you,' said this aged Earl, beginning to understand at last what these rogues were up for; 'I will give no key to you. It all belongs to my boy, Alan. No one else shall have a farthing.'

'Then you may count your moments, lord. The key is in your old cramped hand. One, two; and three, I shoot you.'

I saw that the old man was abroad; not with fear, but with great wonder, and the regret of deafness. And I saw that rather would he be shot, than let these men go rob his son, buried now, or laid to bleach in the tangles of the wood, three or it might be four years agone, but still alive to his father. Hereupon my heart was moved; and I resolved to interfere. The thief with the pistol began to count, as I crossed the floor very quietly, while the old Earl gazed at the muzzle, but clenched still tighter his wrinkled hand. The villain, with hair all over his eyes, and the great horse-pistol levelled, cried, 'Three,' and pulled the trigger; but luckily, at that very moment, I struck up the barrel with my staff, so that the shot pierced the canopy, and then with a spin and a thwack, I brought the good holly down upon the rascal's head, in a manner which stretched him upon the floor.

Meanwhile the other two robbers had taken the alarm, and rushed at me, one with a pistol, and one with a sword; which forced me to be very lively. Fearing the pistol most, I flung the heavy velvet curtain of the bed across, that he might not see where to aim at me, and then stooping very quickly, I caught up the senseless robber, and set him up for a shield and target; whereupon he was shot immediately, without having the pain of knowing it; and a happy thing it was for him. Now the other two were at my mercy, being men below the average strength; and no sword, except in most skilful hands, as well as firm and strong ones, has any chance to a powerful man armed with a stout cudgel, and thoroughly practised in single-stick.

So I took these two rogues, and bound them together; and leaving them under charge of the butler (a worthy and shrewd Scotchman), I myself went in search of the constables, whom, after some few hours, I found; neither were they so drunk but what they could take roped men to prison. In the morning, these two men were brought before the Justices of the Peace: and now my wonderful luck appeared; for the merit of having defeated, and caught them, would have raised me one step in the State, or in public consideration, if they had only been common robbers, or even notorious murderers. But when these fellows were recognized, by some one in the court, as Protestant witnesses out of employment, companions and understrappers to Oates, and Bedlow, and Carstairs, and hand-in-glove with Dangerfield, Turberville, and Dugdale – in a word, the very men against whom His Majesty the King bore the bitterest rancour, but whom he had hitherto failed to catch – when this was laid before the public at least a dozen men came up, whom I had never seen before, and prayed me to accept their congratulations, and to be sure to remember them; for all were of neglected merit, and required no more than a piece of luck.

In the course of that same afternoon, I was sent for by His Majesty. He had summoned first the good Earl Brandir, and received the tale from him, not without exaggeration, although my lord was a Scotchman.

The next thing he did was to send for me; and in great alarm and flurry, I put on my best clothes, and hired a fashionable hairdresser, and drank half-a-gallon of ale, because both my hands were shaking. Then forth I set, with my holly staff, wishing myself well out of it. I was shown at once, and before I desired it, into His Majesty's presence, and there I stood most humbly, and made the best bow I could think of.

'Now, John Ridd,' said the King, 'thou hast done great service to the realm, and to religion. It was good to save Earl Brandir, a loyal and Catholic nobleman; but it was great service to catch two of the vilest bloodhounds ever laid on by heretics. And to make them shoot another: it was rare; it was rare, my lad. Now ask us anything in reason; thou canst carry any honours, on thy club, like Hercules. What is thy chief ambition, lad?'

'Well,' said I, after thinking a little, 'my mother always used to think that having been schooled at Tiverton, with thirty marks a year to pay, I was worthy of a coat of arms. And that is what she longs for.'

'A good lad! A very good lad'; said the King, and he looked at the Queen, as if almost in joke; 'but what is thy condition in life?'

'I am a freeholder,' I answered in my confusion, 'ever since the time of King Alfred. A Ridd was with him in the isle of Athelney, and we hold our farm by gift from him; or at least people say so. We have had three very good harvests running, and might support a coat of arms; but for myself I want it not.'

'Thou shalt have a coat, my lad,' said the King, smiling at his own humour; 'but it must be a large one to fit thee. And more than that shalt thou have, John Ridd, being of such loyal breed, and having done such service.'

And while I wondered what he meant, he called to some of the people in waiting at the farther end of the room, and they brought him a little sword, such as Annie would skewer a turkey with. Then he signified to me to kneel, which I did (after dusting the board, for the sake of my best breeches), and then he gave me a little tap very nicely upon my shoulder, before I knew what he was up to; and said, 'Arise, Sir John Ridd!'

This astonished and amazed me to such extent of loss of mind, that when I got up I looked about, and thought what the Snowes would think of it. And I said to the King, without forms of speech, –

'Sir, I am very much obliged. But what be I to do with it?'

Compelled to Volunteer

BEGINNING to be short of money, and growing anxious about the farm, longing also to show myself and my noble escutcheon to mother, I took advantage of Lady Lorna's interest with the Queen, to obtain my acquittance and full discharge from even nominal custody. It had been intended to keep me in waiting, until the return of Lord Jeffreys from that awful circuit of shambles, through which his name is still used by mothers to frighten their children into bed. And right glad was I – for even London shrank with horror at the news – to escape a man so blood-thirsty, savage, and even to his friends (among whom I was reckoned) malignant.

Lorna cried, when I came away (which gave me great satisfaction), and she sent a whole trunkful of things for mother, and Annie, and even Lizzie. And she seemed to think, though she said it not, that I made my own occasion for going, and might have stayed on till the winter. Whereas I knew well that my mother would think (and every one on the farm the same) that here I had been in London, lagging, and taking my pleasure, and looking at shops, upon pretence of King's business, and leaving the harvest to reap itself, not to mention the spending of money; while all the time there was nothing whatever, except my own love of adventure and sport, to keep me from coming home again. But I knew that my coat of arms, and title, would turn every bit of this grumbling into fine admiration.

Now as the winter passed, the Doones were not keeping themselves at home, as in honour they were bound to do. Twenty sheep a week, and one fat ox, and two stout red deer (for wholesome change of diet), as well as three score bushels of flour, and two hogsheads and a half of cider, and a hundredweight of candles, not to mention other things of almost every variety, which they got by insisting upon it – surely these might have sufficed to keep the robbers happy in their place, with no outburst of wantonness. Nevertheless, it was not so; they had made complaint about something – too much ewe-mutton, I think it was – and they had ridden forth, and carried away two maidens of our neighbourhood.

Before we had finished meditating upon this loose outrage, we had news of a thing far worse, which turned the hearts of our women sick.

Mistress Margery Badcock, a healthy and upright young woman, with a good rich colour, and one of the finest henroosts anywhere round our neighbourhood, was nursing her child about six of the clock, and looking out for her husband. Suddenly, by the light of the kitchen fire, she saw six or seven great armed men burst into the room upon her; and she screamed so that the maid in the back kitchen heard her, but was afraid to come to help. Two of the strongest and fiercest men at once seized poor young Margery; and though she fought for her child and home, she was but an infant herself in their hands. In spite of tears and shrieks and struggles, they tore the babe from the mother's arms, and cast it on the lime-ash floor; then they bore her away to their horses (for by this time she was senseless,) and telling the others to sack the house, rode off with their prize to the valley. And from the description of one of those two, who carried off the poor woman, I knew beyond all doubt that it was Carver Doone himself.

The other Doones being left behind, set to with a will to scour the house, and to bring away all that was good to eat. And being a little vexed herein (for the Badcocks were not a rich couple), and finding no more than bacon, and eggs, and cheese, and little items, and nothing to drink but water; in a word, their taste being offended, they came back to the kitchen, and stamped; and there was the baby lying.

'Rowland, is the bacon good?' one of them asked, with an oath or two: 'it is too bad of Carver to go off with the only prize, and leave us in a starving cottage; and not enough to eat for two of us. Fetch down the staves of the rack, my boy. What was farmer to have for supper?'

'Nought but an onion or two, and a loaf, and a rasher of rusty bacon. These poor devils live so badly, they are not worth robbing.'

'No game! Then let us have a game with the baby! It will be the best thing that could befall a lusty infant heretic. Ride a cock-horse to Banbury Cross. Bye, bye, baby Bunting; toss him up, and let me see if my wrist be steady.'

The cruelty of this man is a thing it makes me sick to speak of; enough that when the poor baby fell (without attempt at cry or scream, thinking it part of his usual play, when they tossed him up to come down again), the maid in the oven of the back-kitchen, not being any door between, heard them say as follows: –

'If any man asketh who killed thee,
Say 'twas the Doones of Bagworthy.'

Now I think that when we heard this story, and poor Kit Badcock came all around, in a sort of half-crazy manner, not looking up at any one, but dropping his eyes, and asking whether we thought he had been well-treated, and seeming void of regard for life, if this were all the style of it; then, having known him a lusty man, and a fine singer in an ale-house, and much inclined to lay down the law, and show a high hand about women, I really think that it moved us more than if he had gone about ranting, and raving, and vowing revenge upon every one.

Now the people came flocking all around me, at the blacksmith's forge, and the Brendon ale-house; and I could scarce come out of church, but they got me among the tombstones. They all agreed that I was bound to take command and management against the Doones. I bade them go to the magistrates, but they said they had been too often. Then I told them that I had no wits for ordering of an armament, although I could find fault enough with the one which had not succeeded. But they would hearken to none of this. All they said was, 'Try to lead us; and we will try not to run away.'

And being pressed still harder and harder, as day by day the excitement grew (with more and more talking over it), and no one else coming forward to undertake the business, I agreed at last to this; that if the Doones, upon fair challenge, would not endeavour to make amends, by giving up Mistress Margery, as well as the man who had slain the babe, then I would lead the expedition, and do my best to subdue them.

And then arose a difficult question – who was to take the risk of making overtures so unpleasant? I waited for the rest to offer; and as none was ready, the burden fell on me, and seemed to be of my own inviting. Hence I undertook the task, sooner than reason about it; for to give the cause of everything is worse than to go through with it.

It may have been three of the afternoon, when leaving my

witnesses behind (for they preferred the background) I appeared with our Lizzie's white handkerchief upon a kidney-bean stick, at the entrance to the robbers' dwelling. I could not bring myself to think that any of honourable birth would take advantage of an unarmed man coming in guise of peace to them.

And this conclusion of mine held good, at least for a certain length of time; inasmuch as two decent Doones appeared, and hearing of my purpose, offered, without violence, to go and fetch the Captain. Those men came back in a little while, with a sharp short message that Captain Carver would come out and speak to me, by-and-by, when his pipe was finished. Accordingly I waited, and at length, a heavy and haughty step sounded along the stone roof of the way; and then the great Carver Doone drew up, and looked at me rather scornfully.

'What is it you want, young man?' he asked, as if he had never seen me before.

In spite of that strong loathing, which I always felt at sight of him, I commanded my temper moderately, and told him that I was come for his good, and that of his worshipful company, far more than for my own. But I begged him clearly to understand, that a vile and inhuman wrong had been done, and such as we could not put up with; but that if he would make what amends he could by restoring the poor woman, and giving up that odious brute who had slain the harmless infant, we would take no further motion; and things should go on as usual.

He made me a bow of mock courtesy, and replied as follows: –

'Sir John, your new honours have turned your poor head, as might have been expected. We are not in the habit of deserting anything that belongs to us; far less our sacred relatives. The insolence of your demands well-nigh outdoes the ingratitude. If there be a man upon Exmoor, who has grossly ill-used us, kidnapped our young women, and slain half a dozen of our young men, you are that outrageous rogue, Sir John. And after all this, how have we behaved? We have laid no hand upon your farm, we have not carried off your women, we have even allowed you to take our Queen, by creeping and crawling treachery, and to come home with a title. And now, how do you requite us? By inflaming the boorish indignation at a little frolic of our young men; and by coming with insolent demands, to yield to which would ruin us. Ah, you ungrateful viper!'

'It is true that I owe you gratitude, sir, for a certain time of forbearance; and it is to prove my gratitude that I am come here now. I do not think that my evil deeds can be set against your own; although I cannot speak flowingly upon my good deeds, as you can. I took your Queen because you starved her, having stolen her long before, and killed her mother and brother. This is not for me to dwell upon now; any more than I would say much about your murdering of my father. But how the balance hangs between us, God knows better than thou or I, thou low miscreant, Carver Doone.'

'I have given thee thy choice, John Ridd,' he said, in a lofty manner, which made me drop away under him: 'I always wish to do my best with the worst people who come near me. And of all I have ever met with, thou art the very worst, Sir John, and the most dishonest.'

So seeing no use in bandying words, nay, rather the chance of mischief, I did my best to look calmly at him, and to say with a quiet voice, 'Farwell, Carver Doone, this time; our day of reckoning is nigh.'

'Thou fool, it is come,' he cried, leaping aside into the niche of rock by the doorway: 'Fire!'

Save for the quickness of spring, and readiness, learned in many a wrestling bout, that knavish trick must have ended me: but scarce was the word 'Fire!' out of his mouth ere I was out of fire, by a single bound behind the rocky pillar of the opening. In this jump I was so brisk, at impulse of the love of life (for I saw the muzzles set upon me from the darkness of the cavern), that the men who had trained their guns upon me with good will and daintiness, could not check their fingers crooked upon the heavy triggers; and the volley sang with a roar behind it, down the avenue of crags.

With one thing and another, and most of all the treachery of this dastard scheme, I was so amazed that I turned and ran, at the very top of my speed, away from these vile fellows; and luckily for me, they had not another charge to send after me.

Without any further hesitation, I agreed to take command of the honest men, who were burning to punish, ay and destroy, those outlaws, as now beyond all bearing. One condition however I made, namely that the Counsellor should be spared, if possible: not because he was less a villain than any of the others, but that he seemed less violent. And I found hard work to make them listen to my wish upon this point; for of all the Doones, Sir Counsellor had made himself most hated, by his love of law and reason.

We arranged that all our men should come, and fall into order with pike and musket, over against our dunghill; and we settled, early in the day, that their wives might come and look at them. And all these women brought so many children with them, and made such a fuss, and hugging, and racing after little legs, that our farm-yard might be taken for an out-door school for babies, rather than a review-ground.

I myself was to and fro among the children continually; for if I love anything in the world, foremost I love children.

Nevertheless, I must confess, that the children were a plague sometimes. They never could have enough of me – being a hundred to one, you might say – but I had more than enough of them.

Yet the way in which the children made me useful proved

also of some use to me; for their mothers were so pleased, that they gave me unlimited power and authority over their husbands; moreover, they did their utmost among their relatives round about, to fetch recruits for our little band. And by such means, several of the yeomanry from Barnstaple, and from Tiverton, were added to our number; and inasmuch as these were armed with heavy swords, and short carabines, their appearance was truly formidable.

Tom Faggus also joined us heartily, being now quite healed of his wound, except at times when the wind was easterly.

Also Uncle Ben came over to help us with his advice and presence, as well as with a band of stout warehousemen, whom he brought from Dulverton. For he, and his partners, when fully assured of the value of their diggings, had obtained from the Crown a licence to adventure in search of minerals, by payment of a heavy fine and a yearly royalty. Therefore they had now no longer any cause for secrecy, neither for dread of the outlaws; having so added to their force as to be a match for them. And although Uncle Ben was not the man to keep his miners idle, one hour more than might be helped, he promised that when we had fixed the moment for an assault on the valley, a score of them should come to aid us, headed by Simon Carfax, and armed with the guns which they always kept for the protection of their gold.

Now it was known that the Doones were fond of money, as well as strong drink, and other things; and more especially fond of gold, when they could get it pure and fine. Hence, what we devised was this; to delude from home a part of the robbers, and fall by surprise on the other part. We caused it to be spread abroad that a large heap of gold was now collected at the mine of the Wizard's Slough. And when this rumour must have reached them, we sent Captain Simon Carfax, the father of little Gwenny, to demand an interview with the Counsellor by night, and as it were secretly. Then he was to set forth a list of imaginary grievances against the owners of the mine; and to offer, partly through resentment, partly through the hope of gain, to betray into their hands, upon the Friday night, by far the greatest weight of gold as yet sent up for refining. He was to have one quarter part, and they to take the residue. But inasmuch as the convoy across the moors, under his command, would be strong, and strongly armed, the Doones must be sure to send not less than a score of men if possible. He himself, at a place agreed upon, and fit for an ambuscade, would call a halt, and contrive in the darkness to pour a little water into the priming of his company's guns.

It cost us some trouble to bring the sturdy Cornishman into this deceitful part; and perhaps he never would have consented but for his obligation to me, and the wrongs (as he said) of his daughter. But right well he did it, having once made up his mind to it; and perceiving that his own interests called for the total destruction of the robbers.

A Long Account Settled

HAVING resolved on a night-assault (as our undisciplined men, three-fourths of whom had never been shot at, could not fairly be expected to march up to visible musket-mouths), we cared not much about drilling our forces, only to teach them to hold a musket, so far as we could supply that weapon to those with the cleverest eyes; and to give them familiarity with the noise it made in exploding. And we fixed upon Friday night for our venture, because the moon would be at the full; and our powder was coming from Dulverton, on the Friday afternoon.

Uncle Reuben did not mean to expose himself to shooting,

his time of life for risk of life being now well over, and the residue too valuable. But his counsels, and his influence, and above all his warehousemen, well practised in beating carpets, were of true service to us. His miners also did great wonders, having a grudge against the Doones; as indeed who had not for thirty miles round their valley?

It was settled that the yeomen, having good horses under them, should give account with the miners' help of as many Doones as might be dispatched to plunder the pretended gold. And as soon as we knew that this party of robbers, be it more or less, was out of hearing from the valley, we were to fall to, ostensibly at the Doone-gate (which was impregnable now), but in reality upon their rear, by means of my old water-slide. For I had chosen twenty young fellows, partly miners, and partly warehousemen, and sheep-farmers, and some of other vocations, but all to be relied upon for spirit and power of climbing. And with proper tools to aid us, and myself to lead the way, I felt no doubt whatever that we could all attain the crest, where first I had met with Lorna.

The moon was lifting well above the shoulder of the uplands, when we, the chosen band, set forth, having the short cut along the valleys to foot of the Bagworthy water; and therefore, having allowed the rest an hour to fetch round the moors and hills, we were not to begin our climbing until we heard a musket fired from the heights, on the left hand side, where John Fry himself was stationed, upon his own and his wife's request, to keep him out of combat. And that was the place where I had been used to sit, and to watch for Lorna. And John Fry was to fire his gun, with a ball of wool inside it, so soon as he heard the hurly-burly at the Doone-gate beginning; which we, by reason of waterfall, could not hear, down in the meadows there.

We waited a very long time, with the moon marching up

heaven steadfastly. But suddenly the most awful noise that anything short of thunder could make, came down among the rocks, and went and hung upon the corners.

'The signal, my lads!' I cried, leaping up. 'Now hold on by the rope, and lay your quarter-staffs across, my lads; and keep your guns pointing to heaven, lest haply we shoot one another.'

'Us shan't never shutt one anoother, wi' our goons at that mark, I reckon,' said an oldish chap, but as tough as leather, and esteemed a wit for his dryness.

'You come next to me, old Ike; you be enough to dry up the waters; now, remember, all lean well forward. If any man throws his weight back, down he goes; and perhaps he may never get up again; and most likely he will shoot himself.'

However, thank God, though a gun went off, no one was any the worse for it, neither did the Doones notice it, in the thick of the firing in front of them. For the order to those of the sham attack, conducted by Tom Faggus, was to make the greatest possible noise, without exposure of themselves; until we, in the rear, had fallen to.

Therefore we stole up the meadow quietly, keeping in the blots of shade, and hollow of the watercourse. And the earliest notice the Counsellor had, or any one else, of our presence, was the blazing of the log-wood house, where lived that villain Carver. It was my especial privilege to set this house on fire. No other hand but mine should lay a brand, or strike steel on flint for it; I had made all preparations carefully for a good blaze. And I must confess that I rubbed my hands, when I saw the home of that man, who had fired so many houses, having its turn of smoke, and blaze, and of crackling fury.

We took good care, however, to burn no innocent women, or children, in that most righteous destruction, for we brought them all out beforehand. For Carver had ten or a dozen wives; and perhaps that had something to do with his taking the loss of Lorna so easily. One child I noticed, as I saved him; a fair and handsome little fellow, beloved by Carver Doone, as much as anything beyond himself could be. The boy climbed on my back, and rode; and much as I hated his father, it was not in my heart to say, or do, a thing to vex him.

We drew aside, by my directions, into the covert beneath the cliff. But not before we had laid our brands to three other houses, after calling the women forth, and bidding them go for their husbands, to come and fight a hundred of us. In the smoke, and rush, and fire, they believed that we were a hundred; and away they ran, in consternation, to the battle at the Doone-gate.

'All Doone-town is on fire, on fire!' we heard them shrieking as they went: 'a hundred soldiers are burning it, with a dreadful great man at the head of them!'

Presently, just as I expected, back came the warriors of the Doones; leaving but two or three at the gate, and burning with wrath to crush under foot the presumptuous clowns in their valley. Just then, the waxing fire leaped above the red crest of the cliffs, and all the valley flowed with light, and the limpid waters reddened, and the fair young women shone, and the naked children glistened.

But the finest sight of all was to see those haughty men striding down the causeway darkly, reckless of their end, but resolute to have two lives for every one. A finer dozen of young men could not have been found in the world perhaps, nor a braver, nor a viler one.

My followers waited for no word: they saw a fair shot at the men they abhorred, the men who had robbed them of home or of love; and the chance was too much for their charity. At a signal from old Ikey, who levelled his own gun first, a dozen muskets were discharged, and half of the Doones dropped lifeless, like so many logs of firewood, or chopping-blocks rolled over. While the valley was filled with howling, and with shrieks of women, and the beams of blazing houses fell, and hissed in the bubbling river; all the rest of the Doones leaped at us, like so many demons. They fired wildly, not seeing us well among the hazel bushes; and then they clubbed their muskets, or drew their swords, as might be; and furiously drove at us.

And one thing I saw, which dwelled long with me; and that was Christopher Badcock spending his life to get Charlie's. It was Carver Doone who took his wife away, but Charleworth Doone was beside him; and, according to cast of dice, she fell to Charlie's share. All this Kit Badcock (who was mad, according to our measures) had discovered and treasured up; and now was his revenge-time.

He had come into the conflict without a weapon of any kind; only begging me to let him be in the very thick of it. For him, he said, life was no matter, after the loss of his wife and child; but death was matter to him, and he meant to make the most of it. Such a face I never saw, and never hope to see again, as when poor Kit Badcock spied Charlie coming towards us. Kit went up to Charleworth Doone, as if to some inheritance; and took his seisin of right upon him, being himself a powerful man; and begged a word aside with him. What they said aside, I know not: all I know is that without weapon, each man killed the other. And Margery Badcock came, and wept, and hung upon her dead husband; and died that summer, of heart-disease.

That was a night of fire, and slaughter, and of very long-harboured revenge. Enough that ere the daylight broke, upon that wan March morning, the only Doones still left alive were the Counsellor, and Carver. And of all the dwellings of the Doones (inhabited with luxury, and luscious taste, and licentiousness) not even one was left, but all made potash in the river.

The Counsellor, and the Carver

CARVER DOONE'S handsome child had lost his mother, so he stayed with me, and went about with me everywhere. He had taken as much of liking to me – first shown in his eyes by the firelight – as his father had of hatred; and I, perceiving his noble courage, scorn of lies, and high spirit, became almost as fond of Ensie, as he was of me. He told us that his name was 'Ensie', meant for 'Ensor', I suppose, from his father's grandfather, the old Sir Ensor Doone. And this boy appeared to be Carver's heir, having been born in wedlock, contrary to the general manner and custom of the Doones.

However, although I loved the poor child, I could not help feeling very uneasy about the escape of his father, the savage and brutal Carver. This man was left to roam the country, homeless, foodless, and desperate, with his giant strength, and great skill in arms, and the whole world to be revenged upon. For his escape the miners, as I shall show, were answerable; but of the Counsellor's safe departure the burden lay on myself alone.

After the desperate charge of young Doones had been met by us, and broken, and just as poor Kit Badcock died in the arms of the dead Charlie, I happened to descry a patch of white on the grass of the meadow, like the head of a sheep after washing-day.

Perceiving me, the white thing stopped, and was for making back again; but I ran up at full speed; and lo, it was the flowing silvery hair of that sage the Counsellor, who was scuttling away upon all fours; but now rose, and confronted me.

'John,' he said, 'Sir John, you will not play falsely with

your ancient friend, among these violent fellows. I look to you to protect me, John.'

'Honoured sir, you are right,' I replied; 'but surely that posture was unworthy of yourself, and your many resources. It is my intention to let you go free.'

'I knew it. I could have sworn to it. You are a noble fellow, John; I said so, from the very first; you are a noble fellow, and an ornament to any rank.'

'But upon two conditions,' I added, gently taking him by the arm; for instead of displaying any desire for commune with my nobility, he was edging away towards the postern; 'the first is, that you tell me truly (for now it can matter to none of you) who it was that slew my father.'

'I will tell you, truly and frankly, John; however painful to me to confess it. It was my son, Carver. If I had been there, it would not have happened. I am always opposed to violence. Therefore, let me haste away: this scene is against my nature.'

'You shall go directly, Sir Counsellor, after meeting my other condition; which is, that you place in my hands Lady Lorna's diamond necklace.'

'Alas, John, the thing is not in my possession. Carver, my son, who slew your father, upon him you will find the necklace. What are jewels to me, young man, at my time of life? When you come to my age, good Sir John, you will scorn all jewels, and care only for a pure and bright conscience. Ah! ah! Let me go. I have made my peace with God.'

He looked so hoary, and so silvery, and serene in the moonlight, that verily I must have believed him, if he had not drawn in his breast. But I happened to have noticed, that when an honest man gives vent to noble and great sentiments, he spreads his breast, and throws it out, as if his heart were swelling; whereas I had seen this old gentleman draw his breast in, more than once, as if it happened to contain better goods than sentiment.

'Will you applaud me, kind sir,' I said, keeping him very tight, all the while, 'if I place it in your power, to ratify your peace with God? The pledge is upon your heart, no doubt; for there it lies at this moment.'

With these words, and some apology for having recourse to strong measures, I thrust my hand inside his waistcoat, and drew forth Lorna's necklace, purely sparkling in the moonlight, like the dancing of new stars. The old man made a stab at me, with a knife which I had not espied; but the vicious onset failed; and then he knelt, and clasped his hands.

'Oh, for God's sake, John, my son, rob me not, in that manner. They belong to me; and I love them so; I would give almost my life for them. There is one jewel there I can look at for hours, and see all the lights of heaven in it; which I never shall see elsewhere. All my wretched, wicked life – oh, John, I am a sad hypocrite – but give me back my jewels. Or else kill me here; I am a babe in your hands; but I must have back my jewels.'

His beautiful white hair fell away from his noble forehead, like a silver wreath of glory, and his powerful face, for once, was moved with real emotion,

'Sir Counsellor, I cannot give you what does not belong to me. But if you will show me that particular diamond, which is heaven to you, I will take upon myself the risk, and the folly, of cutting it out for you. And with that you must go contented: and I beseech you not to starve, with that jewel upon your lips.'

Seeing no hope of better terms, he showed me his pet love of a jewel; and I thought of what Lorna was to me, as I cut it out (with the hinge of my knife severing the snakes of gold) and placed it in his careful hand. Another moment, and he was gone, and God knows what became of him.

Now as to Carver, the thing was this: the band of Doones, which sallied forth for the robbery of the pretended convoy, was met by Simon Carfax, according to arrangement, at the ruined house called the 'Warren', in Bagworthy Forest. The Warren, as all our people know, had belonged to a fine old gentleman, whom every one called 'The Squire', who had retreated from active life, to pass the rest of his days in fishing, and shooting, and helping his neighbours. For he was a man of some substance; and no poor man ever left the Warren, without a bag of good victuals, and a few shillings put in his pocket. However, this poor Squire never made a greater mistake, than in hoping to end his life peacefully, upon the banks of a trout-stream, and in the green forest of Bagworthy. For as he came home from the brook at dusk, with his fly-rod over his shoulder, the Doones fell upon him, and murdered him, and then sacked his house, and burned it.

Now Simon, having met these flowers of the flock of villainy, begged them to dismount, and led them, with an air of mystery, into the Squire's ruined hall, black with fire, and green with weeds.

'Captain, I have found a thing,' he said to Carver Doone himself, 'which may help to pass the hour, ere the lump of gold comes by. The smugglers are a noble race; but a miner's eyes are a match for them. There lies a puncheon of rare spirit, with the Dutchman's brand upon it, hidden behind the broken hearth. Set a man to watch outside; and let us see what this be like.'

With one accord they agreed to this, and Carver pledged Master Carfax, and all the Doones grew merry. But Simon being bound, as he said, to see to their strict sobriety, drew a bucket of water from the well, into which they had thrown the dead owner, and begged them to mingle it with their drink; which some of them did, and some refused.

But the water from that well was poured, while they were carousing, into the priming-pan of every gun of theirs; even as Simon had promised to do with the guns of the men they were come to kill. Then just as the giant Carver arose, with a glass of pure hollands in his hand, and by the light of the torch they had struck, proposed the good health of the Squire's ghost – in the broken doorway stood a press of men, with pointed muskets, covering every drunken Doone. The Doones rushed to their guns at once, and pointed them, and pulled at them; but the Squire's well had drowned their fire: and then they knew that they were betrayed; but resolved to fight like men for it. They fought bravely; and like men (though bad ones) died in the hall of the man they had murdered.

Carver Doone alone escaped. Partly through his fearful strength, and his yet more fearful face; but mainly perhaps through his perfect coolness, and his mode of taking things.

For Lorna's sake, I was vexed at the bold escape of Carver. Yet greatly as I blamed the yeomen, who were posted on their horses, just out of shot from the Doone-gate, for the very purpose of intercepting those who escaped the miners, I could not get them to admit that any blame attached to them.

But lo, he had dashed through the whole of them, with his horse at full gallop; and was out of range, ere ever they began to think of shooting him. Then it appears that Captain Carver rode through the Doone-gate, and so to the head of the valley. There he discovered all the houses, and his own among the number, flaming with a handsome blaze, and throwing a fine light around, such as he often had revelled in, when of other people's property. Now he swore the deadliest of all oaths, and seeing himself to be vanquished (so far as the luck of the moment went) spurred his great black horse away, and passed into the darkness.

How to Get Out of Chancery

THE thing which next betided me was not a fall of any sort; but rather a most glorious rise to the summit of all fortune. For in good truth it was no less than the return of Lorna – my Lorna, my own darling; in wonderful health and spirits, and as glad as a bird to get back again.

What a quantity of things Lorna had to tell us! And yet how often we stopped her mouth – at least mother, I mean, and Lizzie – and she quite as often would stop her own, running up in her joy to some one of us!

'Oh, I do love it all so much,' said Lorna, now for the fiftieth time. 'I am sure I was meant for a farmer's – I mean for a farmhouse life, dear Lizzie' – for Lizzie was looking saucily. 'And now, since you will not ask me, dear mother, in the excellence of your manners, and even John has not the impudence, in spite of all his coat of arms, – I must tell you a thing, which I vowed to keep until tomorrow morning; but my resolution fails. I am my own mistress; what think you of that, mother? I am my own mistress!'

'Then you shall not be so long,' cried I; for mother seemed not to understand her, and sought about for her glasses: 'darling, you shall be mistress of me; and I will be your master.'

In the morning, Lorna was ready to tell her story, and we to hearken.

She had taken advantage of the times in a truly clever manner. For that happened to be a time – as indeed all times hitherto (so far as my knowledge extends), have, somehow or other, happened to be – when everybody was only too glad to take money for doing anything. And the greatest money-taker in the kingdom (next to the King and Queen, of course, who had due pre-eminence, and had taught the maids of honour) was generally acknowledged to be the Lord Chief Justice Jeffreys.

Upon his return from the Bloody Assizes, with triumph and great glory, after hanging every man who was too poor to help it, he pleased His Gracious Majesty so purely with the description of their delightful agonies, that the King exclaimed, 'This man alone is worthy to be at the head of the law.' Accordingly in his hand was placed the Great Seal of England.

So it came to pass that Lorna's destiny hung upon Lord Jeffreys; for at this time Earl Brandir died, being taken with gout in the heart, soon after I left London. Lorna grieved for him, as we ought to grieve for any good man going; and yet with a comforting sense of the benefit which the blessed exchange must bring to him.

Now the Lady Lorna Dugal appeared, to Lord Chancellor Jeffreys, so exceeding wealthy a ward, that the lock would pay for turning. Therefore he came, of his own accord, to visit her, and to treat with her; having heard (for the man was as big a gossip as never cared for anybody, yet loved to know all about everybody) that this wealthy and beautiful maiden would not listen to any young lord, having pledged her faith to the plain John Ridd.

Thereupon, our Lorna managed so to hold out golden hopes to the Lord High Chancellor, that he, being not more than three parts drunk, saw his way to a heap of money. And there and then (for he was not the man to dally long about anything) upon surety of a certain round sum – the amount of which I will not mention, because of his kindness towards me – he gave to his fair ward permission, under sign and seal, to marry that loyal knight, John Ridd; upon condition only that the King's consent should be obtained. His Majesty, well-disposed towards me for my previous service, and being moved moreover by the Queen, who desired to please Lorna, consented, without much hesitation.

Everything was settled smoothly, and without any fear or fuss, that Lorna might find end of troubles, and myself of eager waiting, with the help of Parson Bowden, and the good wishes of two counties. I could scarce believe my fortune, when I looked upon her beauty, gentleness, and sweetness, mingled with enough of humour, and warm woman's feeling, never to be dull or tiring; never themselves to be weary.

However humble I might be, no one, knowing anything of our part of the country, would for a moment doubt that now here was a great to-do, and talk of John Ridd, and his wedding. The fierce fight with the Doones so lately, and my leading of the combat (though I fought not more than need be), and the vanishing of Sir Counsellor, and the galloping madness of Carver, had led to the broadest excitement about my wedding of Lorna. We heard that people meant to come from more than thirty miles around, upon excuse of seeing my stature and Lorna's beauty; but in good truth out of sheer curiosity, and the love of meddling.

Blood Upon the Altar

MY darling looked so glorious, that I was afraid of glancing at her, yet took in all her beauty. She was in a fright, no doubt; but nobody should see it; whereas I said (to myself at least), 'I will go through it like a grave-digger.'

Lorna's dress was of pure white, clouded with faint lavender (for the sake of the old Earl Brandir), and as simple as need be, except for perfect loveliness. I was afraid to look at her, as I said before, except when each of us said, 'I will;' and then each dwelled upon the other.

It is impossible for any, who have not loved as I have, to conceive my joy and pride, when after ring and all was done, and the parson had blessed us, Lorna turned to look at me, with her playful glance subdued, and deepened by this solemn act.

Her eyes, which none on earth may ever equal, or compare with, told me such a tale of hope, and faith, and heart's devotion, that I was almost amazed, thoroughly as I knew them. Darling eyes, the clearest eyes, the loveliest, the most loving eyes – the sound of a shot rang through the church, and those eyes were dim with death.

Lorna fell across my knees, when I was going to kiss her, as the bridegroom is allowed to do, and encouraged, if he needs it; a flood of blood came out upon the yellow wood of the altar steps; and at my feet lay Lorna, trying to tell me some last message out of her faithful eyes. I lifted her up, and petted her, and coaxed her, but it was no good; the only sign of life remaining was a drip of bright red blood.

Some men know what things befall them in the supreme time of their life – far above the time of death – but to me comes back as a hazy dream, without any knowledge in it, what I did, or felt, or thought, with my wife's arms flagging, flagging, around my neck, as I raised her up, and softly put them there. She sighed a long sigh on my breast, for her last farewell to life, and then she grew so cold, and cold, that I asked the time of year.

It was now Whit-Tuesday, and the lilacs all in blossom; and why I thought of the time of year, with the young death in my arms, God, of His angels, may decide, having so strangely given us. Enough that so I did, and looked; and our white lilacs were beautiful. Then I laid my wife in my mother's arms, and begging that no one would make a noise, went forth for my revenge.

Of course, I knew who had done it. There was but one man upon earth, or under it, where the Devil dwells, who could have done such a thing – such a thing. I used no harsher word about it, while I leaped upon our best horse, with bridle but no saddle, and set his head towards the course now pointed out to me. Who showed me the course, I cannot tell. I only know that I took it. And the men fell back before me.

Weapon of no sort had I. Unarmed, and wondering at my strange attire (with a bridal vest, wrought by our Annie, and red with blood of the bride), I went forth just to find out this; whether in this world there be, or be not, God of justice.

With my horse at a furious speed, I came upon Black Barrow Down, directed by some shout of men, which seemed to me but a whisper. And there, about a furlong before me, rode a man on a great black horse; and I knew that the man was Carver Doone.

'Thy life, or mine,' I said to myself; 'as the will of God may be. But we two live not upon this earth, one more hour, together.'

I knew the strength of this great man; and I knew that he was armed with a gun – if he had time to load again, after shooting my Lorna,– or at any rate with pistols, and a horseman's sword as well. Nevertheless, I had no more doubt of killing the man before me, than a cook has of spitting a headless fowl.

Sometimes seeing no ground beneath me, and sometimes heeding every leaf, and the crossing of the grass blades, I followed over the long moor, reckless whether seen or not. But only once, the other man turned round, and looked back again; and then I was beside a rock, with a reedy swamp behind me.

Although he was so far before me, and riding as hard as ride he might, I saw that he had something on the horse in front of him; something which needed care, and stopped him from looking backward. In the whirling of my wits, I fancied first that this was Lorna; until the scene I had been through fell across hot brain, and heart, like the drop at the close of a tragedy. Rushing there, through crag and quag, at utmost speed of a maddened horse, I saw, as of another's fate, calmly (as on canvas laid), the brutal deed, the piteous anguish, and the cold despair.

The man turned up the gully leading from the moor to Cloven Rocks. But as Carver entered it, he turned round, and beheld me not a hundred yards behind; and I saw that he was bearing his child, little Ensie, before him. Ensie also descried me, and stretched his hands, and cried to me; for the face of his father frightened him.

Carver Doone, with a vile oath, thrust spurs into his flagging horse, and laid one hand on a pistol-stock, whence I knew that his slung carbine had received no bullet, since the one that had pierced Lorna. And a cry of triumph rose from the black depths of my heart. What cared I for pistols? I had no spurs, neither was my horse one to need the rowel; I rather held him in than urged him, for he was fresh as ever; and I knew that the black steed in front, if he breasted the steep ascent, where the track divided, must be in our reach at once.

His rider knew this; and, having no room in the rocky channel to turn and fire, drew rein at the crossways sharply, and plunged into the black ravine leading to the Wizard's Slough.

I followed my enemy carefully, steadily, even leisurely; for I had him, as in a pitfall, whence no escape might be. He thought that I feared to approach him, for he knew not where he was: and his low disdainful laugh came back.

A gnarled and half-starved oak, as stubborn as my own resolve, and smitten by some storm of old, hung from the crag above me. Rising from my horse's back, although I had no stirrups, I caught a limb, and tore it (like a wheat-awn) from the socket. Men show the rent even now, with wonder; none with more wonder than myself.

Carver Doone turned the corner suddenly, on the black

and bottomless bog; with a start of fear he reined back his horse, and I thought he would have rushed upon me. But instead of that, he again rode on; hoping to find a way round the side.

Now there is a way between cliff and slough, for those who know the ground thoroughly, or have time enough to search it; but for him there was no road, and he lost some time in seeking it. Upon this he made up his mind; and wheeling, fired, and then rode at me.

His bullet struck me somewhere, but I took no heed of that. Fearing only his escape, I laid my horse across the way, and with the limb of the oak struck full on the forehead his charging steed. Ere the slash of the sword came nigh me, man and horse rolled over, and well-nigh bore my own horse down, with the power of their onset.

Carver Doone was somewhat stunned, and could not arise for a moment. Meanwhile I leaped on the ground, and waited, smoothing my hair back, and baring my arms, as though in the ring for wrestling. Then the little boy ran to me, clasped my leg, and looked up at me: and the terror in his eyes made me almost fear myself.

'Ensie, dear,' I said quite gently, grieving that he should see his wicked father killed, 'run up yonder round the corner, and try to find a bunch of bluebells for the pretty lady.' The child obeyed me, hanging back, and looking back, while I prepared for business.

With a sullen and black scowl, the Carver gathered his mighty limbs, and arose, and looked round for his weapons; but I had put them well away. Then he came to me, and gazed, being wont to frighten thus young men.

'I would not harm you, lad,' he said, with a lofty style of sneering: 'I have punished you enough, for most of your impertinence. For the rest I forgive you; because you have been good, and gracious, to my little son. Go, and be contented.'

For answer, I smote him on the cheek, lightly, and not to hurt him: but to make his blood leap up. I would not sully my tongue, by speaking to a man like this.

There was a level space of sward, between us and the slough. With the courtesy derived from London, and the processions I had seen, to this place I led him. And that he might breathe himself, and have every fibre cool, and every muscle ready, my hold upon his coat I loosed, and left him to begin with me, whenever he thought proper.

I think he felt that his time was come. I think he knew from my knitted muscles; and the firm arch of my breast, and the way in which I stood; but most of all from my stern blue eyes; that he had found his master. At any rate a paleness came, an ashy paleness on his cheeks, and the vast calves of his legs bowed in.

Seeing this, villain as he was, I offered him first chance. I stretched forth my left hand, as I do to a weaker antagonist, and I let him have the hug of me. But in this I was too generous; having forgotten my pistol-wound, and the cracking of one of my short lower ribs. Carver Doone caught me round the waist, with such a grip as never yet had been laid upon me.

I heard my rib go; I grasped his arm, and tore the muscle out of it (as the string comes out of an orange); then I took him by the throat, which is not allowed in wrestling; but he had snatched at mine; and now was no time of dalliance. In vain he tugged, and strained, and writhed, dashed his bleeding fist into my face, and flung himself on me, with gnashing jaws. Beneath the iron of my strength – for God that day was with me – I had him helpless in two minutes, and his blazing eyes lolled out.

'I will not harm thee any more,' I cried, so far as I could for panting, the work being very furious: 'Carver Doone, thou art beaten: own it, and thank God for it; and go thy way, and repent thyself.'

It was all too late. Even if he had yielded in his ravening frenzy, for his beard was frothy as a mad dog's jowl; even if he would have owned that, for the first time in his life, he had found his master; it was all too late.

The black bog had him by the feet; the sucking of the ground drew on him, like the thirsty lips of death. In our fury, we had heeded neither wet nor dry, nor thought of earth beneath us. I myself might scarcely leap, with the last spring of o'er-laboured legs, from the engulfing grave of slime. He fell back, with his swarthy breast (from which my grip had rent all clothing), like a hummock of bog-oak, standing out the quagmire; and then he tossed his arms to heaven, and they were black to the elbow, and the glare of his eyes was ghastly. I could only gaze and pant: for my strength was no more than an infant's, from the fury and the horror. Scarcely could I turn away, while, joint by joint, he sank from sight.

Give Away the Grandeur

WHEN the little boy came back with the bluebells, which he had managed to find – as children always do find flowers when older eyes see none – the only sign of his father left was a dark brown bubble, upon a new-formed patch of blackness. But to the centre of its pulpy gorge, the greedy slough was heaving, and sullenly grinding its weltering jaws, among the flags, and the sedges.

With pain, and ache, both of mind and body, and shame at my own fury, I heavily mounted my horse again, and looked down at the innocent Ensie. Would this playful, loving child grow up like his cruel father, and end a godless life of hatred with a death of violence? He lifted his noble forehead towards me, as if to answer, 'Nay, I will not:' but the words he spoke were these:

'Don' – for he never could say 'John' – 'oh Don, I am so glad, that nasty naughty man is gone away. Take me home, Don. Take me home.'

It has been said of the wicked, 'Not even their own children love them.' And I could easily believe that Carver Doone's cold-hearted ways had scared from him even his favourite child.

It was lucky for me that my horse had lost spirit, like his master, and went home as mildly as a lamb. For, when we came towards the farm, I seemed to be riding in a dream almost; and the voices both of men and women (who had hurried forth upon my track), as they met me, seemed to wander from a distant muffing cloud. Only the thought of Lorna's death, like a heavy knell, was tolling in the belfry of my brain.

When we came to the stable door, I rather fell from my horse than got off; and John Fry, with a look of wonder, took his head, and led him in. Into the old farm-house I tottered, like a weanling child, with mother in her common clothes, helping me along, yet fearing, except by stealth, to look at me.

'I have killed him,' was all I said; 'even as he killed Lorna. Now let me see my wife, mother. She belongs to me none the less, though dead.'

'You cannot see her now, dear John,' said Ruth Huckaback, coming forward; since no one else had the courage. 'Annie is with her now, John.'

'What has that to do with it? Let me see my dead one; and then die.'

All the women fell away, and whispered, and looked at me, with side-glances, and some sobbing; for my face was hard as flint. Ruth alone stood by me, and dropped her eyes, and trembled. Then one little hand of hers stole into my great shaking palm, and the other was laid on my tattered coat: yet with her clothes she shunned my blood, while she whispered gently, –

'John, she is not your dead one. She may even be your living one yet, your wife, your home, and your happiness. But you must not see her now.'

'Is there any chance for her? For me, I mean; for me, I mean?'

'God in heaven knows, dear John. But the sight of you, and in this sad plight, would be certain death to her. Now come first, and be healed yourself.'

For hours, however, and days, Lorna lay at the very verge of death, kept alive by nothing but the care, the skill, the tenderness, and perpetual watchfulness of Ruth. Luckily Annie was not there very often, so as to meddle; for kind and clever nurse as she was, she must have done more harm than good. But my broken rib, which was set by a doctor, who chanced to be at the wedding, was allotted to Annie's care; and great inflammation ensuing, it was quite enough to content her. This doctor had pronounced poor Lorna dead; wherefore Ruth refused most firmly to have aught to do with him. She took the whole case on herself; and with God's help, she bore it through.

Now whether it were the light, and brightness of my Lorna's nature, or the freedom from my anxiety – for she knew not of my hurt;– or, as some people said, her birthright among wounds and violence, or her manner of not drinking beer, – I leave that doctor to determine, who pronounced her dead. But anyhow, one thing is certain; sure as the stars of hope above us, Lorna recovered long ere I did.

On me lay overwhelming sorrow, having lost my love and lover, at the moment she was mine. With the power of fate upon me, and the black cauldron of the wizard's death boiling in my heated brain, I had no faith in the tales they told. I believed that Lorna was in the churchyard, while these rogues were lying to me. In my sick distracted mind (stirred with many tossings), like the bead in a wisp of frog-spawn drifted by the current, hung the black and worthless burden of the life before me. A life without Lorna; a tadpole life. All stupid head; and no body.

One day, I was sitting in my bedroom, for I could not get downstairs, and there was no one strong enough to carry me, even if I would have borne it. Though it cost me sore trouble and weariness, I had put on all my Sunday clothes, out of respect for the doctor, who was coming to bleed me again (as he always did, twice a week); and it struck me, that he had seemed hurt in his mind, because I wore my worst clothes to be bled in.

Presently a little knock sounded through my gloomy room, and supposing it to be the doctor, I tried to rise, and make my bow. But to my surprise, it was little Ruth, who had never once come to visit me, since I was placed under the doctor's hands.

'Can you receive visitors, Cousin Ridd? – why, they never told me of this!' she cried: 'I knew that you were weak, dear John; but not that you were dying. Whatever is that basin for?'

'I have no intention of dying, Ruth; and I like not to talk about it. But that basin, if you must know, is for the doctor's purpose.'

'What, do you mean bleeding you? You poor weak cousin! Is it possible that he does that still?'

'Twice a week for the last six weeks, dear. Nothing else has kept me alive.'

'Nothing else has killed you, nearly. There!' and she set her little boot across the basin, and crushed it. 'Not another drop shall they have from you. Is Annie such a fool as that?'

'Dear cousin, the doctor must know best. Annie says so, every day. Else what has he been brought up for?'

'Brought up for slaying, and murdering. Twenty doctors killed King Charles, in spite of all the women. Will you leave it to me, John? I have a little will of my own; and I am not afraid of doctors. I have saved your Lorna's life. And now I will save yours; which is a far, far easier business.'

'You have saved my Lorna's life! What do you mean by talking so?'

'Only what I say, Cousin John. Though perhaps I over-prize my work. But at any rate she says so.'

'I do not understand,' I said, falling back with bewilderment. 'I do not understand,' was all I could say, for a very long time.

'Will you understand, if I show you Lorna? I have feared to do it, for the sake of you both. But now Lorna is well enough, if you think that you are, Cousin John. Surely you will understand, when you see your wife.'

Before I had time to listen much for the approach of foot-steps, Ruth came back, and behind her Lorna; coy as if of her bridegroom; and hanging back with her beauty. Ruth banged the door and ran away; and Lorna stood before me.

But she did not stand for an instant, when she saw what I was like. At the risk of all thick bandages, and upsetting a dozen medicine bottles, and scattering leeches right and left, she managed to get into my arms, although they could not hold her. She laid her panting warm young breast on the place where they meant to bleed me, and she set my pale face up; and she would not look at me, having greater faith in kissing.

I felt my life come back, and glow; I felt my trust in God revive; I felt the joy of living and of loving dearer things than life. It is not a moment to describe; who feels can never tell of it. But the compassion of my sweetheart's tears, and the caressing of my bride's lips, and the throbbing of my wife's heart (now at last at home on mine) made me feel that the world was good, and not a thing to be weary of.

Little more have I to tell. The doctor was turned out at once; and slowly came back my former strength, with a darling wife, and good victuals.

Today, there is no need for my farming harder than becomes a man of weight. Lorna has great stores of money, though we never draw it out, except for some poor neighbour.

As for poor Tom Faggus, every one knows his bitter adventures, when his pardon was recalled, because of his sally to Sedgemoor. Not a child in the county, I doubt, but knows far more than I do of Tom's most desperate doings. How, being caught upon Barnstaple Bridge, with soldiers at either end of it (yet doubtful about approaching him), he set his strawberry mare, sweet Winnie, at the left hand parapet, with a whisper into her dove-coloured ear. Without a moment's doubt she leaped it, into the foaming tide, and swam, and landed according to orders. Also his flight from a public-house (where a trap was set for him, but Winnie came, and broke down the door, and put two men under, and trod on them), is as well known as any ballad. It was reported for awhile that poor Tom had been caught at last, by means of his fondness for liquor, and was hanged before Taunton Gaol; but luckily we knew better. With a good wife, and a wonderful horse, and all the country attached to him, he kept the law at a wholesome distance, until it became too much for its master; and a new king arose. Upon this, Tom sued his pardon afresh; and Jeremy Stickles, who suited the times, was glad to help him in getting it, as well as a compensation. Thereafter, the good and respectable Tom lived a godly and righteous (though not always sober) life; and brought up his children to honesty, as the first of all qualifications.

I sent little Ensie to Blundell's school, at my own cost and charges, having changed his name, for fear of what any one might do to him. For the bold adventurous nature of the

Doones broke out on him, and we got him a commission, and after many scrapes of spirit, he did great things in the Low Countries. He looks upon me as his father; and without my leave, will not lay claim to the heritage, and title of the Doones, which clearly belong to him.

Of Lorna, of my lifelong darling, of my more and more loved wife, I will not talk; for it is not seemly, that a man should exalt his pride. Year by year, her beauty grows, with the growth of goodness, kindness, and true happiness – above all with loving. And if I wish to pay her out for something very dreadful – as may happen once or twice, when we become too gladsome – I bring her to forgotten sadness, and to me for cure of it, by the two words, 'Lorna Doone'.

Also in Puffin Classics

THE RAILWAY CHILDREN

E. Nesbit

When Father has to go away for a time, the three children and their mother leave London and go to live in a small house in the country. They seek solace in the nearby railway station, making friends with Perks the Porter and with the Station Master himself. But the mystery remains: where is their father, and is he ever going to return?

BLACK BEAUTY

Anna Sewell

The adventures, disappointments and joys of a horse's life are the subject of *Black Beauty*, perhaps the most loved animal story ever written. He is a marvellous animal: sweet-tempered but strong, spirited but with fine instincts. A stirring story, as exciting and moving today as it was over a hundred years ago.

THE SECRET GARDEN

Frances Hodgson Burnett

After the death of her parents, Mary is brought back from India as a forlorn and unwanted child to live in her uncle's great lonely house on the moors. Then one day she discovers the key to a secret garden and, like magic, her life begins to brighten in so many ways.

THE LOST WORLD

Sir Arthur Conan Doyle

Journalist Ed Malone is looking for an adventure, and that's exactly what he finds when he meets the eccentric Professor Challenger: an adventure that leads Malone and his three companions into the Amazon jungle, to a lost world where dinosaurs roam free and the natives fight out a murderous war with their fierce neighbours, the ape-men.

WHAT KATY DID

Susan Coolidge

The moving story of how Katy Carr overcomes her tragic accident and learns to be as loving and as patient as the beautiful invalid, Helen.

MOONFLEET

J. Meade Falkner

Most of the inhabitants of the tiny village of Moonfleet are either smugglers or fishermen, so it's no surprise when 15-year-old John Trenchard gets involved in the smuggling business. Eventually he's forced to leave the country with a price on his head, and only returns to England after a long and difficult period abroad.

THE PRINCE AND THE PAUPER

Mark Twain

Tom Canty and Edward Tudor look alike, but their lives could hardly be more different. For Edward is Prince, and heir to the throne, whilst Tom is a miserable pauper. Until one day fate intervenes and for a while each must see how the other lives ...

THE CHILDREN OF THE NEW FOREST

Captain Marryat

England in 1647: the country is divided as Cavaliers and Roundheads fight bitterly to decide who should rule. The four Beverley children lose their parents in the war and are forced to go into hiding. Ill-prepared for a life on the land, and always at great risk of discovery, they set about hunting and housekeeping with great spirit and courage.

OUR EXPLOITS AT WEST POLEY

Thomas Hardy

The story of two boys who discover how to divert the course of an underground river and play havoc with the lives of the local Somerset villagers. But it's their own lives that are finally most in danger!

KING SOLOMON'S MINES

H. Rider Haggard

The magnificent story of three men who trek north to the remote interior of Africa in search of a lost friend. And how at the end of their perilous journey they find, not just the missing adventurer, but the spectacular diamond mines of Solomon!

KIDNAPPED

R. L. Stevenson

A swashbuckling tale of kidnap and murder, set in the Scottish Highlands after the Jacobite rebellion. It tells of the flight of young David Balfour after he is treacherously cheated of his rightful estate and then wrongly suspected of murder.

THE PRINCESS AND THE GOBLIN

George MacDonald

Princess Irene lives in a castle in a wild and lonely mountainous region. One day she discovers a steep and winding staircase leading up through the castle to a bewildering labyrinth of unused passages – and a further stairway. What lies at the top? Can her ring protect her against the lurking menace of the goblins from under the mountain? And will Curdie, the miner's son, reach her in time to warn her of the goblins' horrifying plot?

POLLYANNA GROWS UP

Eleanor H. Porter

In this sequel to *Pollyanna* (also in Puffin Classics), Pollyanna is home again, but not for long. A trip to Boston is in the offing, with new faces, new friends and new experiences. But then Aunt Polly falls on hard times and even Pollyanna has trouble maintaining her usual cheerful outlook.

THE CALL OF THE WILD

Jack London

This tale of a dog's fight for survival in the harsh and frozen Yukon is one of the greatest animal stories. It tells of a dog born to luxury but sold as a sledge dog, and how he rises magnificently above all his enemies to become one of the most feared and admired dogs in the north.

HEIDI

Johanna Spyri

The classic story of an unwanted child who finds love and happiness against all the odds. Bringing with it the keen scent of mountain air, *Heidi* is a tender, warm-hearted book that never seems to grow stale.

LITTLE WOMEN

Louisa M. Alcott

The March girls – Meg, Jo, Beth and Amy – manage to lead interesting lives despite their father's absence at war and the family's lack of money. Whether they're making plans for putting on a play or forming a secret society, their enthusiasm is infectious. Even Laurie, the rich but lonely boy next door, is swept up in their gaiety.

GOOD WIVES

Louisa M. Alcott

What happened to the March girls when they became young women? Did Meg marry John Brooke? Did Jo and Laurie fall in love? Did Beth's health improve? And did Amy follow the career she'd set her heart on? This sequel to *Little Women* is a touching and rewarding story in its own right.

LITTLE MEN

Louisa M. Alcott

'Think what luxury – Plumfield my own, and a wilderness of boys to enjoy it with me!' This was Jo March's ambition at the end of *Good Wives*, and now it has become a reality. The mother of two boys, and adoptive mother of twelve more, Jo couldn't be happier. The informal school at Plumfield is a haven for poor orphaned boys who thrive on warmth, goodness and the affectionate interest of the entire March family.

JO'S BOYS

Louisa M. Alcott

Ten years on from the founding of Plumfield's school, many changes have taken place. Along the paths once trodden by childish feet tramp busy students attending the college built with a legacy from old Mr Lawrence. All Jo's original boys are grown men scattered round the world, and the girls have become graceful young women with lofty ambitions. A new generation of boys romp at Plumfield, but that doesn't mean the old one has been forgotten.

THE ADVENTURES OF TOM SAWYER

Mark Twain

The famous tale of a boy's life in a small town on the banks of the Mississippi River. Tom skips school and with his friends, Huck Finn and Jim, spends his days on mad adventures – some real, some imagined. Like Tom himself, this is a happy and cheerful book, exciting but also funny.

THE ADVENTURES OF HUCKLEBERRY FINN

Mark Twain

Huck was fourteen when he ran away from home and met old Jim, and together on a raft they tumbled in and out of experiences which sound wildly fantastic today but were just part of the life of the busy Mississippi more than a hundred years ago. A great American classic.